Kitty Hawk
And
The Icelandic
Intrigue

Book Three of the Kitty Hawk Flying Detective Agency Series

Iain Reading

This page is dedicated to all those people who
like books that have a Chapter Zero

To Sarah!

17 Feb 2020

Other books by this author:

Kitty Hawk and the Curse of the Yukon Gold
Kitty Hawk and the Hunt for Hemingway's Ghost
Kitty Hawk and the Icelandic Intrigue
Kitty Hawk and the Tragedy of the RMS Titanic
The Guild of the Wizards of Waterfire
The Hemingway Complex (non-fiction)

www.kittyhawkworld.com
www.wizardsofwaterfire.com
www.iainreading.com
www.secretworldonline.com

TABLE OF CONTENTS

Prologue

Run Like Never Before In My Entire Life

The bullet split the air with a dreadful ripping sound and whizzed past my ear like some horrifyingly angry insect. The experience was completely new and terrifying to me, and it was one that I could have happily lived the rest of my life without having had. After hearing the bullet rip past me (and feeling it, too, since such a terrible sound is felt as much as it is heard) everything that followed seemed to happen all at once in excruciatingly slow motion.

What was that?!? I asked myself as I bolted upright and my brain tried to make sense of what it had just experienced. But I already knew full well what it was. My brain was slow to accept what it already knew to be true, because with that acceptance came the realization that someone was trying to kill me, and had the bullet not missed, I would already be dead.

After accepting what was happening, panic began to set in. People sometimes talk about being frozen in fear—like a deer in the headlights of a car—but for me, the fear had the exact opposite effect. All I could think was that I needed to run; I needed to get out of here—right away—and to anywhere other than the middle of the road where I was exposed and vulnerable to being shot at a second time.

Fortunately, my brain had the good sense not to run *toward* the source of the gunfire, and I managed to scramble down the side of the road and take cover in the ditch. Somewhere up the road, men with guns were pulling themselves out of their wrecked automobile and planning to come after me. If I stopped breathing for a second and strained to listen over the sound of the wind, I could hear them grunting as they pulled themselves free of the car accompanied by the sound of broken glass raining onto the ground.

"You have to get out of here," the little voice in my head reminded me. "You don't have much time!"

I know, I told myself. I tried to breathe normally and stay calm. I didn't have time to make any mistakes. Even the smallest misstep could cost me my life. All I could do was run, but where could I run to when I was on a road in the middle of nowhere? If I got back onto the road, I would be completely exposed, even in the dim light of the early morning.

"The only place you *can* run," the little voice said, "is cross-country."

I lifted my head for a second to see if anyone was coming after me. I couldn't see anyone, but that didn't mean no one was out there, so I kept my head low, ran across the ditch, and scrambled up the rocky ledge on the other side.

Please, God, don't let them shoot at me now, I thought as I climbed up the ledge and out of the ditch.

Once I was at the top, I crouched low and surveyed the way ahead of me. The landscape was rocky and rough—full of places to hide and take cover.

"Maybe that's what you should do," the little voice suggested. "Maybe you should just find somewhere to hide? It's pretty dark out here and there are plenty of shadows you could crawl into. Just hide somewhere until they decide to leave you here."

I shook my head.

"It won't be dark for long," I muttered to myself as I looked toward the brightening horizon where the sun would soon be rising. "And I am not just going to sit around helplessly waiting for them to find me. I am going to get as far from them as I possibly can."

"Then what are you waiting for?!?" the little voice replied, still panicked.

I peered over the ledge and back up the deserted road to where the shot that had barely missed me had come from. I still couldn't see anything—not even the hulk of the wrecked car that I knew was back there—and no one was walking up the road toward me. I closed my eyes and tried to listen for any sound of movement over the howling wind.

"You have to go!" the little voice screamed. "They could be anywhere! They could be standing five feet away from you, ready to grab you again!"

The voice in my head was right. I had to go. But I kept listening, waiting for clarity. Somehow, I felt that I had to have some idea of where they were, because it terrified me much more not knowing anything at all.

And then I heard it—the faint sound of angry voices carried on the wind down the road toward me. They were speaking some foreign language, and they could have been saying just about anything, but I only heard, "That stupid girl is going to pay for this. Let's go get her."

A cold wave of fear washed over me. My heart pounded like a jackhammer, and a sickening chill poured deep into the pit of my stomach.

"Now I run," I whispered to myself, and sprang to my feet. "Now I run like I've never run before in my entire life."

Chapter Zero

Greenland Is Not Very Green

From: Kitty Hawk <kittyhawk@kittyhawkworld.com>
To: Charlie Lewis <chlewis@alaska.net>

Subject: Greetings from Greenland!

Dear Charlie,

Greetings from Nuuk, Greenland!

You wouldn't believe how amazing it is here. It is so much like Alaska in some ways, but also incredibly different, too. Nuuk is a charming little fishing village at the edge of the sea with these perfect little colorful houses that line the rocky shoreline with beautiful mountains across the fjords in the distance.

It's not very 'green', though. The guy at the dock who helped me fuel up told me that Greenland is named how it is because the Viking Erik the Red came here after being exiled from Iceland, and he thought the name would sound pleasant and thus attract settlers. I don't think that really worked. There's not many people here. Fifteen thousand, the guy at the dock told me.

I read somewhere on the Internet that one of the top ten best views in the world is the one you see when flying over Greenland. Pilots on commercial airlines flying back and forth between Europe and North America see this view all the time, and consider it to be one of the most breathtaking in the world. I can now tell you from experience that this is absolutely true. It is a land of blue ice and rocky mountains with tidewater glaciers snaking between the mountain peaks down to ocean bays and inlets littered with icebergs. From the air, it looks a lot like Alaska, but it just stretches on forever and ever and ever into the distance. There is so much ice that I can't help but shiver. It is definitely not a 'green' land at all.

Tomorrow I will fly over the rest of Greenland on my way to Reykjavik. I am looking forward to meeting your friends there. Thank you so much for arranging for me to stay with them for a while so I can explore Iceland. I can hardly wait.

I hope everything is great with you. I will write again as soon as I can.

kh.

Chapter One

First In Flight

W ith my adventures in Key West and the Caribbean at an end and all my goodbyes said, it was time to leave. But I lingered for a couple of days longer to spend some time by myself in the sun at the aptly named No Name Key. I swam, snorkeled, and ate conch chowder and key lime pie. I had to force myself to remember that I had a schedule to keep if I wanted to continue with my around-the-world flight. I needed to get going rather than spend endless days in the sun and sand.

It was difficult to leave, which I am sure you can understand, because where I was headed was going to be a lot colder than the warmth of Key West and its crystal-clear waters. I was heading north to Canada, Greenland, and beyond to Iceland. Just thinking about it made me shiver, even as I baked in the hot midday sun. But of course, I had to do it. I had so many adventures in front of me, most of which I couldn't even begin to imagine yet.

Leaving No Name Key behind and leap-frogging my way up the eastern coast of the United States toward Iceland was going to be a tricky venture. That part of the world has a lot of air traffic, so I had to plan things carefully and always be aware of my location and the classification of airspace I was in. Not that I hadn't encountered such situations before, but it was good practice for me to make sure I stayed on top of things.

When my father and I had first planned my little detour down to the Caribbean to vacation with my him and my mom, I had hoped I might be able to stop in Washington D.C. and New York on my way north. I thought I might be able to see some of the museums in Washington, including the Smithsonian and the plane that Amelia Earhart used to make her historic trans-Atlantic flight in 1932. But it seemed a bit too much, so I dropped the idea.

"We'll go back to D.C. together some time and see all that," my father told me as we sat at our kitchen table in Tofino and planned the whole trip.

"And New York City, too," I reminded him.

"Right," he said. "What was there, again?"

"It's New York City, duh!" I replied. "What more do you need than that?!?"

But I had to stop *somewhere* along the way to refuel and spend the night, somewhere between Florida and Halifax, Nova Scotia—my second-to-last stop in Canada before Newfoundland and the rest of the world. And as fate would have it, halfway between Key West and Halifax was a little town by the sea with a very special name—Kitty Hawk, North Carolina.

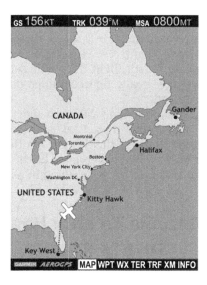

On December 17, 1903, the now famous Wright brothers—Orville and Wilbur—made the first powered aircraft flight in history in the sand dunes just south of the town of Kitty Hawk. The rest, as they say, is history.

It was a powerful moment for me to stand at the top of those dunes with the wind in my face, thinking about how this is where it all started. If I turned my back on the rather obtrusive and enormous white memorial, I could almost imagine what it must have been like on that cold day back in 1903. (Although, even in my imagination, it still looked a lot like jittery old black and white movie footage.)

As I looked out across the expanse, I realized that I owed much more than my name to the place on which I stood. I owed nearly everything that made me who I am to what had happened there more than a hundred years before. From the Wright brothers' achievements on those sandy dunes flowed the entire history of powered flight, from the very first fragile paper and wood airplanes all the way to planes like my own De Havilland Beaver seaplane and beyond.

Flying has become so commonplace in our modern world that we forget that flight was once only a dream to those whom history will never forget: the Wright brothers, Amelia Earhart, Howard Hughes, and all the other great pioneers of flight. All of it started right where I was standing, on some windy sand dunes overlooking the Atlantic Ocean.

I closed my eyes for a moment and spread my arms out like wings. For just one tiny moment, I let the wind try to lift me into the sky. It was easy to imagine that I was soaring through the sky high above, but when I opened my eyes, I was brought back to reality by the enormous white memorial behind me. The pamphlet I'd picked up at the visitor center informed me that it was the largest monument in the United States built for a living person. No big surprise there—it is huge!

Farther down the hill, a boulder marks the spot where the Wright brothers lifted off the ground on their first test flights. First flight, twelve seconds, 120 feet; second flight, twelve seconds, 175 feet; third flight, fifteen seconds, 200 feet; fourth flight, fifty-nine seconds, 859 feet. The Wright brothers must have really figured things out between the third and fourth flights, I guessed.

It was difficult for me to imagine that such short flights were capable of changing history. In less time than it takes me to start the engine on my trusty De Havilland Beaver, the Wright brothers' first flight was already over. But the world would never again be the same.

This is a place I was meant to visit, I thought as I held my iPhone at arm's length and took a picture of myself at the Kitty Hawk town sign.

Welcome To Kitty Hawk
First In Flight

"First in flight," I whispered reverently as I forwarded the photo to my dad back in Tofino.

I was deeply inspired by my visit to this most important and personally significant site. This inspiration helped me through my next daunting task—going through my flight plans for the next day as I continued my flight north and into the maze of airspace that crisscrossed the eastern seaboard of the United States.

"At least the Wright brothers didn't have to deal with all this, I muttered as I scrolled through my GPS and flipped through chart books. I needed to make sure I was 100 percent clear on my flight plan for the next day.

"They didn't have GPS either," the little voice in my head reminded me helpfully.

"Good point," I conceded heartily.

If you think having a GPS is useful when driving a car, you can only imagine how completely invaluable one is when you're up in an airplane.

I continued with my planning, and once I was satisfied that I was ready, I packed away my chart books and GPS for the night and had a quick shower before climbing into bed.

"Amelia Earhart, the Wright brothers—those are some pretty big footsteps you are following," the little voice in my head observed as I lay under the warm covers and thought about my day.

I know it, I admitted to myself. *But I'm not worried. I have my GPS, remember?*

Chapter Two

Perfect Little Towns

Virginia, Delaware, Pennsylvania, New York, Massachusetts; Norfolk, Washington, Philadelphia, Albany, and Boston: The familiar state and city names flowed past left and right across the screen of my GPS as I made my way north. Finally, the Canadian border appeared in the distance, and I headed for the city of Halifax.

Landing my trusty De Havilland seaplane in the harbor, I tied up to the dock and talked to the fueling attendant before checking in with Canadian Customs. As usual, the fuel guy was a helpful source of information and was able to give me some interesting facts and advice about the city. He told me about the horrific Halifax Explosion that happened in 1917 during the height of the First World War. He described how a French cargo ship carrying explosives collided with another ship and set off an explosion so unbelievably huge that it was the largest man-made explosion in history until the first atomic bombs were tested in 1945. Buildings were completely flattened by the shock of the explosion, a fifty-foot tidal wave washed ashore into the nearby city and caused further destruction, and even buildings farther away that weren't destroyed were scorched black by the blast on the side facing the explosion. He said the black scorching is still visible on many older buildings.

Sadly for Halifax, that was not the first major disaster the city had experienced. Five years earlier the city had also been closely involved with the doomed maiden voyage of the *Titanic*, which had sunk into the deep Atlantic Ocean a thousand kilometers offshore of Halifax. The bodies that were recovered from the water at the site of the disaster were brought back to Halifax to be claimed by their loved ones or buried. In this way, Halifax became the final resting place of more than a hundred of the victims of the tragedy; most of them were laid to rest in a nearby cemetery called Fairview Cemetery.

As I wandered along the rows of headstones, I noticed that many had no names on them—only a marker number and the date of death: April 15, 1912. I was reminded of the cemetery that I had seen back in Dyea the previous summer with the victims of the Palm Sunday avalanche. The grave markers in that cemetery had shared a common date of death as well, revealing to the uninformed that some terrible disaster must have occurred to take so many lives on the same day.

A couple of the gravestones caught my eye because of the fresh flowers that had been laid at them. One of these had a headstone that read *Erected to the memory of an unknown child whose remains were recovered after the disaster.* The other was a smaller headstone that simply read *J Dawson Died April 15, 1912.*

J Dawson? I thought. *Like Jack Dawson—Leonardo Di Caprio's character in the* Titanic *movie?*

I asked one of the groundskeepers about this, and he told me that the J Dawson buried there was actually Joseph Dawson who had worked down in the ship's boiler rooms and had nothing to do with the Hollywood movie at all. The character from the movie wasn't real, he said, but that didn't stop people from leaving flowers at the gravesite anyway.

The next morning I flew out of Halifax for a short flight to Gander, Newfoundland, my final stop in Canada before heading out across the ocean toward Greenland and Iceland. I was stopping there for the exact same reason that thousands of flights over the years had also stopped there. And that reason was fuel.

Gander is a town that is close to the northeastern corner of the North American continent, and in the early days of aviation when airplanes didn't have the long fuel ranges that they do now, it was a perfect spot to stop and refuel for the long flights over the Atlantic Ocean that connected Europe and North America. And with the limited range of my De Havilland Beaver, that was the exact same reason that I was stopping there, too.

As it turned out, some bad weather over the North Atlantic forced me to spend a few days in the quiet little town of Gander while I waited for a safe opening to make the flight onward to Greenland. I didn't mind, however, and took the time to wander the town and make some new friends.

One afternoon I visited a tiny residential street with a very special name. Many streets and roads in Gander are named after famous people in the history of aviation including Charles Lindbergh, Chuck Yeager, and of course, Amelia Earhart. It probably sounds silly, but one of the most powerful moments on my entire journey was standing there on an out-of-the-way street corner surrounded by sleepy little streets lined with bungalow houses. I took out my iPhone to take a photo of the simple street sign with EARHART STREET painted in black letters on a white background. My flight around the world was following the spirit of Amelia Earhart, and somehow that simple little sign in a tiny town in the middle of nowhere made everything real for me all over again.

In addition to exploring the town, I spent a lot of time talking with some of the town's residents in the nearby Tim Horton's doughnut shop where I would drop in for a coffee and spend some time reading books on my Kindle e-reader.

Day after day, I made friends with a few of the coffee shop regulars and heard their many stories.

One early-morning regular, on hearing that I was on my way to the land of the Vikings in Greenland and Iceland, told me about her research work at various archaeological sites in Newfoundland. One morning she brought in some photo albums, and we sat together flipping through them while she explained to me the various types of evidence they'd found of Viking settlements in Newfoundland hundreds of years before Columbus supposedly discovered America.

Some of the older residents had some slightly more modern stories to tell. They told me what the town was like a few decades back in the 20th century when Gander was at the crossroads of the aviation world. In those glamorous days of airline travel, the planes would come every day carrying passengers, including movie stars and other celebrities, back and forth between Europe and America. But eventually aviation technology advanced enough to allow planes to fly longer distances without refueling, and the golden era of the town came to an end because stopping in Gander was no longer necessary.

All of this was ancient history to most of the people I met, but nearly every regular excitedly told me about a much more recent event that they referred to as "the day the planes came": September 11, 2001. On that infamous day (one that I can vaguely remember, as I was very young at the time), North American airspace was completely shut down following the terrorist attacks in New York City and Washington. More than forty international flights were diverted and had to land in tiny little Gander. Once on the ground, the hundreds of passengers were stuck there and had to spend the next three days far from where they had expected to be. It was difficult, but they were warmly welcomed by the local residents who opened their homes and kitchens to the stranded passengers and did their best to make them feel at home.

I could relate to that. With the weather not cooperating, I had also become temporarily and unexpectedly trapped in Gander. But the experience taught me that perhaps it's good to sometimes get stranded somewhere for a little while. Too often in life, we rush from place to place, and perfect little towns like Gander get forgotten along the way. Joking and laughing with the locals gathered around my booth in Tim Horton's doughnut shop and learning about their histories and stories was one of the most rewarding experiences of my life. Between that and exploring the town, and seeing that plain little Amelia Earhart street sign, I realized that sometimes the simple moments in life can be the most important and special. And I would have missed it all if the weather had been better. I would have stopped to refuel and continued on my way, just like so many planes had done decades before me.

By the time the weather cleared and I was ready to set out for Greenland, a small group of my new friends gathered to see me off. With hugs all around, they gave me a box of Tim Horton's TimBits and some homemade Bakeapple and Partridge Berry Jam to remember my time in Newfoundland.

After waving goodbye to the small group of locals on the shoreline, I powered up my trusty De Havilland Beaver and was soon airborne heading east with tears in my eyes, a boxful of TimBits on the seat next to me, and a collection of memories from my long journey across the great continent that I called home. But it was time to leave Canada behind and head to the far north. Up ahead of me was Greenland, where I would stop to refuel before heading onward toward the first major stop on my epic flight around the world. I was headed to a land of Vikings and volcanoes—and ice.

Iceland.

Chapter Three

Welcome To Iceland

Flying over the vast emptiness of Greenland was like flying over the surface of some distant icy planet in a faraway galaxy. The mountains and glaciers and endless ice looked like something from another world—a cold, alien world where there could not possibly be any life.

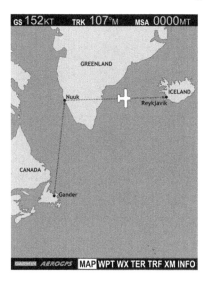

And yet there *was* life. I had just left the capital city of Nuuk a few hours earlier, and although the term 'city' probably isn't what one would normally apply to a place with a population of sixteen thousand people, by Greenland standards it was a metropolis. Snuggled between the array of colorful little houses and apartment blocks scattered across the rocky peninsula, Nuuk has an airport, a university, office buildings, museums, and all the things you normally associate with cities. (I am not sure if there is an escalator anywhere in Nuuk, however. I have always believed that real cities always have an escalator somewhere. If you don't have an escalator, then you're not a real city.)

Since leaving Nuuk, I hadn't seen a single sign of life on the desolate landscape of rock and ice beneath me. Humans had been living in Greenland for more than a thousand years, but apparently, they stuck to the coastlines, because the enormous ice cap down below hardly looked suitable for human habitation, except maybe for scientists on some kind of extreme expedition.

As I passed over the eastern coastline of Greenland, I was dazzled by the millions of white-blue icebergs littering the inlets and waters below me. In the bright sun, they sparkled like tiny diamonds and sapphires floating on the water. It was such an astonishingly beautiful sight that I couldn't resist taking my trusty De Havilland Beaver down to a lower altitude for a closer look.

As I got closer, I could see that what had appeared to be tiny icebergs from thousands of feet in the air were actually enormous frozen castles set adrift in the waters after breaking loose from the ice packs and glaciers that make up the coastline. In the sunlight, these fortresses of ice were a blinding blaze of white light that made me shield my eyes from the glare. The white faded to an exquisite and ethereal blue that I was quite familiar with from the glaciers I'd seen in Alaska the previous summer.

Greenland was a lot like Alaska in many ways, but it was also very different. Alaska is hardly what you would call a densely populated area of the world, but compared to what I was experiencing in Greenland, it was crowded and teeming with people. The isolation and desolation of Greenland was like nothing I had ever experienced before.

Leaving Greenland behind, I climbed back up to cruising altitude and continued across the open ocean toward Iceland. Below me was a different kind of desolation—nothing but water as far as the eye could see. Although the seas looked calm from high up in the air, I could tell from the whitecaps on the surface far below that there was a lot of wind and waves down there.

As I continued across the open water, I turned my mind to what waited for me up ahead. I was flying into Iceland's capital city of Reykjavík where I was meeting the family of a friend of Charlie's who had graciously offered to let me stay with them for a couple of weeks while I explored the country.

I didn't like the idea of imposing myself on other people, but when I told Charlie that I was planning to stop in Iceland to explore for a while, he insisted on calling up his friend and arranging for me to stay with his family. They were delighted to have me, Charlie said, but I was still reluctant.

"You can't experience a country or its culture properly if you're sleeping in some hotel," Charlie said.

"I wouldn't sleep in a hotel," I replied. "My plane is outfitted so I can sleep in the back whenever and wherever I need to."

"Nevertheless," Charlie replied insistently. "My point is still valid. In order to truly experience a culture you have to get down into it—get dirty—and spend time with some locals."

He was right, of course. I did want to get down and dirty into every country and culture where I planned to stop on my way around the world. So I forced myself to put my stubborn pride aside and decided that accepting the generosity of others didn't always mean I would be imposing myself on them. It was like Charlie said: They would be as interested in meeting me and hearing my stories as I would be in meeting them and hearing theirs.

Konrad was the name of Charlie's friend, and he and his family were somewhere down below waiting for me as I approached Iceland's western shore and flew past rocky fields of lava and mountains toward the capital city. As I continued down toward Reykjavík, I could see that it was definitely a real city. I don't know if there were any escalators down there, but the city is sprawling and huge, and spans countless inlets and peninsulas along the rocky shoreline.

Dominating the skyline of the central downtown core of Reykjavík is the towering spire of a strangely shaped white church. It is more or less in the form of what you would consider a normal church, but there is something dramatic and unusual about the way the spire seems to swoop up into the sky in a dazzling tower of white. It is perched atop a hill with a commanding view of the city spread out all around it, and this only adds to its dominance over the surrounding landscape.

I brought myself in for a windy and bumpy landing at the harbor next to the downtown area and taxied into my pre-arranged mooring place in the nearby marina. As I pulled in, I could see a family of four waiting for me on the dock.

The father of the group was a handsome man in his late forties with a healthy collection of gray in his dark brown hair and beard, and a smile that had *welcome* written all over it. His wife was a beautiful and stately woman in her early forties with dark blonde hair and a somewhat serious expression on her face that broke easily into a wide smile when she saw my plane approaching. Their daughter looked to be around twenty years old with long, straight, jet black hair and dark blue eyes and a similar sort of serious expression that she had clearly inherited from her mother. The littlest of the group was a young boy about four or five years old, with messy brown hair that blew around in the strong wind that was buffeting the harbor. He looked like a miniature version of his father.

The four of them smiled and waved excitedly as my plane pulled up to the dock. I shut down my engine and coasted in. Konrad tied me up to the dock like a pro before I had even fully climbed out of the cockpit. Charlie had mentioned to me that Konrad had worked in Alaska on fishing boats when he was younger, and the ease with which he fixed my mooring lines showed that he surely hadn't forgotten his earlier life as a fisherman.

"Welcome to Reykjavík!" he cried as he strode over to shake my hand firmly with his big strong hands. "Konrad Cooper—nice to meet you."

"Nice to meet you," I replied, shaking his hand in return as vigorously as I could.

"And this is Ásta, my wife," he said, gesturing to the stately blonde woman standing next to him. The pronunciation of her name sounded strange to my ears—something like '*outschta'*.

"We are so thrilled to see you!" Ásta said, also stepping forward to shake my hand with as much enthusiasm as her husband but with considerably less force.

"I am thrilled to be here!" I replied excitedly. Their enthusiastic welcome was contagious.

"I'm Kristín," the beautiful dark-haired girl said quietly as she leaned forward to shake my hand. The pronunciation of her name was a little easier, sounding something like '*krishteen*'.

"And this is Pétur," Ásta said, patting the head of the young boy with messy hair who was hiding timidly behind her while holding tightly onto her hand. Pétur's name was another tough one to pronounce, sounding something like '*pyetur*'. Clearly, I was going to have to see all of their names written down and hear them pronounced a few more times before I got them right.

I kneeled down on the dock in front of the young boy and extended my hand in greeting. He shyly slipped behind his mother's leg, and we all laughed. I smiled at him brightly, and after a moment, he gave me a faint smile in return.

I'll take that, I thought as I rose to my feet again. *That's good enough for me.*

I was now officially welcomed to Iceland.

"It is a pleasure to meet all of you—Mr. and Mrs. Cooper, Kristín, and Pétur," I said, turning to each in greeting as I said their names. I made a funny face at Pétur as I struggled to pronounce his name, and he smiled and giggled.

"It is a pleasure to meet you too," Ásta replied with a warm smile. "But please call us Konrad and Ásta."

Fair enough. I nodded in agreement. But older people always say that, don't they? They don't seem to understand that it feels impolite to address someone you just met as anything but Mr. or Mrs. I suppose it's the same as how younger people don't understand that calling them that makes them feel old, which is precisely why they tell people to call them by their first names instead.

"There are a couple of things you probably should know about Icelandic names," Konrad said with a grin. "They are a bit different than we're used to in North America. I know when I first came here it took me a while to get used to it."

"Oh, I'm sorry," I replied, hoping that I hadn't made some kind of cultural gaffe so soon after arriving. "But aren't you from Iceland?"

He laughed heartily. "Goodness, no," he replied. "Didn't Charlie tell you? I'm from Alaska, the same as him."

I wrinkled my forehead, thinking this over.

"He said that he used to work on your family's fishing boat when he was younger," I replied, embarrassed. "I guess I never put two and two together, and just assumed you were from Iceland."

"I suppose I *am* from Iceland nowadays, after living here so long," Konrad replied, giving his wife a rough hug around her shoulders. "When

I first came over to work, I only planned to stay a couple of years, but I just fell in love with this place and with this beautiful girl here and ended up staying."

"It is amazing here," I agreed, gesturing across the harbor to the distant snow-peaked mountains beyond. They were unlike the kind of mountains I was used to back home in Canada or in Alaska. They had an unfamiliar look and tint to them, but they were beautiful all the same.

"It certainly is," Konrad agreed. "But now it's time for your first lesson in Icelandic culture."

"Ok," I replied. "Hit me with it."

"I am Konrad Cooper," he said, patting himself on the chest. "My wife is Ásta Einarsdóttir, my daughter is Kristín Ástasdóttir, and this little guy down there is Pétur Ástasson."

"Huh?" I asked, confused. Why did everyone have a different last name? Did they all have different parents? That wasn't possible, was it? I struggled to imagine the complicated family tree that would explain such a scenario.

"In Iceland," Konrad explained. "They don't use family names as last names like we do in North America. Instead they have a system that uses the names of their parents to make their last names."

I was confused.

"For example, my father's name was Einar," Ásta said, seeing my confusion and taking over the explanation. "And I am his daughter so my name is Ásta Einarsdóttir. 'Einarsdóttir' means 'daughter of Einar'."

I nodded, still confused. I wasn't sure I understood.

"Kristín is Ásta's daughter," Konrad continued. "So she becomes Kristín Ástasdóttir—or 'daughter of Ásta'. And Pétur is Pétur Ástasson—'son of Ásta'."

The four of them looked at me optimistically, hoping that I understood. I nodded again as my brain thought it over. I hoped that I was finally starting to understand.

"Normally in Iceland we would use the father's name to form our children's last names," Ásta said. "Like with mine: Einarsdóttir. But it's not a strict rule, and since Konrad was a foreigner and there were difficulties with the Mannanafnanefnd, we decided to just use my name instead."

"The Mannanafnanafund...?" I asked, unable to replicate the pronunciation of the strange word she had just said.

"The Mannanafnanefnd," Konrad said, both of us laughing at my terrible pronunciation. "The Icelandic Naming Committee."

This was getting more confusing by the second.

"The Icelandic Naming Committee?" I asked with what was surely a look of confused desperation on my face.

"Exactly," Konrad replied. "It's a committee that decides which names are allowed in Iceland and which are not."

"You're kidding," I replied in disbelief.

Konrad shook his head. "I'm one hundred percent serious," he replied. "In order for a name to be allowed in Iceland, it must approved by the Mannanafnanefnd. And in order for that to happen it has to be on their list of acceptable Icelandic names or submitted for approval as a new name."

"And for a name to be accepted by the Mannanafnanefnd," Ásta explained, laughing at my confusion, "it must be proven to have occurred at least three times in Icelandic history. If not, then it is evaluated by the committee who will decide whether it is compatible with Icelandic tradition and culture and whether it is consistent with the Icelandic alphabet and grammar."

My facial expression became even more disbelieving and confused, and increasingly desperate.

"My name is actually Conrad Cooper, both with a C," Konrad said. But when I came here and planned to stay, I had to change my first name to Konrad with a K because there is no C in the Icelandic alphabet."

"Are you serious?" I replied, raising my eyebrows. "And what about your last name? Kooper with a K?"

Konrad shook his head and laughed. "I wish," he replied. "My last name actually became Jónsson—son of Jón—because my father's name is John."

"So your name in Iceland is Konrad Jónsson?" I asked as I tried to sort out the incredibly complicated twists and turns of what they were telling me.

Both Ásta and Konrad shook their heads.

"Unfortunately not," Ásta said. "The naming committee ultimately rejected the name Konrad as being un-Icelandic, so Conrad chose the closest thing we could think of, and he became Karl instead. So now he is Karl Jónsson."

I stared at them blankly, trying to decide whether they were being serious of just playing some complicated practical joke on me.

Konrad stuck out his hand toward me in a mock greeting. "Hello," he said sarcastically. "I am Conrad Cooper—oops, I mean, Karl Jónsson."

"That is completely crazy," I replied, still unsure that I understood.

"Fortunately," Konrad said with a sigh of relief, "a few years after I arrived they relaxed the naming laws for foreigners, and I was allowed to use my real name again, although I kept the spelling of my first name as Konrad with a K just to keep things simpler in my day-to-day life. So now, I am myself again—almost. I am Konrad Cooper."

I wrinkled my forehead and nose as I thought all of this through. "So Kristín and Pétur," I said slowly, "should be Kristín Karlsdóttir and Pétur Karlsson?"

"Exactly!" Ásta replied brightly. "But in Iceland, it's also acceptable to use a mother's name as well, even though it's less common."

"And we liked the idea of using Ásta's name since she's Icelandic," Konrad said. "It just felt better that way. So we used her name for the kids instead."

"I think I've got it," I said after I finished working the whole thing through in my head one last time. "But it's really strange."

"You ain't seen nothing yet," Konrad said mysteriously as he clapped me on the shoulder. "Welcome to Iceland."

Chapter Four

What A Strange And Amazing Country

After stuffing a change of clothes into my backpack, I left the harbor with Konrad and his family, and immediately we found ourselves in downtown Reykjavík.

The streets of Reykjavík are lined with cute little colorful houses and buildings, which gave them a very European look to me. (Of course, I had no idea what European should look like since this was the first time I'd been outside of North America, but to my inexperienced eyes, that's how they looked.)

We stopped in front of a building at the corner of a small square, where we climbed through a door and up some stairs to a tiny restaurant perched on the floor above a wool shop. Konrad seemed to know the owner, who greeted him enthusiastically before leading us up another flight of stairs to a small narrow side room with windows overlooking the square below.

"This is amazing," I said as the owner took all of our jackets and left us to our own private dining room. "But you didn't have to go to all this trouble."

"Don't be silly," Ásta replied with a wave of her hand. "It's no trouble at all."

"This is your welcome to Iceland," Konrad said. "How can you expect us to not celebrate the occasion appropriately?"

As I sat down, I noticed on the other side of the table that Pétur was smiling shyly across at me as he clutched a piece of newspaper. He tugged on his mother's sleeve and whispered in her ear.

"Pétur wants to know if you will sign an autograph," Ásta said.

"An autograph?" I asked, surprised.

"You're famous," Kristín said, reaching across the table to borrow Pétur's newspaper clipping. Carefully unfolding the paper, she leaned over to show it to me.

"What is this?!?" I asked in shock as I read the article.

CANADA'S YOUNG NEW AMELIA EARHART
SETS OFF ON AROUND-THE-WORLD SOLO FLIGHT
By Iain Reid of the Vancouver Sun

She's hard to miss in her brightly painted red and white De Havilland seaplane roaring across the harbor of Tofino, a small fishing village overlooking the Pacific Ocean on Vancouver Island off the western coast of Canada. A hundred or so excited local supporters and tourists turned out to see eighteen-year-old Kitty Hawk off in style as she began her attempt to make a solo flight around the world. They cheered loudly as her heavily fuelled and specially equipped seaplane lifted up off the waters of the harbor and into the clear blue skies on the first leg of a flight that will take her across Canada and the United States, and then to Europe, Africa, Asia, and Australia before returning home again to North America.

"It's not a race," Kitty says humbly of her ambitious undertaking. She is not trying to set any speed records, nor is she promoting any causes or trying to raise funds for charity. She simply wants to do what most young people her age want to do after leaving high school. She's just doing it in her own unique way. "I just want to see the world," she says. "I want to see what's out there."

While some might have concerns about such a young pilot making a potentially dangerous flight as this one, Kitty's parents are not worried.

"Kitty's been flying with me since before she was in kindergarten," her father says. "She had hundreds, if not thousands, of flying hours before she even applied for her official pilot's license. And she's a natural at it. I think there are very few pilots better than her in the entire world."

Kitty's flying skill will be tested during the long journey ahead of her. Her plan is to make her way around the globe in a series of short flights from one stop to the next, pausing at each not only to refuel her plane but also to accommodate her endless curiosity about our planet.

Follow Kitty's progress around the world on Twitter @kittyhawkworld.

Next to the article was a photograph of me leaning against my plane back home in Tofino with a caption that read: "Teenage pilot Kitty Hawk with her seaplane as she prepares for her flight around the world."

"This is unbelievable," I said as I read the article for a second time. When I had spoken to the reporter back in Tofino, I'd known that he would write something about me for the local newspaper, but I had no idea it would go beyond that. "Where did you get this?" I asked.

"We clipped it from the *International Herald Tribune*," Kristín said. "This article was in every major newspaper in the world."

I couldn't believe it. "I'm sorry," I said after I read the article for a third time and searched my pockets for something to sign the article for Pétur. "This is just a bit overwhelming for me."

"See?" Kristín said, handing me a pen. "You're famous."

I took the pen and tried to think of something clever to write. It wasn't easy.

Thank you for the warm welcome to your cold country, I wrote in some of the dead space at the corner of my picture and signed my name.

"Takk," Pétur said quietly as I handed the newspaper clipping back to him.

"Pétur says 'thank you'," Kristín told me as the food began to arrive. The waitress set down bowls of soup and steaming plates of fish in front of us.

"The soup is chilled pea," Konrad explained. "And the fish is salted cod with some herb skyr on the side, which is a kind of Icelandic yoghurt that they've been eating here for more than a thousand years."

"It's not yoghurt, Konrad," Ásta scolded.

"Sorry, dear," Konrad replied. He raised a hand to his mouth to stage whisper an aside to me. "Icelanders don't like their national food to be called yoghurt," he explained.

"That's because it's *not* yoghurt," Ásta said.

"How else am I supposed to describe it to someone who's never had it?" Konrad protested. "As Icelandic semi-liquid whipped cheese? Mmmmm... that sounds enticing."

Everyone laughed.

"You'll have to learn to love skyr," Kristín said. "Everyone in Iceland eats it."

I reached over to scoop a bit of the thick white yoghurt-like substance onto the tip of my spoon, and tasted it cautiously.

"Oh," I said, surprised by the thick, rich texture and taste. "That's so good! It's like yoghurt, only better."

"It's not yoghurt!" Ásta and Kristín both said in unison, and everyone laughed again.

Whatever it was, the skyr was delicious and went perfectly with the flaky white fish. The soup was also amazing—salty and meaty—although I admit that I was a bit uncertain about eating cold soup at first. Where I grew up, soup was always served and eaten hot.

The main course for the night was roasted lamb, which Konrad assured me was something that was as Icelandic as you could get. The meat was soft and tender, and by the end of the meal, I had eaten far more than I should have. It was a good thing I was still wearing my flying sweats—the yoga sweatpants I always wore when flying—because I had plenty of extra room to expand. I normally wouldn't be caught dead leaving the house with them on, but when I know I'll be sitting in an airplane cockpit for eight to twelve hours a day, I always choose comfort over style.

We lingered for a long time over dessert and coffee, talking and laughing in our private little dining room. Pétur curled up on the floor on a pile of jackets and fell asleep while the rest of us continued talking.

I didn't realize how late it was or how long we had been sitting there because it was still light outside. At some point, I looked at my watch and was stunned to see that it was almost eleven o'clock at night.

"It's so late!" I said in surprise, looking at the other's puzzled faces.

"How is it still daylight when it's eleven at night?"

"We're so far north that it stays quite bright for most of the day at this time of year," Konrad explained, also looking at his watch.

"In a few weeks the sun won't even have set by this time of night," Kristín added. "In mid-June it doesn't set until around midnight."

"The sun sets at midnight?!?" I asked in amazement.

Everyone nodded as though this were the most normal thing in the world.

"And then rises again a few hours later," Kristín said.

"Unbelievable," I said. I'd experienced almost endless summer days the previous summer in Alaska, but this was really remarkable.

"We need all the daylight to make up for the lack of sun in winter," Ásta explained. "In winter, we go to work and school in total darkness. The sun rises sometime around eleven in the morning, then sets again a few hours later."

"Unbelievable," I said again, and then the restaurant owner appeared, gently reminding us that he was ready to close for the night. Konrad paid the bill while Ásta collected the sleeping Pétur from his nest on the floor.

After we left the restaurant, Konrad dropped off Kristín and me at her nearby apartment. The family had arranged for me to stay with her for the duration of my time in Iceland. I didn't even bother protesting and explaining to them that I was perfectly happy to sleep in my plane. I knew that it was a lost cause because Kristín had a spare bedroom, and besides, I have to admit that I was dying for a shower.

Kristín's apartment was small but comfortable, and again, it looked very European to my eyes. She showed me to my room and the bathroom, and soon I was standing under the hot bliss of a steaming shower of water and washing away the sweat and grime of my day.

As I showered, I noticed a rather pungent smell in the air overwhelming the scent of my Rock Star soap from Lush. It smelled like something rotten—rotten eggs, to be exact. I sniffed around and decided that it was the smell of sulphur, and it was coming from the tap water.

After I toweled myself off and changed into some appropriate sleeping clothes, I mentioned this to Kristín.

"I don't even notice it," Kristín said with a laugh and a shrug. "In Iceland, almost all the hot water for showers and heating comes from underground geothermal sources. They just drill a hole and out comes enough hot water to meet everyone's needs. It just smells a bit, that's all."

What a strange and amazing country, I thought as I lay awake that night trying to fall asleep. It was well past midnight, and outside my window, the sun finally had managed to set.

After lying in the darkness for a few minutes, wide awake, I switched on my iPhone to check my Twitter account. I was astounded to see that my number of followers had jumped from seven (Mom, Dad, Skeena, Skeena's dad, Charlie, Will, and Jay, but not Buck—he didn't believe in Twitter, he told me) to over four hundred. More than four hundred people were now following me as I made my journey around the world.

"You'd better tell them something," I said to myself and typed in a message.

Kitty Hawk @kittyhawkworld
Arrived in Reykjavik! Ate cold pea soup and salted cod with skyr. The sun never seems to set but now I have to sleep. Goodnight, everyone.

Chapter Five

This Is So Cool

"This is so cool," Kristín said as she pulled herself up into the co-pilot's seat of my plane. I pulled myself in next to her and tried to move some of my junk out of the way so she could sit properly. "I can't believe you have your own plane and you're flying around the world," she said as she looked around the inside of the cockpit, her eyes wide open in amazement. "I think you might be the coolest person I have ever met."

"I guess it's pretty cool, yah," I shrugged, blushing bright red. To me this was a major compliment because Kristín was twenty years old and studying environmental engineering at the University of Iceland. She was stunningly beautiful, dressed incredibly stylishly, and seemed very grown up compared to me. It was hard to believe that she thought *I* was the cool one.

Kristín and I were climbing into my plane in preparation for a flight across Iceland to the village of Húsavík where her family had a house. Konrad's job required him to split his time between Reykjavík and Húsavík, so the family maintained houses in both locations.

Konrad, Ásta, and Pétur had left early in the morning to make the long drive to the northeastern part of the island. Meanwhile, Kristín and I slept in and were now going to cross the island by air and catch up with the rest of them in Húsavík.

"I want you to explain everything to me," Kristín said as she strapped herself in. "Tell me every step of what you have to do to fly this beautiful machine."

"Okay," I replied, smiling like crazy and flattered that she was so interested in what I was doing. "You already saw me do a walk-around outside the plane to make sure everything was working, and now I'll go through my pre-ignition checklist before I start up the engine."

Kristín listened intently as I explained each step of my pre-flight procedures, and then I started up the engine. We taxied out of the Reykjavík harbor and into open water where I powered up the engine and started my takeoff run. It was a windy day with a lot of chop, so it was quite bumpy even once we got airborne.

"Look down there. It's Viðey Island," Kristín said, pointing out her window as we pulled up into the air and made a slow turn to the northeast. "That's where the John Lennon Imagine Peace Tower is located."

"Where is it?" I asked as I looked out her window to the island below. I couldn't see a tower anywhere.

"Well, we can't see it now because it's a huge tower of light that Yoko Ono comes over every year to light on John Lennon's birthday on October ninth," Kristín explained. "And it stays on every night until December eighth, which is the day he was killed. Then it's turned on again for a while at Christmas and New Year, and sometimes on other special occasions as well."

"It's a tower of light?" I asked.

"Yeah," Kristín replied. "Like a huge beam of light that shines directly up into the sky for thousands of meters. When it's switched on you can see it from just about everywhere."

Passing over the island, I leveled out my turn and set a course for Húsavík as we climbed to a decent cruising altitude. The landscape was unlike anything I'd ever seen before: rocky and harsh, and painted by nature in varying shades of black, brown, and mossy green. Up ahead of us, a fourth color was added to the palette as an enormous ice cap came into view on the horizon. According to my GPS, this huge field of ice is called Langjökull, and is only one of many massive frozen plateaus that comprise more than ten percent of Iceland's topography.

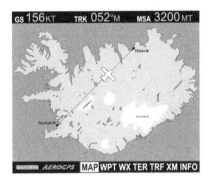

"There aren't many roads down there," I observed as we continued over the harsh landscape of rock and ice.

"No, not really," Kristín agreed. "But you can see the Ring Road off there to the left." She pointed out my window to a highway off in the distance.

"What's the Ring Road?" I asked.

"It's a road that basically makes a circle all the way around Iceland," Kristín replied. "They built it back in 1974 to celebrate the 1100th anniversary of human settlement in Iceland, although not everyone was happy about it."

"What do you mean?" I asked, unable to imagine why anyone would be unhappy about building a nice road so that people could get around the country.

"Before they built the roads," Kristín explained. "the villages on the coastlines around Iceland were kept supplied by regularly scheduled boats and ferries. But when they put in the road, it was obviously a lot easier to deliver supplies by truck. Gradually the supply boats stopped running, and many villages ended up being disconnected to the outside world. Eventually, they were just abandoned.

I laughed at the irony of this. "So they built roads to connect the country and ended up disconnecting it instead," I observed.

"Parts of it, anyway," Kristín agreed. "Some of the people from those disconnected areas moved to other villages, but a lot of them also ended up moving to Reykjavík. Iceland used to be a very rural country, but now more than half the population lives in Reykjavík."

"Half the population?" I asked, surprised. "How many people live in Iceland?"

"About three hundred twenty thousand, I think," Kristín guessed.

"And how many in Reykjavík?" I asked.

"Depends on how you count it, but probably as many as two hundred thousand people live in the greater area of the city."

Looking down at the desolate landscape below, it wasn't hard to believe that so many of the country's people lived in Reykjavík—more than sixty percent of them, leaving much of the rest of the island barren and empty.

As we flew on, I thought about this a bit more and was surprised by how few people there are in Iceland. By North American standards, the population of the entire country is barely enough to qualify as a decent sized city.

"But if your population is only around three hundred thousand people," I said, thinking aloud, "how many understand English? Because even though I've only been here for a day, it seems like everyone can speak perfect English."

Kristín thought about this for a moment. "I'm not sure," she replied slowly. "But I think most people do. Everyone I've ever met speaks English."

We flew in silence for a few moments as I thought about this.

"Then why are so many English books translated into Icelandic?" I asked. Earlier that morning when Kristín and I walked through the city, I had seen bookstores with a lot of English-language books translated into Icelandic. That seemed like an awful lot of effort for a mere three hundred thousand people, most of whom probably read English anyway. I mean, I know it's nicer to read a book in your native language, but surely it costs a lot of money to get a book translated, right? Could it possibly be worth it to translate so many books?

"Aha! That I can explain," Kristín replied proudly. "That's because Iceland has a one hundred percent literacy rate. And not only can everyone in Iceland read; they also read *a lot*."

"So I guess it makes sense to make the effort to translate books into Icelandic," I said, "even though so many people can read English."

"Exactly," Kristín replied with a grin. "Icelanders read more books per capita than any other population in the world. I guess we have to in order to survive the long, cold winter nights."

"You read more books per capita than the rest of the *world*?" I replied. "That's impressive."

Kristín nodded. "It's true," she replied with a weak smile. "But we also drink more Coca-Cola per capita than the rest of the world, too, and I'm not sure that's what you'd call a very impressive statistic."

Chapter Six

That's Where It Gets Complicated

The next morning Konrad, Kristín, and I found ourselves bouncing along the rough back roads of northeast Iceland in their Land Rover. Konrad was taking me up to see one of the places where he worked—a vast dam-building project along the Jökulsá á Fjöllum River in the northeastern highlands. (Don't even ask me to pronounce *that* one. It was hard enough trying to spell it.)

We drove out of the village of Húsavík where I'd spent the night with Konrad's family after flying out the previous day with Kristín. Húsavík is a cute little fishing village nestled on a long inlet at the foot of some mountains and cliffs that plunge directly into the ocean.

As we drove out of the town, we passed by some colorful houses and wooden churches before leaving the ocean behind us and climbing steadily into the hills. The landscape was covered in dark rock and red soil with green grasses and moss that spread like a carpet into the distance toward great sloping cliffs and mountain peaks. Although it was quite desolate and barren, the sheer power of the landscape was spectacular, and it left me breathless.

"Look over there!" I cried out, pointing off to the left where clouds of white smoke in the distance rose up over green fields dotted with grazing sheep. "Is something on fire?!?"

"Steam," Konrad replied calmly, "from inside the ground."

I took a second look at the billowing clouds and saw that he was right. It wasn't smoke. It was far too white and clean, and it evaporated into the atmosphere as it was carried downwind.

As we drove closer, I could see tiny wisps of steam rising from cracks and fissures in the ground all around us. The entire area was alive with geothermal activity.

"This area is called Þeistareykir," Konrad said. "And it was once the location of the biggest sulphur mine in Iceland. You can probably smell the sulphur, actually."

"I sure can," I replied. I sniffed the air cautiously and recognized the same odor that I'd noticed when I took a shower in Kristín's flat in Reykjavík. I wrinkled my nose and tried to block it out.

"Back when Denmark controlled Iceland," Konrad said, "this area was a very important place because sulphur was needed for making gunpowder. And with all the wars that Denmark was fighting in those days, they needed a lot of gunpowder."

"And nowadays?" I asked.

Konrad shook his head and grinned. "Well, Denmark doesn't fight wars anymore as far as I know," he said. "And I guess there are better places to get sulphur these days anyway. But the thing about this place that people are now interested in is the geothermal energy. This whole area is being developed, and they are building a huge geothermal power plant up here."

Konrad turned the steering wheel, and we bounced off one rough-and-tumble road onto another. I grasped the shoulder strap of my seatbelt and hung on as best I could as the Land Rover pitched and heaved around the corner.

"There's a lot of intense heat and steam under the ground here in Iceland," Konrad explained. "So if you drill a deep enough hole, you get an inexhaustible supply of free steam that can be used to drive turbines and generate electricity."

"And this is what you work on?" I asked. "I mean, this is your job?"

"Let me put it this way," Konrad said. "When I was a kid, my favorite thing was playing with LEGO."

"Mine too," Kristín said from the back seat. She had insisted I sit in the front so I could have the best view.

"And my favorite thing to do with LEGO," Konrad said, "was to design and build my own creations—buildings, machines, spaceships, whatever. You name it. So I guess it's not much of a surprise that I became an engineer."

"Except that the work you do right now is not exactly engineering, is it Dad?" Kristín said, reaching forward to pat her father on the shoulder.

"Yeah, thanks for reminding me," Konrad replied, shaking his head sadly. "It's more like babysitting."

"How do you mean?" I asked.

"I'm a liaison officer between the various parties who have interests in the different construction projects we're doing out here," Konrad explained, ticking them off on his fingers as we drove. "The various aluminum companies, the Icelandic energy companies, environmental groups, the government offices and ministries, the general public, and so on. I need my background in engineering to do my job, but Kristín is right, at the moment it basically boils down to being a glorified babysitter."

"But what do you mean by babysitting?" I asked. "Are all those people not able to get along?"

Kristín and Konrad both burst into laughter. "I'm sorry," Konrad said, looking over with a grin. "I shouldn't laugh. But let's just say no, they don't get along at all."

"What's the problem?" I asked.

"The problem is this right here," Konrad said, gesturing out of the window as he pulled off to the side of the road and switched off the engine so we could get out of the car. We were overlooking a rugged river valley. As soon as I opened my door, I could hear the distant roar of a river far below us.

Looking down toward the noise of the water, I saw a fast-moving river cutting its way through a majestic canyon with dark, sheer cliffs spotted with green moss on either side. Scattered along the length of the canyon were a variety of different earth-moving machines, bulldozers, and backhoes standing idle next to the scarred faces of the rock and earth that they were carving their way through.

"The energy companies are building a hydroelectric dam," Kristín explained, pointing down to the construction site below. "And it will flood this entire area and create a giant lake up here."

"And that's a problem," Konrad continued, "because not everyone is exactly thrilled about it."

"The locals don't like it?" I asked.

Konrad looked around at the barren landscape. "There aren't really any locals up here except the reindeer," he said. "But across Iceland in general, even though some people are in favor of projects like these, there are many who are not. Part of my job is to facilitate communication between the different groups and keep everyone honest."

"And to try and do what's best," Kristín added.

Konrad sighed heavily. "Yeah," he said, "to try to do what's best, because I believe that these projects are good for the environment. If I didn't believe that, I wouldn't support them."

"Wait a second," I said, holding up my hand to interrupt. I wasn't sure that I'd heard him correctly. Did he say that he thought this dam-building project was *good* for the environment? As I looked around at the pristine and dramatic landscape surrounding us, I tried to imagine what it would look like if it were flooded as the result of building an enormous dam. "How can building a dam and flooding this entire area be *good* for the environment?" I asked.

Konrad smiled a thin smile. "That's where it gets complicated," he said.

Chapter Seven
It's The Elves Again

"Complicated in what way?" I asked, pressing Konrad for an explanation. "Isn't it pretty simple? You build a dam, it floods the valley, and it hurts the environment."

"Unfortunately, it's not as simple as that," Kristín said.

"When we're talking about the various energy projects in this part of Iceland—this river dam or the geothermal plants—it all comes down to aluminum," Konrad said.

"Aluminum?" I asked. "What does that have to do with anything?"

"Aluminum," Konrad explained, gesturing dramatically. "Is is one of the great substances of the universe. It's very strong. It doesn't corrode. It can easily be worked into whatever shape or form you need. And as everyone knows, it is extremely lightweight. That's why they make so many different things out of it, from soda cans, to iPads, to deodorant, to airplanes. But, best of all, it is incredibly abundant. In fact, it is the most abundant metal on earth."

"But?" I asked. I sensed there was a big 'but' coming up in Konrad's story. "What's the catch?"

"The catch," Konrad said, "is that aluminum almost never occurs in its pure form in nature. You can't just dig a hole in the ground and pull out pure aluminum."

I was confused. "What do you mean? How can it be the most abundant metal on Earth if you can't find it?"

"Because," Konrad said, "when it's chemically combined with other elements, you can find it almost anywhere. It just isn't pure aluminum."

"Oh," I replied. This was starting to sound hauntingly familiar, like something I had learned in high school chemistry class.

"Fortunately for all the iPad and airplane owners of the world," Konrad continued, winking at me, "it is possible to extract pure aluminum from the compound aluminum oxide, which in turn can be extracted from bauxite ore using a chemical process called the Bayer process, where you immerse the ore in a solution of sodium hydroxide and then take the..."

"Dad!" Kristín interrupted. "Are you serious? This is starting to sound like chemistry class!"

"Yes, I'm lost too," I said, laughing. "I'm sorry; I don't mean to be rude, but Kristín's right. You're starting to lose me with all this chemistry."

"Okay, fine, you yokels," Konrad replied, pretending to be upset. "Long story short, you take some aluminum oxide, dissolve it in some other chemicals, run electricity through it, and voila! You get pure aluminum. And that is how they have made aluminum for the last one hundred and thirty years, including the aluminum they used to build everything from your iPad to your beautiful De Havilland float plane."

"But?" I asked again, still waiting for the big 'but' in the story.

"But," Konrad said slowly, "it takes a lot of electricity. And by a lot, I really mean a *LOT* of electricity."

"And that is where the geothermal power plants and hydroelectric dams come in?" I asked.

"Exactly!" Konrad answered, jabbing his finger in the air to punctuate his answer. "The dams are built to supply electricity for a huge aluminum smelter that is being built near Húsavík."

It was all starting to make sense, despite Konrad having skipped over his detailed explanation of the chemical processes (for which I was thankful). But there was still one thing I didn't understand.

"How does all this help the environment?" I asked. "All this construction and industry sounds pretty *bad* for the environment."

"Because it's clean, renewable energy," Konrad said. "And right now most of the world's aluminum is produced using electricity from coal-burning power plants that dump millions of tons of pollution into the atmosphere. In comparison to that option, the power alternatives that Iceland has to offer are a thousand times cleaner, even if they do cause a limited amount of damage to the environment here. And that is why I support these projects."

I nodded and thought this over as I looked around at the surrounding landscape that would soon be completely underwater. I tried to imagine a giant coal power plant in its place with its towering smokestacks belching poisonous smoke into the air, or worse yet, the ominous cooling towers of a nuclear power plant up here on the summits of Iceland.

"I hadn't thought of that," I said. "I guess I forgot where electricity comes from."

"Most people do forget that," Konrad agreed. "Everyone thinks inventions like electric cars will solve all the world's problems, but no one ever thinks where the electricity to charge those cars would come from. Eighty-five percent of the world's electricity comes from burning fossil fuels. How does it make sense to burn more fossil fuels in power plants to provide electricity for electric cars?"

"I hadn't thought of that either," I agreed.

Konrad stood at the edge of the canyon looking down at the river below.

"It's beautiful here," he said, staring out across the river canyon. "I am the first to admit that building a hydroelectric dam up here will cause damage to the environment. But I am also a realist, and I know that for every ton of aluminum we can produce here using clean, renewable energy, that's one less ton that has to be produced in Russia or China or anywhere else using electricity that was produced by burning fossil fuels."

I looked out across the valley and tried to think of alternatives to both of these options.

"Wait a minute," I said. "What about recycling? Couldn't people just recycle more, and then we wouldn't need to build more power plants anywhere?"

Konrad laughed cynically.

"I'm sorry for laughing," he said. "But maybe Kristín should answer this question. This is what she's studying, after all."

"Of course people could recycle more," Kristín said. "And if they did, that would be great, but they don't. In fact, when it comes to recycling things like aluminum cans, people are actually recycling *less* of them than they were ten or fifteen years ago."

"Less?!?" I asked, surprised. "I thought the big trendy thing nowadays was being 'green' and saving the environment."

"It is," Kristín said, shrugging. "But that's what seems to be happening."

"When this huge new aluminum smelter is built," Konrad said, "and it's running at full capacity, it will produce more than half a million tons of aluminum per year. But that's just a fraction of how much aluminum is wasted every year and not recycled. Three or four times that amount of aluminum goes straight into landfills around the world just from aluminum cans alone."

"And of course aluminum isn't just used for aluminum cans," Kristín said. "It's used in all sorts of consumer packaging, building materials, and in wiring, and even things people don't think about, such as Nespresso coffee pods."

I felt a bit bad. I had a Nespresso coffee machine at home, and I wondered whether my family recycled the little aluminum coffee pods. I was fairly sure that my mother probably did, but standing up there at the edge of that beautiful, rugged river canyon and imagining the bulldozers and other construction equipment carving away at the nature far below me, the consequences of just tossing those little coffee pods in the garbage was suddenly made very real to me. When Konrad had invited me to see a bit of the countryside with him, I hadn't expected it to turn into such a heavy discussion about the environment.

"As I said, I'm a realist," Konrad concluded. "We all know that recycling helps the environment, and yet most people still don't do it. But the solution isn't to pretend that the world can be saved if only we recycled more, because most people aren't going to. Right here, right now I believe that I can make a difference by helping to build power plants that will produce clean energy and that will reduce the need to produce aluminum elsewhere using energy produced with fossil fuels. Damaging the environment here is a bad thing, there is no doubt about it, but the world isn't going 'green' as much as people like to think it is, and I believe that on a global scale, the benefits of building a power plant here far outweigh the negative aspects."

We stood there for a few moments in silence, each of us thinking our own thoughts as we looked out on the spectacular view in front of us and listened to the roar of the river far below. After a few minutes, I noticed a Land Rover off to my left grinding its way down the road toward us from the direction of the construction site.

"It's so strange to think about," I said. "That hurting the environment can actually help it."

"You don't have to take my word for it," Konrad said, looking over as the Land Rover pulled closer. "In a couple nights there's a town hall meeting back in Reykjavík between some of the locals, the energy and aluminum companies, and some environmental groups. Why don't you come along and hear from all the different sides of the argument?"

The three of us turned to watch the approaching Land Rover pull off the road close to us and skate to a halt on the dirt and rocks. The driver's door opened and a tall, rugged-looking man stepped out. He had a grim expression on his face as the wind blew the bangs of his dark grey hair across his forehead.

"This fellow right here will be at that meeting, in fact," Konrad said, smiling a broad smile as our visitor walked toward us. "This is Magnús."

Konrad and Magnús shook hands and Konrad introduced me. "This is Kitty Hawk," Konrad said as I stepped forward and shook Magnús's rough and callused hands.

"Good to meet you," Magnús said, his expression still grim as he released my hand from his powerful grip.

"Don't always look so serious," Konrad said, smiling and clapping Magnús on the shoulder. "What can possibly be so important that you had to drive up here instead of waiting for me to get down to the site?"

"It's not good news, I'm afraid," Magnús said, his serious expression unchanged. "It's all the heavy equipment back at the site. Every single machine broke down all at once this morning."

Konrad's grin evaporated quickly upon hearing the news. "*All* of them? At the same time?!?" Konrad asked in disbelief, looking down into the valley where all the machines were standing idle.

"Every single one," Magnús replied, hesitating for a moment and looking over at me before completing his sentence. "It's the elves again."

Chapter Eight

The Elves Are Very Accommodating

The elves? I thought incredulously. My ears perked up immediately when I heard Magnús attribute widespread engine failure to elves. Kristín explained it to me after we'd all jumped back into the Land Rover and continued down the rough road toward the construction site. I climbed into the back seat so that Kristín and I could speak without disturbing Konrad, who was busy talking in Icelandic to someone on his cell phone.

"In Iceland many people believe in elves and other invisible beings," Kristín said. "We call them the Huldufólk—the Hidden People."

"The Huldufólk," I repeated, struggling a bit with the pronunciation.

"There are different stories that tell how they came to be," Kristín explained. "But the explanation that I've heard the most is that somewhere in some long lost book of the bible there is a story about Eve and her children. God tells Eve that he will visit her, so she hurries to wash and clean all of her many children before God arrives. By the time he appears, however, some of the children are still unwashed, so in embarrassment, Eve hides them out of sight behind the house or something. But of course God isn't fooled by this, and as a punishment, he hides those children and all their ancestors from human sight for all eternity."

"That's harsh," I said, "if it's true."

Kristín nodded, laughing. "But that's the story, anyway, whether it's true or a myth."

"But why would these Hidden People or elves want to sabotage the construction equipment at the site?" I asked.

Kristín shrugged. "In Iceland," she said, "sometimes road works or construction projects encounter unexplained breakdowns or bad luck because the human plans interfere with the homes or lives of the hidden world. When that happens, there is trouble for a while, but in the end, they always work it out somehow. Maybe they have to change the road to avoid a certain area or move some boulders or rocks to a different location, or something like that, but they always seem to work it out."

Kristín could see the skeptical look on my face and turned to give me a grin. "The elves are very accommodating," she explained. "And much more understanding than humans are."

"What about you?" I asked. "Do you believe in the Hidden People?"

Kristín shrugged. "Maybe it's just nonsense," she replied, turning to look me in the eye. "But you never know, so I don't take any chances."

Konrad pulled our Land Rover to a stop next to some machines and a portable office trailer in the middle of the vast construction site. We all stepped out of the car into a cold, stiff wind and walked over to where Magnús was waiting with a couple of construction workers wearing hardhats.

As the group of them held a heated conversation in Icelandic, I wandered a bit to have a look around. The landscape in Iceland was fascinating to me. It was like nothing I'd ever seen before. It was like the surface of some far distant planet in a different galaxy—rugged and beautiful in its harshness. I thought about the existence of a hidden world here in Iceland, and it was easy to believe that such a landscape was home to beings other than humans.

I walked over toward one of the bulldozers and kicked with my boots at the rocks and mud on the ground surrounding it. It had rained the night before, and there were plenty of footprints in the muddy soil from the various workmen who'd tried to get the machine working that morning. You could almost feel their frustration by looking at the chaotic pattern of boot prints in the mud.

Maybe I can find some elf prints! I thought suddenly, smiling to myself at the thought of it.

I scanned the ground for any unusual traces that the invisible creatures might have left behind on their mission to sabotage the construction equipment. A number of different people had been walking around this particular machine that morning. I could make out tracks from various different types of deep-treaded work boots and running shoes. I could even see from the impressions that my own boots were leaving in the mud that someone at the construction site had been wearing the same kind of Blundstone boots I was wearing, except theirs were a larger size. I couldn't find anything that looked remotely like elf footprints, though. Not that I knew what elf footprints looked like, but I guess I was imagining some tiny pointy magical boot prints or something like that.

"Why would elves have tiny magical boots on?" the little voice inside my head asked me. "It's muddy and wet out here. Why wouldn't they be wearing normal shoes?"

"What exactly *are* normal shoes for an elf?" I asked myself, but the little voice didn't have an answer for that. "Maybe they are barefoot?"

"What are you looking for?" Konrad asked with a smile as he, Kristín, and Magnús walked over toward me. "Elf prints?"

Busted!

I blushed red in embarrassment and shrugged my shoulders as they approached.

"Maybe," I replied, sheepishly. "But I don't even know what that would look like."

"You won't find any prints left behind," Magnús explained. "They never leave any trace except the broken machinery."

"But what will you do?" I asked. "What do they want?"

"We'll have to wait until tomorrow to find out," Magnús replied. "We've called in a special psychic who knows about these things, and she will come out here tomorrow and talk to the elves for us."

"A psychic?" I asked, raising my eyebrows skeptically, but Magnús didn't seem to notice. "Do you mean a sort of... elf negotiator?"

"Já, exactly," Magnús replied. "Maybe some elf house is in the way and needs to be moved, or something like that, but whatever it is, she will sort it out with them and we can continue building."

"The elves are very accommodating," Kristín whispered to me again with a grin.

I couldn't help but smile broadly at the thought of all this. I was definitely learning a lot about the construction business, Icelandic style.

"My guess is that the problem is with this stone right up here," Magnús added, pointing toward a large black boulder off to the left of our group. I looked over to see a towering stone rising up out of the rocky landscape like a dark finger, its surface jagged and dark with patches of green moss covering its face. "I've always had a bad feeling about that one," Magnús said, nodding earnestly. "Up here in these mountains is where the trolls live."

Trolls too? I thought to myself. *This just keeps getting better and better.*

Chapter Nine
We Don't Even Notice Our Own Blindness

"The elves and the Hidden People are not the same," the short, squat woman sitting across from me said. "And the trolls are something else entirely as well."

Her name was Halldóra Sæfinnsdóttir, and she was the psychic that Konrad and his company had asked to come out to the construction site to speak to the elves. She was a small but strong-looking woman in her late thirties with dark blonde hair, which she wore cut short (a bit like an elf), and she had a flat but kind face etched with the first shallow wrinkles of age from a life spent in the wind and snow. We were sitting next to each other in the back of Konrad's Land Rover as we bounced along the rough back roads up to the construction site for the dam. For me it was my second trip there in as many days, but I couldn't resist the opportunity to speak to Halldóra in person and watch her negotiate with the elves, so Konrad had arranged for us to ride together on the way out so we could chat.

"What is the difference between the elves and Hidden People?" I asked.

Halldóra smiled and put her hand on my knee. "They are hardly much different from you and me," she replied brightly. "They are humanoids, just like us. In fact, the Hidden People look so much like you and me that I don't always recognize them for what they are. Their style of dress usually gives them away. They dress simply, like farmers or shepherds, and they are simple folk who take care of their families and live happy, uncomplicated lives."

"And the elves?" I asked enthusiastically.

"The elves are different," Halldóra replied. "And they come in all sorts of shapes and sizes. There are tree elves that stand ten meters tall and tiny little house elves that are barely taller than a large dog. There are even smaller ones, like flower elves, and so on. What sets them apart the most, for me, is how colorful they are. They often dress in colorful clothing and I can usually spot them from quite a distance."

"So you can see them?" I asked enthusiastically.

"Of course I can!" Halldóra replied with a laugh, her eyes sparkling. "In fact, I can see dozens of them right now, lining the sides of the road. They must know that I am coming out here to talk with them."

I turned my head to look at the ragged landscape scrolling past us outside the window. The weather was overcast and gray, and a light mist was clinging to the distant cliffs and mountains—perfect conditions to lend an air of mystery to the day—but as hard as I tried, I couldn't see anything or anyone lining the sides of the road as we rumbled past.

I turned back to face Halldóra and saw her waving out of her window at some unseen being at the side of the road. "Hello, little one!" she called out, laughing.

"But why can't I see them?" I asked after Halldóra turned back again. "Can you see them because you have special awareness and abilities that most people don't have?"

Halldóra took a deep breath and thought this over. "I think so," she replied, nodding.

"My friend told me a story about a lost book of the bible," I said, thinking back to what Kristín had told me the day before. "And God and Eve and her children being hidden from sight."

Halldóra nodded along as I spoke. "Yes, yes, I know the story," she said. "But that's all just fairytales and storytelling."

It was funny to hear a woman who had just been waving out the car window to some invisible elves dismiss this explanation as a fairytale.

"What do you think it is, then? I mean, what are they?" I asked.

"I think the explanation is much more scientific," Halldóra replied, surprising me by saying this. "Do you know those optical illusion tests you can take to find the blind spot in your vision?"

I shook my head. "I don't think so," I said. I wasn't sure what she meant.

"It doesn't matter," she replied, with a wave of her palm. "You can check it out later on the Internet. But the important thing is this: Every person has a blind spot in the middle of his vision where he cannot see anything—nothing at all—right in the very center."

I crossed my eyes to check my vision for this but couldn't see what she meant. I had no idea what she was talking about.

"What do you mean?" I asked, confused. "I can see perfectly well."

"You only *think* you can because your mind compensates for it," Halldóra replied, pointing a finger directly at my right eyeball. "But in actuality, there is a blind spot right in the dead center of your vision where the light that comes in goes straight back to a point on your retina where the optic nerves that lead to your brain are located. At this one small spot, there are no receptors, and therefore you and I and everyone else has a blind spot there."

I crossed my eyes again, pulling them back in my head and struggling to see what she was talking about. "That's impossible," I said. "I can't see any such thing."

Halldóra laughed. "Of course you can't see it. No one can," she said. "But you can't always believe what you see—or what you don't see, for that matter—but something is there whether you see it or not; trust me."

"But how is it that I can't see it?" I replied, still stubbornly crossing and un-crossing my eyes trying to see what she was talking about.

"Because your mind is a very powerful thing," Halldóra replied, tapping her right temple with the tip of her finger. "Much more powerful than most people realize. It uses the information it receives from the other areas of your vision to compensate for the blind spot. It automatically makes a best guess as to what it *assumes* is supposed to be there and just fills in the information it needs. As a result, we don't even notice our own blindness."

"I'm going to have to do this blind spot test later," I said as I struggled to understand this concept.

Halldóra laughed. "The point I was trying to make is that the mind is a powerful thing. It makes us see things that are not there, like the blind spot in our vision, but it also makes us *not* see things that *are* there."

"Like the elves," I said, stopping the fooling around with my eyes and turning to look at Halldóra again.

"Exactly," Halldóra said with a nod. "You always hear people talking about how we humans only use ten percent of our brains. That's true, but there is a reason for it. I don't think we could handle our brains operating at a higher level. We would simply overload before too long. So our minds have developed the ability to slow down and filter out most of the information that is available to us through our senses. And as children we learn even further how to filter things out until we just don't see some things at all anymore."

"Like the Hidden People," I whispered, nodding to myself.

"Children see everything," Halldóra said, leaning over to put her arm around me. "You can just tell by looking into their eyes and watching how they look at the world that they can see things that other people cannot. But they are also constantly learning and developing as well. At no other point beyond childhood do we learn so much, so fast."

I continued nodding. "Or so well," I said. "What we learn as children we often have learned for life."

Halldóra leaned back again, laughing and smiling. "Exactly!" she cried out. "And how long do you think it takes children to stop seeing things that no one else around them can see? The human mind is very practical and concentrates on only the most important things. Young children assume that these things that no one else can see must not be very important, so their minds simply learn to filter them out as if they aren't even there."

"Just like the blind spot," I said, "except in reverse."

"Exactly," Halldóra said.

It was incredible. In the course of that short drive, bouncing along the rough back roads of the Icelandic highlands, Halldóra the psychic had been dismissive of the fairytale explanations for the Hidden People and had revealed herself to be a believer in a more scientific explanations.

Twenty minutes earlier, I would have dismissed the entire concept of the existence of elves and hidden people as crazy fairytales. But now I didn't know what to think anymore. Maybe there was something to this whole elf thing after all?

Chapter Ten
You Find Evil In Every Kind Of Being

"The elves are very accommodating," I muttered under my breath, thinking back to what Kristín had said the day before. I was looking out of the window of the car at the passing landscape, struggling to see even a glimpse of some unseen beings standing along the sides of the road.

"Pardon me?" Halldóra asked, leaning over across the back seat of the Land Rover to hear me better.

"Oh nothing," I replied, turning back to face her. "I was just thinking about something that my friend said yesterday about the elves: that they were very accommodating when humans came along wanting to build something that affected their homes."

Halldóra nodded knowingly, a wistful smile on her face. "They have to be, I suppose," she said. "What other choice do they have? Sometimes they move off to where there is no one else around, but humans are always building, always expanding, so what else can they do?"

"Are there elves and hidden people in other countries as well?" I asked, only realizing after I said it how crazy it would sound to any of my friends back home if they could hear me talking like this. "Or are they only in Iceland?"

"Oh goodness, of course there are," Halldóra laughed. "The hidden beings exist in a world that is parallel to our own but that is offset from ours just the tiniest little bit, which is why most people cannot see them. There are hidden beings everywhere in the world. But of course it is true that some cultures are more sensitive to them and more aware of them."

"Then what happens in other countries when human beings want to build a road or a house over a spot where the elves are already living? At least in Iceland, where there is an awareness of this other world, it seems that some kind of compromise or agreement can be reached between the elves and humans."

"Their presence can be felt in different ways," Halldóra explained, nodding again. "Maybe a human family builds a house over top of the home of an elf family without even realizing it. But maybe once the humans move into the house they find themselves feeling very unhappy, and they don't know why. Perhaps they are feeling a part of the unhappiness that was caused by building their house over someone else's home."

"Like a dark presence," I replied.

Halldóra thought this over for a moment.

"Maybe not a dark presence," Halldóra said, trying to find the right words to explain. "Not a dark or evil manifestation from the spirit world, like ghosts or poltergeists or some such thing, but we all know that bad moods are contagious, and if you spend enough time around someone who is unhappy, then you will probably become unhappy too, even if you don't even realize that the unhappy beings around you are even there. You still pick up on the vibe."

That made sense to me somehow. There were plenty of times in life when I'd felt feelings of unhappiness for no particular reason.

We drove on a while in silence as I looked out the window again and thought about what Halldóra had told me.

"Are there evil elves?" I asked. "One of the men at the construction site mentioned something about trolls."

Halldóra smiled. "Elves and hidden people are just what they are, neither good nor bad," she replied. "Like humans they come in all sorts of different moods and temperaments—although in my experience they tend to be more understanding than human beings. But trolls are something else entirely."

"What are the trolls, then?" I asked.

Halldóra thought for a moment, staring distantly out of the window at the passing landscape as if she were trying to catch a glimpse of a troll. "I haven't seen them very often," she began slowly, "because they tend to live in isolated areas up in the rocks and mountains like we're driving through right now. They come out mostly at night."

"Are the trolls evil?" I asked.

"Maybe evil is too strong a word," Halldóra replied, turning back to face me. "But they don't tend to be very kind to human beings, either, or to the elves and Hidden People, for that matter. They are usually slow and dim-witted and just generally unpleasant, but without being actually evil in nature."

"Grumpy?" I suggested.

"Yes!" Halldóra replied, smiling. "That might be a good word for it. They are grumpy and not very smart, and not at all like the bright and happy beings that the elves are."

"When I was younger," I said, thinking back to the stories about trolls I'd heard as a child, "we learned a story about three goats that needed to cross a bridge where a nasty ugly troll lived underneath, and they had to trick him in order to get across."

"Yes, yes, I know it well," Halldóra nodded. "I think there are many such stories in many different cultures because human roads in remote areas often tend to pass through or over the dwellings of the trolls."

This got me thinking. "Maybe sometimes when people are driving down a road or a highway," I said, thinking aloud, "and they suddenly get an unpleasant feeling for no particular reason, they have just driven over the lair of trolls."

"Maybe," Halldóra laughed. "But let me tell you a story about the road between Reykjavík and the international airport out at Keflavík. There is a certain part where the road curves, and there are many accidents there. And some of the people who run off the road there say that just before they crashed, they saw a figure at the side of the road waving at them and distracting them just as the road began to curve. Many people believe that at this spot the road was built over the house of a troll, and sometimes he just gets tired of the cars rumbling overhead all day and goes out to cause some trouble."

I shivered at the thought of how many times I had been driving home at night back home in Tofino and was startled when I thought I'd seen something at the side of the road. How easy it would be to skid off the road if that happened in wet or icy conditions.

"That sounds kind of evil to me," I said.

Halldóra thought about this for a moment then slowly began to shake her head. She took my hands in hers and leaned close in toward me with a grim and serious expression on her face.

"I think your word is better," she replied. "This kind of behavior is more grumpy and mischievous than evil. Evil is something far worse. And you find evil in every kind of being, whether hidden or otherwise."

Chapter Eleven
The Elf Negotiator

K onrad parked his Land Rover next to the portable office trailer at the main construction site where Magnús was already waiting for us with a large group of construction workers gathered around him.

Konrad jerked the parking brake into position and turned around to say something to Halldóra in Icelandic before the two of them opened their doors and stepped out onto the wet gravel and mud.

After waiting a few moments, I stepped out of the Land Rover, but kept my distance as Halldóra spoke with Magnús and the other workers. She talked with them briefly before walking off toward the towering black boulder that Magnús had commented on the day before.

Halldóra walked slowly up to the face of the jagged rock and touched it with the palm of her hand before turning away and raising her hands in greeting to an unseen group of beings standing nearby.

"You're a long way from Kansas now, Toto," Konrad said quietly as I walked over to the group and stood next to him.

I smiled in reply and positioned myself between Konrad and Magnús to use their bodies as a shield against the wind. A short distance away, Halldóra was holding a conversation with an unseen group of beings around her. Sometimes she craned her neck to look up at some of the taller ones, and at other times crouched down to listen to some of the shorter ones. Occasionally she spoke to them, her voice barely audible over the sound of the howling wind. But mostly she just listened to them, nodding and shaking her head as she did so.

"What do you think will happen?" I asked Konrad. "Do you think she will be able to work something out?"

Konrad smiled and nodded. "I am sure she will," he said. "I've never heard of a situation where they weren't able to resolve things somehow. Maybe we have to move some rocks or boulders out of the way, or build around some things. But somehow we'll figure it out."

"I can't believe I'm having this conversation," I muttered to myself, and Konrad laughed.

"I sometimes can't believe it myself," he observed with a wry smile. "And maybe it's all just a big joke, but I think everyone just feels better after being told that they aren't messing around with the unknown. Out here in the boonies, it can be a bit frightening sometimes. You hear strange sounds in the wind, and your mind starts to trick you into seeing things in the different shapes of the rocks all around."

Over by the dark tower of stone, Halldóra continued listening intently to her unseen hosts. I squinted my eyes and tried to blur them in and out of focus in the hope that I would be able to see something—anything. But as hard as I tried I couldn't see a thing.

There's probably nothing to see there in the first place, I thought. *And I'm standing here in the cold wind with a group of grown men watching a lunatic woman hold a conversation with thin air.*

"Do you think she can really see something?" I asked Konrad. "How does she know what they are saying? Can she hear them?"

"I think she *believes* she can see something," Konrad replied tactfully. "And as for how she knows what they are saying, she once told me that she doesn't hear them through her ears but in her mind instead. She said that many of the elves have psychic abilities, as she has, and it is through those abilities that she is able to communicate."

I nodded as Konrad explained.

"That makes sense," the little voice in my head commented. "Assuming that we're all agreed that this entire thing is completely insane."

We all watched for a few more minutes until Halldóra finally reached the end of her discussion with whomever she was talking to. She raised her palm in farewell to the unseen beings and walked back toward us with a grim expression on her face. As she drew closer, she shook her head to signal that the news wasn't good.

"What is it?" Magnús asked. "What's wrong?"

Halldóra paused for a moment to take a deep breath, and then she looked at each of us before speaking.

"This place is sacred to the elves," Halldóra said, gesturing with her hand to the surrounding area and the black tower of rock behind her. "It is a special place in their mythology because it was here that a battle took place a thousand years ago and the elves defeated a race of trolls who had tormented them."

Out of the corner of my eye, I saw Magnús quickly tap Konrad on the elbow and give him a sharp nod. "Trolls," he said simply, gesturing with his thumb toward the dark finger of jagged rock that he'd had a bad feeling about.

"The elves have a significant presence here," Halldóra continued, speaking slowly and earnestly. "There is a museum and university here; homes and schools; sacred monuments and temples. They have come here to escape the endless advance of humans and are disappointed that even here, so far away from everything, they cannot find peace."

Some of the men, including Magnús, dropped their eyes and looked at the ground in an uncomfortable moment of silence, kicking the dirt awkwardly with the toes of their boots.

"So what did they say about our building project here?" Konrad asked. "How will we come to an agreement about building this dam?"

Halldóra looked at Konrad with sadness in her eyes. "This place is sacred to them," she said simply. "They do not want you to build here."

"Okay," Konrad replied calmly. "But we *are* building here. So what can we do to reach an understanding with them?"

"That's just it," Halldóra said. "There is no understanding to be reached. There are no agreements to be made. They do not want you to build here, and they absolutely will not move."

Chapter Twelve
Different Songs, Same Language

The next morning I found myself back aboard my trusty De Havilland Beaver flying over the rugged and icy landscape of Iceland. Konrad and the rest of his family had headed back to Reykjavík by car earlier in the morning so they could stop along the way to visit some relatives before arriving in the city later in the day. I would meet up with Konrad and Kristín in the evening at the town hall meeting that Konrad had mentioned was being held between the environmental groups and aluminum companies. But first I was taking the scenic route to Reykjavík. The weather was forecast to be clear for most of the day, and on an island as wet and windy as Iceland, I had to take every opportunity I had to see the island from the air.

After pulling up out of Húsavík harbor, I stayed low for a few minutes to circle around and take a closer look at a pair of humpback whales who had wandered into the bay. Húsavík was a popular spot for whales, Kristín had told me, and they could frequently be spotted swimming in the protected waters just outside of the town's main harbor.

Seeing the sleek wet backs of those beautiful creatures as they came to the surface to breathe, I was reminded of the previous summer that I'd spent studying their Alaskan counterparts, and I instinctively put my plane into a hard turn as I'd done a thousand times before so I could get a better look at them. The only difference was that now I didn't have to worry about whether my cameras were working properly or whether I was lined up correctly. I just circled around them and enjoyed watching the gentle giants swimming peacefully down below me.

How different are these Icelandic humpback whales from the ones I studied in Alaska? I wondered. The human beings in both locations were quite different, after all. What kinds of different rituals did these humpback whales follow in their day-to-day lives? Did they sing different songs from their Alaskan counterparts?

As I made a lazy circle in the air around the whales, I thought back to my adventures the previous summer and a discussion I'd had with one of the researchers I knew from the University of Alaska. She had spent the previous winter in Hawaii taking part in a study of humpback whale songs that involved researchers located in various places around the Pacific Ocean.

"Humpback whale song is constantly evolving," she told me. "Over the course of a few years, we hear the songs change and develop gradually into something completely new. But what is really amazing is how the changes are communicated between different groups separated by thousands of miles. Our team in Hawaii would notice some small changes to a common whale song there, and within a few days the changes would be repeated in the whale populations in Japan, Baja, and the Philippines as well."

"Does that mean that humpback whales all around the world sing the same songs?" I asked. "Do they all speak the same language?"

"Different whale populations in different areas sing different songs," she told me. "We have found that the whales in the northern Pacific Ocean sing many of the same songs, but those in the South Pacific or Atlantic Oceans sing songs that are completely different. But whether these are completely different languages or just regional dialects, we aren't sure yet."

I looked down below and saw the pair of humpback whales surface, take a breath, arch their backs, and make a deep dive. I knew that they would stay beneath the surface for a while now, so I turned back to continue my climb out of Húsavík.

While I watched their tails slice back into the dark water below me, I had the feeling that they probably weren't much different from the whales I'd seen the previous summer in Alaska. Maybe they sang different songs, but I was sure that they all spoke more or less the same language. Human beings seem to be a lot better at finding differences among themselves than animals are.

With my head full of philosophical thoughts, I continued south and soared over the harsh Icelandic landscape I'd visited previously on ground level. Down below me were the powerful glacial rivers that the Icelandic energy companies wanted to dam to create hydropower for aluminum smelters. I followed the rivers up into the mountains to the source of their power—the enormous Vatnajökull ice field.

Kristín had explained to me that *jökull* is the Icelandic word for *glacier*, and that *Vatnajökull* literally means *the glacier of rivers*. It was called this because dozens upon dozens of enormous winding rivers of ice snaked down from it on all sides, melting into powerful rivers and waterfalls that eventually flowed into the sea.

Kristín and some late-night Wikipedia research had prepared me for how enormous Vatnajökull would be, but as I approached it from the air and its vast incredible whiteness filled my entire view, I was completely overwhelmed. It was absolutely colossal, and I felt as though I were back in Greenland once again, flying over its endless fields of ice and snow.

Kristín also explained that Vatnajökull is more than just an ice field. Buried beneath the glacier—under hundreds of meters of ice—are several active volcanoes that periodically come to life in an apocalyptic clash of fire and ice.

"When the fire gods begin to stir in Iceland, the whole world takes notice," Kristín said with a hint of pride in her voice that made me laugh.

She was referring to the horrifically difficult to pronounce Eyjafjallajökull volcano that erupted in 2010, bringing European air traffic to a standstill for weeks on end.

Turning west toward Reykjavík, I continued across the blinding icy surface of Vatnajökull, and then I flew back out again over the rock and frozen lava fields. Letting my thoughts wander, I thought back to the events of the previous day at the construction site.

"The elves do not want you to build here," Halldóra had said. "And they will not move."

"What will you do now?" I asked Konrad after we'd driven back from the site and dropped Halldóra at the airport so she could fly home.

Konrad shrugged. "We'll put the construction on hold for a day or two while we discuss it with the companies back in Reykjavík," he replied. "Maybe we'll have Halldóra come back out again for another try at negotiations, but we can't keep things on hold forever. Eventually the construction will have to go ahead, elves or no elves."

Was any of it real? Were there really elves there, or was it all just coincidences and delusional thinking?

Before setting out on my flight around the world, my mother and I had taken a long drive together, weaving our way through the mountains from Tofino to Port Alberni where we had lunch together at the closest McDonald's. We talked a lot and laughed along the way, pulling off the side of the road whenever we felt like it to pick berries or go for a hike.

Sitting across from each other over McDonald's Happy Meals, my mom turned serious for a moment and gave me a speech that I could tell she had been planning in her head for days.

"You are going on an adventure," she said. "And along the way you will see amazing things and meet amazing people, and most of all you will encounter cultures that will seem very strange and beliefs that are very contrary to yours."

I nodded.

"And you have to respect those different cultures and beliefs," my mother said, gesturing at me with her cheeseburger. "Don't resist them! Embrace them! They are the whole point of going out and seeing the wide world in the first place. Otherwise, you might as well just stay here and eat McDonald's cheeseburgers for the rest of your life."

Chapter Thirteen

Wash Your Zones!

A fter parking my plane at its berth in the Reykjavík harbor, I decided that I would go for a swim. Why not, after all? I had no plans until the town hall meeting that evening, and I was eager to swim a few laps in one of Reykjavík's public swimming pools kept a perfectly warm temperature by geothermal heating.

After walking up from the dock and through downtown Reykjavík, I stopped in at Kristín's apartment to grab a bathing suit and do some quick Internet research to find a nearby public pool. I found what I was looking for at a place called Laugardalslaug, which boasted an Olympic-sized lane pool and was near enough that I could walk to it.

It was a beautiful day, and even though the pool was nearby, it was still far enough away that I could enjoy a nice long walk along the waterfront path system to soak in a bit of Reykjavík.

I noticed that although Iceland still felt European to me, somehow, there was also something distinctly North American about it. There were Wendy's restaurants and Subway restaurants, and I'd even stopped into a North American style convenience store called 10-11 for a bottle of water. It wasn't quite the same as a 7-Eleven store—its logo and color scheme were different, and it sold all sorts of strange things such as Skyr and snacks made from dried fish—but it still felt overwhelmingly familiar and North American to me.

It shouldn't be a surprise that Iceland feels both European and North American, I thought. *It is, after all, at the crossroads between the two continents.*

It had been a crossroads for a thousand years or more. In school, we'd learned how the Vikings had sailed from Iceland to Greenland to Canada more than a thousand years before and erected settlements there. My recent discussions with one of the coffee regulars in the doughnut shop back in Gander, Newfoundland had reminded me of this fact.

I pulled up my collar to block the wind and continued my brisk walk along the edge of the bay with Mount Esja rising over me across the water to my left.

I remembered that in Social Studies we had learned that Iceland was where the great chess player Bobby Fischer had defeated his nemesis, the Russian Boris Spassky, for the World Chess Championship. I remembered laughing at the time that there was actually something called a 'World Chess Championship. (No offence to all you chess enthusiasts out there, but it's kind of funny.)

We had also learned about the Cold War, and of a famous summit meeting between US president Ronald Reagan and Soviet Premier Mikhail Gorbachev that was held in Iceland. I walked past the actual house in Reykjavík where it had taken place—an imposing white building standing alone in an open field overlooking the bay—but I must confess that . (But don't be too impressed by my cleverness. I looked it up on the Internet at Kristín's apartment before I left and I was planning an interesting walking route to the pool.)

But all of those things seemed old and mothy and tattered—like pulling a gigantic history book off the shelf and blowing the dust off the ragged covers. None of it really meant anything to me. I barely knew how to play chess—the Stanley Cup meant far more to me than who the winners of the World Chess Championships were. And the Cold War, along with Mikhail Gorbachev's Soviet Union, had ceased to exist long before I was even born. To me all of these things were just theoretical concepts. They were things learned about on Wikipedia pages and depicted in period movies. Was there something about Iceland that was relevant to me personally—something that I could understand and feel with my own hands and heart?

"Let's see," I thought. "What did we learn about Iceland that at least happened in my lifetime?"

A few years earlier, Iceland's biggest banks had collapsed as a result of owing more money than they had and being unable to borrow more money to cover themselves. I'd seen a documentary about that once, and Konrad and Ásta had mentioned it at dinner a few days earlier. That had happened in my lifetime, but I could remember it vaguely. But that didn't mean that I understood any of it. Maybe I should have gone to university after high school and studied economics, because "big banks = bad" was about all that the documentary had conveyed to me, and that much I had already known from listening to my mother's various rants on the topic over the years.

But all of this history, from chess championships to Cold War summits, was not particularly Icelandic. Iceland was just the stage onto which the actors in foreign dramas had stepped. Even the financial crisis, a critical event in recent Icelandic history, was not itself particularly Icelandic.

If I want to find something distinctly Icelandic, I will obviously have to look further than the history books, I thought as I reached my destination and paid the entrance fee before heading to the locker rooms to change.

As it turned out, perhaps finding something distinctly Icelandic was all in the small details. Things like dried fish snacks and Skyr were certainly Icelandic, after all. And as I was about to discover, so was something as simple as taking a shower before going for a swim.

"Bathing suit off!" the woman standing guard at the entrance to the pool's showers told me. I turned to see a stern-looking woman in her late forties with high cheekbones and greying blonde hair pulled into a tight bun at the back of her head.

"Pardon me?" I asked, not even sure she was talking to me.

"You must shower without bathing suit," the stern-faced woman repeated, pointing at a sign on the wall. "And wash your zones."

I looked up at the sign she was pointing to. It pictured a genderless humanoid figure standing with six various shaded areas colored to indicate where you were supposed to concentrate your washing efforts— head, armpits, feet, and so on. Next to the figure, the following was written in no less than five languages:

Observe!
Every guest is required to wash thoroughly without a swimsuit before entering the pools. Thank you.

I laughed out loud and wished that I had my iPhone with me so that I could take a picture. But my smile quickly faded as I remembered the signs back in the changing room warning against the use of cameras and camera phones in the changing room areas. No doubt, the stern-faced naked-shower-enforcer woman would not have looked kindly upon that.

Looking around the shower room, I tried to find a stall of some kind, but there was none. It was all completely wide-open with plenty of exposed skin and soaping going on by my fellow pool-goers. It was all very naked and uncomfortably foreign to me, but I took a deep breath and steeled myself to just do it.

You wanted something distinctly Icelandic, remember? I told myself as I stripped off my bathing suit. *And as they say, 'When in Rome, do as the Romans do.'*

"Don't worry," the little voice in my head told me. "Most of the exposed skin you're trying to avoid looking at in here is hanging pretty low anyway. I don't think you have anything to worry about."

After finishing my shower, I reunited with my bathing suit and wrapped a towel around me as a thin barrier against the cold for the short walk to pool. At the edge of the pool, I stripped off the towel and quickly plunged into the water to let it surround me with its delicious warmth.

"Just think," the little voice in my head observed snobbishly. "Thanks to the strict showering regimen, this water is much cleaner than those disgusting broths of human sweat and filth back in North America."

That's definitely true, I agreed as I dropped beneath the surface with my eyes closed, bubbles flying from my nose as I dove deep like a humpback whale.

Breaking the surface again, I wiped the water from my eyelids and dogpaddled for a while, looking around the pool and the sky and clouds above me.

What a great place this would be in winter, I thought, *with snow falling, northern lights glowing in the sky above, and your body safely insulated from the freezing air by the amazing water warmed by the power of the earth itself.*

I'd come there to swim some laps, but instead I just relaxed and lay on the surface of the water, watching the clouds floating overhead as I floated aimlessly around the deserted lane pool. All the other visitors to the pool were sitting and talking over at some circular hot pools far away from me on the opposite end.

I felt a bit like I did when I was surfing—close and connected to the planet.

What a strange and wild place Iceland is, I thought. *It's no wonder they have elves here.*

Chapter Fourteen
Flying Is A Hobby Of Mine

I t took me a while to find the location where the so-called town hall meeting was scheduled to take place. It wasn't in the town hall, of course, but rather in one of the lecture halls at the University of Iceland. Unfortunately for me, however, finding my way around the campus was like navigating a maze, and it took me half an hour to figure my way through the labyrinth of various buildings.

Once I finally found it, I pushed through a pair of doors leading to the glassed-in foyer. To the left was a large sign on an easel pointing the way onward to the meeting hall.

Public Meeting on Land and Energy Development
Hosted by Alcoa, Landsvirkjun, and the University
of Iceland

An additional maze of hallways brought me to the right place—a small lecture theatre with rows of seats and desks facing a long table set up at the front of the room with a projection screen behind it. The meeting hadn't started yet, and various small groups of people were scattered around drinking coffee and chatting together in low voices. Off to the side of the hall I spotted Kristín standing with two men. She smiled and waved, said something brief to the two men, and walked over to greet me.

"Good to see you!" she said enthusiastically, giving me a quick hug. "I'm glad you were able to find the place."

I laughed. "I wasn't sure I'd actually be able to for a while there," I admitted as I unzipped my jacket. "It's a bit confusing."

Kristín took my jacket and hung it on a nearby coat rack. "Let me introduce you to everyone," she said as we walked back to her two acquaintances who were still at the side of the hall engaged in a spirited discussion. "This is a fellow student of mine, Erík Grettirsson," Kristín said, "and this is one of the university's associate professors, Albert Ørsted."

Erík was tall, in his early twenties, with a perfectly coiffed wave of red hair and close-trimmed beard. He looked exactly as I'd always imagined a Viking would look if you could somehow magically pluck him from the rudder of an oar-driven long ship riding the North Sea a thousand years ago, give him a bath and a haircut, dress him in some modern clothes (in this case a funky green shirt and a hipster scarf), and drop him into the middle of present-day Reykjavík.

"And this," Kristín said to them, opening her palm toward me, "is Kitty Hawk."

"I'm surprised we haven't run into each other already," Erík said, his body language confident as he leaned over to shake my hand. "My flat is just a few doors down the street from Kristín's, and she and I see each other all the time, coming and going."

Albert was shorter, in his mid-thirties and skinny almost to the point of being gangly, with thick-rimmed glasses and a badly fitting suit that made him look exactly the way modern-day Hollywood has taught us a nerdy scientist should look. He was nervously folding a blue sheet of paper into a complicated shape, but he paused long enough to reach over and shake my hand.

"It is a pleasure to meet you both," I said.

"Kristín has also been telling us about your around-the-world flight," Erík said with a handsome smile as he poured a cup of coffee and offered it to me along with a plastic stir-stick and packages of sugar and cream. "It's very impressive, I must say; very, very impressive."

"Thank you," I replied with a shrug, unsure of what else to say.

There was something unusual about the way Erík spoke. He spoke quite formally, as though he was reciting poetry from an unseen book in his hands. And although I'd only been in Iceland a few days, I had already heard enough of Icelanders speaking English to know that something about his pronunciation and inflection was a bit strange—but there was something very familiar about it as well.

"What part of Iceland do you come from?" I asked. "There's something about your accent that is quite different from what I've heard so far."

Erík laughed such a big, friendly, resounding belly laugh that I couldn't help but laugh along with him.

"Oh no, I'm from Reykjavík, " he replied, still laughing infectiously. "But when I was growing up, my family lived in Australia for quite some time—the United States, too. So that's left me with a bit of a confused accent, I'm afraid."

Australia. That explained it. That's why it sounded familiar. He sounded just like that crazy wildlife guy I used to watch on TV.

"And how about you, Albert?" I asked, turning to face him. "Are you from Reykjavík?"

"Canada, actually, same as you," he replied simply in an accent that I was more familiar with. His nervous paper folding never stopped as he spoke.

"Albert is on loan to us from the University of Toronto," Kristín explained. "He's here to work on some various research projects for the university and some private companies."

Erík looked up from his coffee and over my shoulder, apparently seeing someone entering the lecture hall that he recognized.

"I do apologize for being such a bore," he said suddenly. "But I need to speak to someone quickly before all this begins." He set down his paper cup and turned to face me, holding out his hand. "It was a pleasure to meet you, Ms. Hawk," he said with another handsome smile. "And if I don't see you again, I wish you all possible success on your world flight."

I nodded and smiled in return, shaking his outstretched hand. "Thank you," I replied. And with that, Erík was off, striding grandly across the room as though he were an actor on a stage.

"I'll be right back too," Kristín said as she also set off toward the opposite side of the lecture hall.

I watched them as they both walked across the room in separate directions—Erík toward a group of young men who looked like students, and Kristín toward an older couple who she greeted with kisses and hugs.

"These things are just awful, aren't they?" I heard Albert say behind me. I turned to face him just as he was putting the finishing touches on his complicated folded blue paper. As he made the last folds, his creation was revealed: It was a paper airplane, but not like any paper airplane that I'd ever seen. Most paper airplanes are fairly simple affairs, but this was something far more advanced, sleek and streamlined. It looked like something that was really built to fly—like something that *wanted* to fly.

Albert used his index finger and thumbnail to press down and secure the final fold. He looked up at me with a bright, relaxed smile as he held the blue paper plane up and gestured for me take it.

"For you," he said simply. "From one flier to another."

"You're a pilot too?" I asked as I took the airplane from him, holding it gently in my hands as I examined it from all sides.

He laughed. "Only in the paper world, unfortunately," he replied. "It's a hobby of mine. But I'm not a real pilot like you are."

"This is beautiful," I said, turning it carefully and examining the miraculous paper construction in my hands.

"You don't have to be so gentle," Albert said, taking the plane from me for a moment and shaking it around roughly. "It can take plenty of abuse, see?"

"Will it really fly?" I asked.

Albert handed the plane back to me. "Or course it will," he said. "Give it a try."

I looked around the crowded room at the various groups of people standing around.

"In here?" I asked, embarrassed. "In front of all these people?"

Albert scoffed. "Forget about all of them," he said. "They're all too busy with their own selfish agendas—corporations, government, environment. They don't know how to just let go and fly and be free."

I looked around the room again, still uncertain, but looking for a suitable open area through which to throw the plane.

"Just do it," Albert said, pointing along a long, narrow stretch of open space between the mingling groups of people.

I pulled my hand back, and then with a grin, I thrust it forward again, releasing the plane at the end of my arm's trajectory.

It nose-dived straight into the floor.

Albert and I looked at each other for a moment then burst into laughter, drawing startled looks from everyone in the room.

"I guess it doesn't know how to fly and be free either," I said.

Albert was still laughing as he bent to pick up the plane from the floor. "Of course it does," he assured me. "But just like in life, you sometimes have to find the right trick in order to set yourself free."

He held up his hand and demonstrated how to flick the plane off at the last moment using my wrist. I did a couple of test flicks, and then I was ready to try again, pulling my arm back and lining up along the stretch of open space in front of me.

"Just gently flick it; don't try to throw it," Albert said quietly as I pulled my arm back again.

In one smooth fluid motion, I swung my arm forward and flicked the plane into the air at the last possible instant. I watched in amazement as it soared gracefully across the room, bucking and riding the tiny air currents as it climbed toward the ceiling over the heads of the oblivious groups of coffee drinkers below. Near the ceiling, the plane reached the end of its climb and slowly arced back down again, cruising silently through a canyon of people before coming to rest underneath the long table at the front of the room.

I turned to Albert, taking a breath for the first time since the plane had left my hand.

"That was amazing!" I cried, smiling from ear to ear.

Albert shrugged. "Like I said, it's a hobby of mine," he replied, laughing. "You should come after the meeting and see my lab. I have a gigantic mess of planes all over the place.

"I'd love to see your collection of paper planes," I said, nodding enthusiastically.

Albert looked surprised and somewhat startled. It took a few moments for him to regain his composure. "R-r-really?" he stuttered in reply. "I mean, it's nothing special—just a bunch of folded paper."

"Of course I'm sure!" I replied. "As you know, flying is a bit of a hobby of mine as well."

Chapter Fifteen

The Secret Is In The Shoes

"Good evening everyone," a tall man in a sweater vest addressed the crowd of people scattered throughout the small lecture hall. He was standing at a podium in the center of a long table where various panel members were seated to face the audience. "Thank you all for joining us tonight," he continued, speaking too closely to the microphone for a moment and causing a brief squeal of feedback. "My name is Tómas Finnsson, and I am a representative of the Icelandic Ministry for the Environment and Natural Resources. To my right is my colleague, Mr. Dagur Týsson, who represents the Icelandic energy company, Landsvirkjun."

He continued to introduce the other members of the panel, which included representatives from energy companies, architectural and engineering firms, Alcoa Aluminum, environmental groups, and researchers from the University of Iceland. Konrad was included in the panel, barely recognizable in a suit and tie. Albert was also included, and he was seated at the far right with the university researchers.

"As you all know," Tómas continued after introducing everyone, "the purpose of this meeting is to continue the practice of keeping the public informed about the ongoing development of the northeastern highlands for energy and industrial production."

"The ongoing *rape and pillage* of the northeast highlands, you mean," a powerful voice behind me bellowed over the heads of the audience members. I turned to look and saw that the voice belonged to none other than Erík, Kristín's student friend whom I'd met only minutes earlier. Kristín and I were seated in the front row of the hall, and many rows behind us at the back sat Erík, arms folded defiantly across his chest as he stared grimly down at the panel members below.

Tómas briefly looked up in Erík's direction but ignored him and continued with his remarks. "For the benefit of those who might have missed previous meetings, I will first ask Mr. Konrad Cooper to update us on the progress of the Arnardalsvirkjun dam and Bakki aluminum smelter construction projects."

"*Destruction* projects would be more like it," Erík bellowed again from the back of the audience, and everyone turned again to look at him.

Tómas looked increasingly uncomfortable with Erík's outbursts. He shuffled the papers in front of him to buy himself some time, and then he looked up at Erík over the rims of his reading glasses.

"I believe most of us here are already aware of your feelings on these projects, Erík," Tómas said calmly, still arranging his papers on the podium in front of him. "But it would be greatly appreciated if you could kindly hold your questions and comments until after the presentation."

"Perhaps I could even hold off on my comments even longer," Erík said sarcastically. "Perhaps I could wait until you and all your friends have completely destroyed every bit of the beautiful and pristine wilderness that this country has left."

"I would not characterize it that way, Erík," Tómas said quietly. "It is not destruction of wilderness. It is merely a reduction of it in some limited areas."

Several members of the audience chuckled at this remark, including me.

"Reduction by means of complete destruction of the living habitats of countless species of plants and animals," Erík countered.

At this comment, Konrad sprang to his feet and leaned across the podium to address Erík through the microphone.

"As you know full well, Erík," Konrad said, "we are taking every possible measure to minimize the environmental impact of every single one of these projects, not only in their final completed form, but also at every stage of construction as well."

"A lot of good that will do for the rare species of moss and lichen that you'll be condemning to extinction when you flood the river valley and submerge them under twenty meters of water."

Konrad's face turned slightly redder, but his voice remained calm and even. "No offence to the indigenous plant life of the eastern highlands," Konrad replied. "But you cannot possibly expect a project of this magnitude to be cancelled on account of a species of moss that no one even knew existed until the very companies seated before you tonight went up the valley to assess the environmental impact of building there in the first place."

"That is precisely what I expect!" Erík replied, his voice booming across the hall and echoing off the walls. "And not just the mosses and lichen, but the fish and geese and reindeer and every other animal that calls the area home."

"All of which will easily find places to live and flourish nearby," Konrad snapped, his voice rising and his face turning redder by the second. "For god's sake, the reindeer aren't even from Iceland in the first place! The Vikings brought them here three hundred years ago. If they can adapt to life in Iceland after coming here all the way from Norway, I'm willing to bet they can cope with the change of having to graze and breed one river valley over."

"Until you build a dam on that river too," Erík replied. "And the next one and the next, until every last bit of our beautiful, untouched wilderness is gone." Erík rose to his feet as he spoke and passionately addressed the panel members and the entire audience. "You know perfectly well that the energy needs of every single Icelandic citizen are easily met with just a handful of small geothermal power plants," he said. "You know that all of these extra dams and power plants have only one purpose—to provide enormous amounts of cheap energy for foreign industry. So instead of being the greenest and most environmentally friendly country in the world, we sell out to these foreign corporations and they come over here, set up shop, pollute our air and water, and destroy Iceland forever."

As Erík was speaking, Tómas walked over to the side of the stage and held a quick and whispered conversation with one of the university security guards standing there.

"And what kind of future do you imagine for all these Icelandic citizens?" Konrad asked. "We are trying to develop Iceland's abundant natural resources to provide clean renewable energy so that we can create jobs and build for the future."

"The future is exactly what I am talking about!" Erík shouted, his sudden outburst startling me. "Because once you build these dams and destroy our waterfalls and rivers, there's no going back! There is no future!"

Konrad shook his head in resignation and sat down in his chair again, relinquishing the podium and microphone to Tómas. A pair of security guards had appeared at the back of the hall and now stood on either side of Erík, and were politely but firmly gesturing for him to follow them outside.

"We thank you for your comments," Tómas said from the front of the room as the two guards took Erík by the elbows and steered him toward the exit. "But I am afraid that we will once again have to ask you to leave."

Erík smiled defiantly as he was guided up the steps and out of the lecture theatre. "Yeah, I know the drill," he shouted back over his shoulder as the two guards led him away. "But mark my words: There is no future for us if we destroy everything we have for the sake of these foreign companies! No future!"

And with that, Erík and his two escorts disappeared from view at the back of the theatre. After a few seconds, we heard the sound of a door closing heavily, and Erík's voice could be heard again, albeit muffled and bellowing indistinctly. After a few moments, all was quiet.

At the front of the room, Tómas paused, leaving the uncomfortable silence hanging in the air for a moment, and then he shuffled his papers and continued with the business of the meeting.

"I apologize for that interruption," Tómas said quietly, clearing his throat. "As I mentioned earlier, we will start tonight with a project update from Mr. Konrad Cooper, but first I wanted to take the opportunity to allow one of the new faces on our panel to introduce himself. Please welcome one of the researchers from the University of Iceland, Professor Albert Ørsted from Canada, who is doing some work in the field of energy development and aluminum production techniques."

Tómas stepped back from the microphone, and to a smattering of applause, Albert got to his feet and walked over to the podium.

"Thank you; good evening," Albert said. "As Mr. Finnsson has already said, my name is Albert Ørsted, and I am here in Reykjavík from Canada doing research at the University of Iceland. My research involves a variety of disciplines, but there are two main topics I would like to share with you tonight. The first is the development of a type of efficient, low-resistance, long-range, high-voltage, underwater cable to allow access by the United Kingdom and Europe to Iceland's abundant and clean energy resources. The second, and maybe more relevant to tonight's discussion, is the development of a more advanced aluminum smelting process to help reduce the greenhouse gasses and fluorine emissions that result from aluminum production, to reduce the energy required for production, and on the whole, to make the process much cleaner and more cost-effective. I am happy to say that we have had considerable success in both of these areas in recent months."

"Blah, blah, blah," the little voice in my head commented as Albert continued speaking. "This meeting was a lot more interesting when that red-haired guy was still yelling."

To be honest, I actually wasn't really listening. I was too busy thinking about Erík's shoes.

Chapter Sixteen
Solving A Problem Is Like Finding A Place To Land

Thanks to the theatre-like design of the lecture hall and the arrangement of seats rising up from the central podium at an angle, I'd had a pretty good look at Erík's shoes as he was being escorted outside. I was sitting at the front at a lower level than where he was seated near the back, so his shoes were basically at eye-level with me as the two security guards led him away.

If nothing else, I mused as he bellowed and complained about being led away from the meeting, *he definitely has good taste in footwear.*

He was wearing a simple pair of black leather Blundstone 370 work boots: steel-toed, slip-resistant soles, heat-resistant, electricity-resistant, oil- and acid-resistant, made in Australia, and incredibly comfortable to boot (no pun intended). Overall, the Blundstone 370 is an exceptional work boot that is perfect for nearly every kind of working situation and environment.

And if this sounds like an advertisement for Blundstone boots, it's only because I know how great they are from experience. I wear the exact same boots myself (a fact for which my toes and the rest of my body are eternally grateful since I regularly drop heavy equipment on my feet by accident, or I slip while walking along the slick wet pontoons of my seaplane).

It was the fact that Erík's boots were the same as mine that made me take notice of them in the first place. I recognized them instantly. I would know a pair of Blundstones anywhere. I'd been wearing them for half of my life. When Erík leaned over to grab his backpack, I was able to read the distinctive Blundstone text on the back strap of one of the boots: *Since 1870.*

There was no doubt about it. Erík was wearing the exact same boots that I was. My mind was racing as I realized the obvious implication of that, which was that he would leave the exact same boot prints in the mud as I would, if, for example, he had walked around the construction site up at the river dam and sabotaged their machinery. I'd seen boot prints just like that two days earlier, identical to my own, and just a few sizes larger.

"Whoa, whoa, whoa, now wait just a minute," the voice inside my head cautioned me. "What are you implying with all this?"

What I am implying is quite simple, I explained. *That when we were* up at the construction site along at the river, and I was nosing around the sabotaged bulldozers, I saw footprints in the mud left by someone wearing Blundstone boots. And now, lo and behold, only two days later, I encounter someone wearing Blundstone boots who also just happens to be rather strongly opposed to the construction of the dam.

The voice in my head was skeptical. "How sure are you that the footprints you saw were from Blundstones? There must have been dozens of pairs of footprints in the mud up there."

Maybe more than dozens, I admitted. Maybe hundreds, but the zigzag pattern on the soles of my boots is very distinctive.

"Maybe it was your own boot prints that you saw," the little voice replied, still playing devil's advocate.

Not possible, I thought, shaking my head. The prints I saw were much larger than my prints. I am sure of it.

The little voice in my head went silent for a moment, pondering the evidence. "That doesn't mean it was Erík up there messing around with the construction equipment," it finally replied. "You said yourself that they are excellent work boots. Where else would people be wearing excellent work boots than at a construction site—right?"

Maybe, I replied, conceding the truth of this. But back in Canada you don't see very many people wearing Blundstones, and I'm willing to bet that it is the same here in Iceland. I'll bet they are pretty rare here.

That seemed to settle the argument for the moment, and my inner voice fell silent once again. Up at the podium at the front of the room, Albert had already finished his science talk and Konrad was finishing off his progress update on the various construction projects.

"So what do we do now?" the little voice in my head asked. "Do we call the police?"

I chuckled to myself. As if I would do that, I replied sarcastically. I'm not THAT sure about it.

Konrad finished his presentation and turned the podium over to one of the representatives of the Icelandic energy company.

"Then what?" the little voice asked. "Do we talk to Konrad or Kristín about it?"

I thought about this for a moment. "Maybe," I muttered under my breath, hoping that no one heard me. "Probably."

I tried to listen to what the various speakers were saying, but my thoughts kept returning to Erík and his boots. Whenever I have a problem to solve, I tend to think about it in terms of flying an airplane. Solving a problem is a lot like finding a safe place to land. There are many different ways you can approach it, and many different factors—wind, waves, and weather, for instance—that influence the outcome. By thinking the situation through from different angles, I can usually find the answer that I am looking for.

Navigating through life is a bit different from flying a plane, though. In a plane, you eventually have to land. But in life, you can often keep thinking about problems forever without ever doing anything about them, circling overhead, searching endlessly for a place to land.

My thoughts continued circling while more speakers gave brief presentations. Before I knew it, the town hall meeting was over and people were slowly making their way to the exits. Up at the front of the room some of the speakers from the evening, including Konrad and Albert, were talking to various members of the audience who apparently had further questions for them.

"I'll grab our coats," Kristín said. "And I'll tell my dad that we can just walk home from here. He looks a bit busy and will probably be here a while."

I nodded in reply and watched Kristín glide gracefully down the lecture hall steps toward the front of the room.

Walking up the stairs past her, a red-haired girl about my age approached me and held out her hand in greeting.

"Hello, there," she said. "I'm Avery Parker, Dr. Ørsted's assistant. And you are Kitty Hawk, correct?"

I stood up and shook her hand. "Yes, yes," I replied, nodding. "That's me."

It took me a moment to realize who 'Dr. Ørsted' was. She meant Albert.

"Dr. Ørsted is a bit busy at the moment, as you can see," Avery said, gesturing to the front of the room where Albert was deep in conversation with several groups of people. "He wanted me to catch you before you left," Avery continued, "and find out if you were free tomorrow for an appointment to stop by his lab."

At that moment, Albert glanced up toward us. He waved and smiled.

"Sure," I replied, waving back at Albert. "Tomorrow would be perfect."

Avery pulled an iPad from her shoulder bag, and after pushing her glasses up on her face, she made a frenetic series of motions, dragging her finger across the iPad screen until she found what she was looking for—Albert's appointment diary, apparently.

"Okay," she replied, studying the screen and frowning in concentration. "He has a fairly busy day tomorrow, but he has open appointments from 7:30 to 7:45 a.m., just before his first lecture. He's also free from 9:15 to 9:30 a.m." She flicked her finger across the screen, scrolling down to look at time slots later in the day. "And then nothing is open again until after his last lecture, which ends at 7:25 p.m."

"The evening appointment would be the best for me," I said, grinning at the idea of making a formal appointment to see paper airplanes.

Avery nodded and looked down again at her iPad screen.

"Okay, sounds good," she said, tapping the screen. "I will put you down for 7:45 p.m."

"Perfect," I replied.

"May I also put down what the meeting is relating to?" Avery asked, gesturing at her iPad screen.

I laughed. "Put down *consultation regarding aeronautical design and engineering using formed cellulose construction materials*," I replied.

Avery looked confused.

"Paper airplanes," I said, grinning.

Avery still looked confused and stared blankly at me for a few more seconds, the thick lenses of her glasses distorting her eyes and intensifying her look of incomprehension.

"He's showing me his collection of paper airplanes," I explained, still grinning.

After a few more seconds, Avery finally understood and blushed deeply.

"Oh, I am so sorry," she said, turning redder by the second.

"Don't worry," I replied, the two of us laughing.

"Okay," she said, typing again on her iPad and reaching in her pocket to hand me a small square of paper. It was a map of the campus showing the location of Albert's lab. "Okay, 7:45 p.m. it is, then," Avery said, "for consultation on paper airplanes."

Avery shook my hand again and we said goodnight as she descended the stairs and made her way toward the front of the lecture theatre. Kristín had retrieved our jackets and was winding her way through the seats back toward me.

"So what will you do about Erík?" the little voice in my head asked as Kristín approached. "Talk to Konrad about it? Talk to Kristín?"

I nodded to myself. *I will definitely talk to them*, I said to myself, *but not yet. I have an idea first.*

Chapter Seventeen
I Bet I Know Exactly Where

E arly the next morning, I found myself sitting in a café just down the street from Kristín's apartment, drinking a cup of coffee and eating a kind of chocolate cake that the menu referred to as *skúffukaka*. I had woken early after Kristín had left for school and was sitting at a table next to the window where I had a clear view of the street in both directions. This commanding view was important to my plan of getting to the bottom of the explanation behind Erík and his suspicious footwear.

Erík had said the night before that he lived just a few doors down the street from Kristín. I didn't know where that was, exactly, but it certainly had to be visible from where I was currently sitting in the café because I could basically see anyone coming and going from any of the houses along both sides of the entire street. If Erík came out of any of the houses nearby, I would definitely see him.

"And then what?" the little voice in my head asked, always the pessimist.

And then we follow him, I replied. *Duh! What else?*

"And then what?" the little voice asked persistently. "Where do you think he's going to go?"

I have no idea where he will go, I snapped. *That's why we're going to follow him!*

Sometimes these voices inside our heads can be difficult, can't they, not to mention unsupportive of our ideas. But after my fourth cup of coffee (and third piece of skúffukaka), even I was starting to have doubts about my clever stakeout plan. Erík was nowhere to be seen.

Maybe he left the house really early this morning before I got here, and I missed him? I muttered under my breath as I pressed my face up against the glass and scanned up and down the street.

"I was wondering the same," the little voice in my head commented. "Maybe we should just finish our coffee and go find something more interesting to do."

I pressed my face closer to the glass and squinted at a figure emerging from one of the doors on the opposite side of the street a short way down—a figure with a familiar shock of red hair.

"Bingo!" I whispered triumphantly as the figure turned around to lock his door and headed off down the street away from me. It was Erík. There was no doubt about it.

Grabbing my backpack off the chair next to me, I walked quickly to the exit of the café and stepped onto the sidewalk just as Erík rounded the corner and disappeared. Either he was a naturally fast walker, or he was in a hurry to get somewhere. I would have to hustle if I wanted to keep up with him.

Keeping that in mind, I pulled my backpack higher up onto my shoulders and jogged down the street to the corner that Erík had disappeared around a few moments earlier. Poking my head around cautiously, I spotted Erík's bright red hair off in the distance, still heading away from me down the hill in the direction of the University of Iceland.

"He's probably late for class," the little voice in my head observed as I continued walking briskly down the hill after him. "That's why he's in a hurry."

Oh, yeah? I asked as Erík reached the bottom of the hill and disappeared out of sight around a corner in the opposite direction from the university. *Then why'd he just turn left?*

I half-jogged down the rest of the hill with my backpack thumping against me at every step. At the next corner, I again poked my head around to make sure the coast was clear before heading after Erík. He was continuing to walk briskly away from the university and in the direction of a strange looking UFO-like restaurant and exhibition hall overlooking Reykjavík in the distance that was called the Perlan.

"Where the heck is he going?" I mumbled to myself as I continued to follow him, keeping a discreet distance as he continued down along some cycling paths and up a pedestrian bridge that crossed over a busy road.

I was worried that Erík might turn around suddenly and see me following him. If I could see his bright red hair so well from a distance, the odds were good that he could spot my red hair as well, so I pulled the hood of my jacket up to cover my head and face and disguise myself as much as possible. I don't know how effective it was, but at least it helped protect me from the biting wind coming from the direction of the ocean.

Off in the distance to my right, a small propeller plane roared down the runway of the small Reykjavík city airport.

Is that where he's going? I wondered. *The city airport?* It was impossible to know, but the farther in that direction we went, the more likely that possibility became, as there wasn't much else out there.

"Wherever he's going, you'd better be careful that he doesn't see you," the little voice in my head worried. "He's off the bike track now, and there's no sidewalk. And when people walk along the side of the road like that, they tend to look behind them to make sure a car isn't coming."

Good thinking, I replied, and slowed down considerably to put some distance between Erík and me. We were both out in the open with hardly any buildings around, so there was no danger that I would lose sight of him, even if he were far away. In the meantime, I would just continue to walk as innocently as possible in case he did happen to glance over his shoulder.

As it turned out, I didn't have to worry. Erík never once looked back in my direction, and after a couple of minutes, it became obvious that my hunch had been right. He was heading for the airport.

Erík turned right, headed across the parking lot of the airport, and disappeared around the corner of the terminal building. I grabbed the straps of my backpack and ran the rest of the way to the terminal.

It was a tiny airport, but it was fairly busy with various people walking around and standing in lines. I couldn't spot Erík anywhere.

He must have known I was following him, I mused, *and he ducked in here just to throw me off his tail.*

Then I spotted him on the opposite side of the hall. He was talking (and flirting) with a woman at one of the service desks for Eagle Air Iceland. (It's funny how flirting can be so obvious, even when it's in a different language and is taking place across a crowded room.)

I pulled my hood up a bit and tried to stay invisible as I watched Erík bring his flirting to an end (when it had accomplished its purpose, no doubt) and walk over to the security checkpoint. The line there wasn't long, and within minutes, Erík emptied his pockets and walked through the metal detector into the secure area of the airport where he soon disappeared into an area where I could no longer follow him.

"So, what now?" the little voice in my head asked after I'd stood there a few long moments in the middle of the crowded airport. "He's gone and is obviously flying somewhere."

"Exactly," I muttered under my breath. "And I bet I know exactly where."

Chapter Eighteen
The Westman Islands

I was willing to bet a million dollars that Erík was going to Húsavík. I was sure of it. It made perfect sense. It was the closest city to the sabotaged construction sites at the river dam, and I was betting that he was planning to fly in and then drive out to the construction site in the middle of the night to sabotage the equipment.

Maybe he even meets up with some co-conspirators in Húsavík, and the whole group of them is responsible for the sabotage, I thought to myself as I threaded my way through the groups of people in the small airport, heading for the television monitors that showed information for the departing and arriving flights. *He's probably part of some crazy militant environmentalist group or something. In fact, he's probably their leader.*

When I reached the monitors, I scanned the list of departing flights. There weren't many on the screen, and I scanned the list several times to be sure, but there was no Eagle Air flight to Húsavík. In fact, there were no flights to Húsavík at all throughout the entire day. And the only upcoming Eagle Air flight for the next few hours was to a place called Vestmannaeyjar—a name that seemed familiar to me somehow, although I wasn't sure why.

"So much for that theory," the little voice in my head observed wryly. "Unless the screen is broken...."

I thought about this for a moment, and then I walked quickly over to the closest Eagle Air service desk.

"Pardon me," I asked the woman in the airline uniform who was standing behind the counter. "Can you tell me when your next flight to Húsavík is?"

"Unfortunately, we don't fly to Húsavík on Sundays," she replied, smiling. "Our next flight to Húsavík is tomorrow morning at eight."

I was stumped. Erík must not be going to Húsavík after all. He must be going to Vestmannaeyjar, whatever that was.

"And what about this ten-thirty flight?" I asked, pointing to the screen. "To Vest-man-nae-y-jar?" I winced apologetically at my incredibly poor pronunciation as I tried to sound out each syllable of the difficult long name.

"Vestmannaeyjar," the woman replied with a chuckle, pronouncing it something like *west man nye year*. "Those are the Westman Islands," she said.

Oh! I thought brightly. *The Westman Islands! I've heard of those.*

Thanking her, I retreated from the counter and stared blankly at the departure screen while I continued pondering the situation.

Vestmannaeyjar was the Westman Islands, a series of small islands off the south coast of Iceland. I knew them because they were one of the places I had planned to visit on my various sightseeing trips around the country. But the more important question was what was Erík planning to do there?

There's only one way to find out, I thought to myself. *I have to follow him there.*

"And how are you planning to do that?" the little voice in my head inquired. "Are you going to buy a ticket and follow him on the plane? He'll recognize you for sure. It can't be a very big aircraft, after all."

That was my first thought, actually, I admitted. *But you forget that I have a plane of my own.*

My inner voice seemed to think about that a moment before answering.

"You'll never make it in time," it replied after a few long seconds.

Sure, I will, I thought. *It's more than half an hour before Erík's flight leaves. That gives me plenty of time to get back to my plane, check the navigation plan I already prepared for my visit to the islands, and be airborne in no time. In fact, I might even beat him there if I am fast enough.*

The little voice in my head didn't seem to have an answer for that, but it didn't matter anyway because I was already headed for the exit, walking quickly and making my way toward the row of taxis.

Jumping into the back of the first available taxi, I asked the driver to take me downtown to the harbor. The ride took longer than I expected, but I was soon behind the wheel of my trusty De Havilland seaplane with the engine warming up and checking my GPS for the navigation plan that I'd already prepared.

After flipping through my GPS for a minute, I was confident that my flight plan was okay and that everything on my plane was running the way it was supposed to. There was nothing left to stop me, and soon I was roaring across the waters of Faxaflói Bay and climbing into the sky.

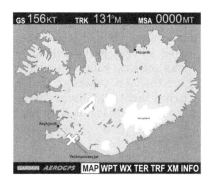

After heading west for the first few minutes, I soon turned southeast and put myself on a safe course for the main inhabited island of the Westman Islands—an island called Heimaey. It was at the airport there that Erík's flight would be landing shortly before me. It was a short flight, and I had hoped to beat him to the island, but it didn't look like that was going to happen after all.

It was a beautiful day with visibility for miles in every direction but with some uncomfortably high winds that I had quickly learned were a part of daily life here in Iceland. Soon the spiky black lava fields passing beneath me gave way to the ocean as I crossed over the coastline and headed out over the water. Up ahead I could see the jagged and rocky island of Heimaey jutting up green and black from the dark waves. I could also see a small commercial plane coming in for a landing at the island's airport. I assumed that was the flight that Erík had taken.

I circled around the majestic cliffs at the northern end of the island and made my final descent past thousands of nesting puffins and other seabirds lining the cliffs off to my right-hand side. After touching down in the protected harbor, I taxied loudly up to the public visitor's dock where a grizzled, weather-beaten man with a large beard was walking toward me. I assumed he was the harbormaster.

Shutting my engine down after the short flight, I glided slowly up to the dock and stepped out onto the pontoon float of my seaplane. The weather-beaten man grunted at me through his beard and pointed down toward the end of the dock to a place where I could tie up.

"Thanks," I said after I'd tied off the mooring lines and secured my seaplane to the dock. I pulled out some Icelandic bank notes from the zipper pocket on my jacket to pay the mooring fee.

The harbormaster grunted at me again and held up the palms of his hands to wave my money away. *It's free,* he was apparently saying.

"Are you sure?" I asked. "I'll be here a few hours, at least."

He grunted again and gestured for me to put my money away.

"Well, thank you," I replied, and nodded my appreciation as I stuffed the money back into my pocket.

With one final grunt, the harbormaster pointed me in the direction of the town, and I headed down the dock, waving to him in thanks. He waved back and probably grunted again, too, but I was too far away with the wind in my ears to hear it.

"This isn't going to be as easy as I thought," I said to myself as I stepped up from the docks and into what appeared to be the center of the town. It was a lot bigger than I'd expected, and a quick glance at my watch confirmed that Erík's flight had already landed, so it was too late for me to make it there to pick up his trail. By now, he might have caught a ride with someone or taken a taxi somewhere, or maybe he was just walking into town on his own.

Wherever he was, I had to figure out how I was going to find him, or else this entire excursion would be nothing more than a sightseeing daytrip for me.

"Not that there's anything wrong with that," the little voice in my head observed optimistically. It was a beautiful sunny day in Iceland, and I was on a tiny island in a charming little fishing town nestled at the foot of some dramatic cliffs that towered above it. That seemed like a pretty good day to me, even if I didn't manage to find Erík.

But I'd still like to find Erík, I reminded myself. *And that café across the street looks like the perfect place to sit and figure out exactly how to do that.*

Chapter Nineteen

The Fire Mountain

"When I was a boy, that mountain over there didn't exist," the gray-haired owner of the café told me as he gestured out the window across a dark lava field to a great reddish-black mound rising in the distance. "None of this land off to the left was there, either. When I was a boy, the ocean was just a few hundred meters away from here. But ever since the eruption, the coastline is at least a couple of kilometers away."

I was sitting with a warm cup of seafood chowder in my hands by the windows of a cozy little café with its owner—Ármann—telling me about the volcanic eruption in 1973 that had nearly destroyed the entire town.

"It was the dead of winter," Ármann said, taking up the story once again. "And there were terrible storms that whole week, so the entire fishing fleet was moored down in the harbor and the men were warm and safe at home with their families.

"Late one evening, the Earth began to stir from a five-thousand-year slumber, and those who were still awake felt a few minor earthquake tremors here and there, but nothing that caused any alarm. We are used to such things around here.

"And then it happened. Sometime past midnight, the Earth awoke, and out past the eastern end of town, the ground literally split open, creating a gaping hellish chasm more than a kilometer long. Fiery fountains of lava sprayed more than a hundred meters into the air, creating incredible curtains of fire along the entire length of the fissure.

"Thanks to the storms and the fact that the fishing fleet was at home, we were able to evacuate the town quickly and safely. By sunrise, the five thousand residents of the island had been ferried to safety on the mainland, but some men stayed behind to tame the volcano and save the town.

"Day after day, the eruption continued. Volcanic ash filled the skies and covered the island like a filthy heavy snow more than a meter deep. Workers scrambled to clear the ash from the streets and reinforce the roofs of the houses to support the immense weight of the ash until they had time to clean it off.

"The fountains of lava continued, and a great mountain rose up from deep within the Earth. Rising from the depths of the world alongside its sister, the ancient but dormant volcano of Helgafell, it rose higher and higher, eventually becoming the mountain that you can see out there, which we call Eldfell—the Fire Mountain.

"For weeks and months the eruption continued and the lava flowed. Cold seawater was pumped in from the ocean and sprayed onto the advancing lava to keep it from consuming the town. This cooled and hardened the lava, which formed a barrier against the still molten lava farther beyond. Sometimes these measures prevailed, and the lava was forced off in another direction. But at other times, nature had her way whether we liked it or not, and the lava flowed right over these improvised dams and on into the town, consuming homes and buildings as it went.

"If you go just down this street here along the edge of town," Ármann said, gesturing out the window again, "you can see a few houses that are half covered in lava and ash. That was where the lava was finally stopped. But there are many more houses farther beyond that you can't see anymore because they are buried underneath the lava."

I turned my head to look down the street and tried to imagine what it must have been like.

"If you go for a walk on the paths through the lava field," Ármann said. "You can see the remnants of the houses that once stood there: pipes, bathtubs, radiators, wires, that kind of thing. And there are little plaques showing the buried houses and telling about the people who once lived there."

"Are they all dead?" I asked, horrified. "Buried under the lava?"

"No, no, goodness no," Ármann replied with a hearty laugh. "No one died. Many homes were destroyed, but the people of the town were all safely evacuated."

I looked out of the window once again and tried to imagine it. Curtains of lava spraying into the air, glowing lava crawling slowly down into the town, consuming the town street by street as locals with black, ash-covered faces struggled desperately to save their homes.

"But it was not just the town that was under threat," Ármann continued. "The lava was also flowing into the sea, slowly creating new land and threatening to close off our harbor. And that was a real problem, because without the harbor for our fishing boats, there would be no reason to stay here.

"An enormous seawater pumping operation was put into action, and special pumps were brought in that could spray thousands of liters of water every second onto the advancing wall of lava. Slowly but surely, the lava was brought to a halt a mere hundred meters before it would have sealed off the entrance to the harbor forever.

"The eruption continued for almost six months, gradually getting less and less intense, and it finally burned itself out completely and the Earth fell silent once again. The harbor and the town had been saved, and the local people were happy, despite the fact that hundreds of homes had been consumed.

"Mother Nature had been defeated—or had she? Perhaps this had been her plan for the humans all along. After all, the harbor is far superior now compared to before the eruption. It is deeper and more protected from the winter storms thanks to the enormous tracts of newly created land off the eastern side of the island that were formed by the lava flows."

Ármann leaned back in his chair and shrugged his shoulders.

"We'll never know," he said simply, ending the story. "But for now she has allowed us to continue living and working here on this island. And for that we are grateful."

"Unbelievable," I whispered in awe.

Behind me, I heard the sound of the bell above the door jingling as another customer stepped into the café.

"And now you must excuse me," Ármann said with a smile, rising from his chair to attend to the new customer. "Please enjoy your soup. I will return to see if you need anything else."

"Thank you; it's delicious," I said as Ármann walked away, heartily greeting the newly arrived customer.

I took another sip of my soup, relishing the warm salty broth as it flowed down deep into my stomach. It tasted like the sea, which sounds like a stupid thing to say since it was seafood chowder, but it seemed to me that everything here on this island smelled and tasted like the sea—a comforting fragrance of gritty earth and ocean. Everything here seemed more real and authentic than the outside world. Even the air.

It was as though this small island was some magical place where all the elements existed all together at once. In fact, it seemed to me that the entire country of Iceland was like this—. More connected to nature somehow. More fundamental. And more elemental. Iceland is the very essence of earth, air, fire, and water.

They certainly have the fire part, that's for sure, I thought to myself, glancing out of the window as I took another sip of soup, and gazing up toward the rising forms of the island's two volcanoes—Eldfell and her older sister, Helgafell.

"Ja, ja, ja," I heard Ármann saying from across the room, clapping his newly arrived customer on the back and reaching over the worn, wooden counter to grab a large, thin book.

Tilting my head a bit, I looked closer at the book as Ármann handed it over. It looked like a phonebook, although a thin one.

"A phone book," I whispered to myself. That gave me an idea.

Chapter Twenty

Totally Busted

"Can I see the phone book too?" I asked Ármann after his other customer had finished with it.

"Of course," he replied cheerfully, bringing the book over to my table. "Do you want some more bread with your soup?"

I shook my head. "No, no more bread, thank you," I replied. "This soup is incredible, but I will barely finish it as it is. I had too many pieces of skúffukaka this morning."

Ármann laughed loudly, a strong and vibrant laugh straight from his belly. "I know exactly what you mean," he whispered, leaning over to pat me on the shoulder before walking toward the kitchen with my empty bread plate.

Maybe Erík is visiting family here on the island, I thought as I opened the phone book and flipped to the G section. *If I remember correctly, Erík's last name is Grettirsson. Let's see if there are any Grettirssons living on the island.*

Running my finger down the page, I searched for Grettirsson.

Grettir Aðalbjarnarson
Grettir Dagfinnsson
Grettir Eiríksson
Grettir Grímólfsson
Grettir Njálsson
Grettir Njarðarson

There were several Grettirs, but no Grettirssons. I guess he wasn't visiting family after all.

"So much for that idea," I muttered as I stared at the open page. I couldn't help but think that something was not quite right about the phone book, but I couldn't put my finger on it, and I just sat there staring at the names on the page.

Then finally, I understood.

And I felt like an idiot.

It was sorted alphabetically by first name, not last name, as I was used to in Canada. The page I was looking at was the section for everyone on the island with the first name Grettir.

I thought back to what Konrad and his family had told me when I first arrived in Iceland about their use of first and last names. In Iceland, a person's last name isn't a family name. It is a name formed using the father's or mother's name to indicate that the person was his or her son or daughter.

After a few minutes of feeling so stupid that I might cry, I actually started to feel rather proud of myself for being so clever and figuring it out.

"You *should* be very proud," the little voice in my head commented sarcastically. "I'm sure you're the first person to ever figure out the Icelandic phone book. But how does this help us? Now there's no way to figure out whether Erík is visiting family on the island or not."

The little voice was right, but I was still proud of myself. I reminded myself to tell my dad about it. (He is the kind of person who finds this kind of thing interesting.) And thinking about my dad reminded me of why I had come to Iceland in the first place: to see the country and experience it, not to chase around crazy half-baked theories.

"So what do we do now?" the little voice asked. "How are we going to find Erík?"

We're not, I replied, pushing the phone book off to the side and picking up my cup of soup again. *We're going to enjoy ourselves here. We'll take a walk around the town and out onto the lava to see these ruined houses that Ármann was talking about. And then we're going to fly home to Reykjavík.*

"And what about Erík?" the little voice asked.

If it's meant to be, we'll bump into him, I replied. *But I won't count on it. I plan to just have a nice, pleasant day looking around the island.*

Slurping down the last of my soup, I put the cup back on the table and grabbed the phone book to close it again. But as I picked it up, something caught my eye.

I'd opened the book to the page where the names started with G, but halfway down the page, the H names began and one of them caught my eye.

Halldóra Sæfinnsdóttir húsmóðir Hásteinsvegur 14

Halldóra?!? Seeing her name was like a light bulb going off inside my head, and I struggled to remember what Halldóra the Elf Lady had said her last name was when we were introduced. It was something complicated and strange sounding that I couldn't understand, much less spell, but I was pretty sure it had started with S.

You are so busted, Erík, I thought as the implications of this new piece of the puzzle washed over me like a tidal wave.

"Halldóra, too," the little voice in my head helpfully reminded me. "She's busted, too."

Yes, Halldóra, too, I agreed, my face turning red as my heart began to pound faster and faster at the enormity of my discovery.

Ármann passed by on his way back from delivering a plate of food to his other customer, and I waved him over.

"All finished?" he asked.

I nodded. "It was amazing; thank you so much," I replied as he cleared the dishes from in front of me. "But can I ask you a question about an address?" I slid the phone book over toward him with my finger on the entry for Halldóra Sæfinnsdóttir. "Do you know where this address is?" I asked. "Husmodir Hasteins-vegur?"

Ármann leaned back and laughed another one of his hearty belly laughs. "Húsmóðir means housewife. In Iceland, we put people's occupations alongside their names in the phone book."

"Oh," I replied, blushing and chuckling along with his infectious laugh. "That's weird."

"And I certainly do know where Hásteinsvegur 14 is," Ármann continued, pointing out the window and down the street. "Just follow this road down here and take the second right once you reach the park. Ten minutes' walk, maybe."

"Thank you," I said as I pulled some Icelandic money from my pocket to pay for my bread and soup. Then a thought occurred to me: *Shouldn't Halldóra's occupation in the phone book be Elf Specialist or Paranormal Advisor or something like that? If this Halldóra is a housewife, then maybe she's not the same person.*

"Are you going for a psychic reading?" Ármann asked. "Or are you a friend of Halldóra's?"

I wasn't sure that I'd heard him correctly.

"Pardon me?" I asked, my heart pounding like a jackhammer once again.

"Halldóra," Ármann said. "Are you going to see her for a psychic reading or an elf consultation or something like that? Or are you a just a friend?"

"About the elves," I told Ármann as the light bulb in my head lit up again like a supernova.

Bingo! Erík and Halldóra were both totally busted.

Chapter Twenty-One
What Kind Of Housewife Is She?

Halldóra's house was a cute little red wooden house on the corner of a street filled with cute little multi-colored houses of all shapes and sizes. Some of the houses were painted white, but even those had their own touch of color, with roofs in blues and greens and reds, and in various shades of terracotta.

As I walked past Halldóra's house on the opposite side of the street, I could see no signs of activity inside. I continued past and tried to find somewhere unobtrusive to sit and watch the house. It didn't take me long to realize that it was going to be difficult to stake the house out without being seen. There was nowhere to hide unless I climbed over the fence into someone's yard. But of course that would be far too suspicious looking, and it would cause more trouble than it solved.

After crossing the intersection, I found a spot along a fence kitty-corner from Halldóra's house where I could sit on the ground and have a clear view of both the front door and the back yard. Sitting down and pretending to read a book would keep me low and out of sight, half-hidden behind a car that was parked nearby, and I would appear fairly inconspicuous. Reading something would also keep me from getting bored while waiting for something to happen. Who knows how long I would have to wait, after all.

I sat down and pulled a book from my backpack—Ernest Hemingway's *To Have and Have Not*—one of the books I'd bought in Key West. I'd been keeping it in my backpack for just such an occasion as this—not a stakeout, *per se*, but an occasion where I could just sit outside in the fresh air and warm sun and read.

With my hood over my head and hair and my face buried in the book, I found I was able to read and still surreptitiously roll my eyes up every minute or two to scan the house for any activity. I did this time and time again, but there was nothing to be seen and no sign of life anywhere, and not just at Halldóra's house. There were no signs of life anywhere else on the street, either. Other than the *very* occasional passing car and the sound of children playing at some distant playground, there were no indications of life at all in this sleepy little town.

I thought back to when I'd bought my book at the Hemingway House Museum bookstore in Key West.

"Hemingway called this book 'a piece of junk'," the lady behind the counter had told me. "Apparently he was not happy with it at all. And that's exactly why you should read it. You already have his best works in that pile of books you're planning to buy. You also need the ones he considered his worst to give yourself a little perspective."

I looked down at the book in my hands and flipped it over to read the back cover text.

"And what about you?" I asked. "What do you think of it?"

The lady laughed. "I think it's a wonderful piece of work," she announced loudly to no one in particular before leaning over toward me and dropping her voice to a conspiratorial whisper. "It's not very good, if you ask me. But I meant what I said about it—about having perspective."

I had liked the sound of that: perspective. So I'd added the book to my growing stack of Hemingway novels next to the cash register.

But as it turned out, perspective was something difficult to come by, because after a couple dozen pages of reading, I began to understand Mr. Hemingway's negative feelings about his own book. The story didn't really do anything for me, so after a while, I used the book to make it look like I was absorbed in the story rather than actually reading it.

"Why are we even waiting here, anyway?" the little voice in my head asked as I sat and listened to the lonely wind blowing across the island. "Don't you have enough proof already to convince you that the whole 'elves sabotaging the construction site' thing is a lie?"

"I have to be absolutely sure," I said under my breath. "I have to be one hundred percent certain that Erík knows Halldóra, and that this Halldóra is the same Halldóra I met a couple of days ago—and that all of this is not just some very odd coincidence."

"An odd coincidence—are you serious?" the little voice responded incredulously. "What else do you need to convince you?"

A fragment of motion out of the corner of my eye caught my attention, and I looked up from the pages of my book to see a lone figure walking briskly up the street toward me. Actually, striding would be a better word for it, and I had seen that stride before.

"Something just like that right there," I said to myself, trying to bury my face in even deeper in my book so the fast-approaching figure wouldn't notice me. The figure was Erík, and he was walking right up the street toward Halldóra's cute little red house.

"He sure took a long time getting here," the little voice in my head observed. "He must have walked into town from the airport or something."

"Yeah, maybe," I thought. "I guess he just likes walking."

With my heart pounding up into my throat, I tried to make myself as small as possible as Erík came closer and closer.

"Please don't look over here," I whispered to myself. "Please."

I didn't have to worry, as it turned out, because Erík didn't even so much as glance over in my direction as he strode up to Halldóra's front door and pulled on the bell.

"That's it, then," the little voice in my head said as I sat there terrified and afraid to move a single muscle, waiting for Halldóra to answer the door. "Now we can get out of here."

Just wait, I said to myself. *I have to wait for the right moment. I don't want to draw attention to myself while he's still standing there.*

I stayed there for what seemed like an eternity, frozen in place in plain sight while Erík stood just a few dozen meters away. His back was turned, but there was always the possibility that he might turn around at any second and look straight at me.

What the heck is Halldóra doing? I wondered, feeling desperate and panicky as each second ticked by heavily. *Why isn't she answering the door?*

More seconds passed, and I really started to panic. I glanced over at the nearby car and considered crawling over to it and out of Erík's line of sight. Halldóra was clearly not at home, and I had no idea what direction Erík would take once he finally gave up and left. If he continued walking down the street toward me, it would be nearly impossible for him not to notice me. If that happened, I could only hope that he wouldn't recognize me with my hood up over my face and red hair. He'd only met me once, after all. Maybe he wouldn't remember what I looked like? Maybe it would probably be okay.

Maybe... probably... I hope....

"That's not very reassuring," the little voice commented as I heard the clicking sound of a lock opening, and my eyes darted up just in time to see the front door of Halldóra's house swing open.

With the door open, I could see that this was definitely the same Halldóra I'd met in the highlands a few days earlier. I recognized her kind face and short blonde hair, and I had the same impression as the first time I saw her: that she looked just like an elf, or at least an elf wearing nothing but a towel wrapped around her.

"That confirms it," I said to myself, gritting my teeth and smiling in satisfaction. The two of them definitely knew each other, and that had to mean that they are working together to sabotage the construction site.

"It looks like they're in on more than just that," the little voice in my head remarked as Erík wrapped his arms around Halldóra's neck and waist and pulled her close for a deep, wet kiss.

"Oh, my god," I gasped as Halldóra wound herself around Erík, her left leg lifting up and twisting behind him passionately. "Oh, my god."

The pair of them kissed deeply for a few seconds then broke apart. Pushing herself backward, Halldóra grabbed both ends of Erík's scarf provocatively and pulled him in through the doorway, closing the door with a solid clunk behind them.

"What kind of housewife is she?" I said under my breath, my mouth still hanging open from the shock of seeing the two of them together. "I wonder if her husband knows about *that*?"

Chapter Twenty-Two
A Town Under The Frozen Lava

Having successfully confirmed my theory that Erík and Halldóra knew each other (or, actually, knew each other plus a little extra), there was no reason for me to stake out the house any longer and run the risk of being spotted. I climbed carefully to my feet, keeping my eyes on Halldóra's little red house the entire time, and slowly backed away. As I walked down the street away from them, I couldn't help but glance nervously over my shoulder to see if I was being followed. It was only after I rounded the corner of the next street over that I was able to relax and breathe a sigh of relief.

With every step that put more distance between them and me, I felt more confident and relaxed. But I knew that I would feel a lot better once I told someone what I had seen, so I pulled my cell phone out of my backpack to call Konrad or Kristín.

Kristín, I remembered, was in classes until later in the evening, so I scrolled through my phone to dial Konrad instead. After pressing the green Call button, I lifted the phone to my ear and waited.

For a moment, nothing happened, but then I heard a series of tones and a robotic female voice speaking Icelandic. I had no idea what she was saying, and yet I knew exactly what she was trying to tell me: *The person you are trying to reach is not available, please try again later.* That kind of message is recognizable in every language.

I pressed the End Call button and dialed again.

"The person you are trying to reach is not available. Please try again later," the robotic Icelandic voice said again after a few seconds' pause.

Staring at my phone, I tried to think of what to do next. Not having any particularly good ideas, I just kept walking. I wasn't sure where I was heading, but the most important thing was to keep putting distance between Erík and me.

"What about sending a text message?" the little voice in my head suggested.

I shook my head and immediately rejected the idea. "This is something that I need to tell them in person," I said to myself.

"You're right. Besides, what's the hurry?" the little voice replied. "You'll see them tonight anyway. Just tell them then."

Exactly, I thought. But then I wondered what I should do between now and then. I planned to visit Albert at his lab and then meet Konrad and Kristín for a late dinner in Reykjavík, but until then, the entire day was mine.

Under normal circumstances, I would have been keen to stay on the island and have a look around, particularly to venture out to the area where the lava flow had covered the town. But the idea of staying on this small island with Erík so close by made me a little nervous.

"Don't be stupid," the little voice in my head told me. "He's quite preoccupied at the moment. I don't think you have anything to worry about."

That was absolutely right, of course, so I adjusted my walking route to take me back toward the east.

The lava field wasn't difficult to find. I just walked toward the two volcanic peaks ahead of me—Eldfell and Helgafell. As I approached the eastern edge of town, a wall of black volcanic rock seemed to rise up suddenly from straight out of the ground. At the very edges of this barrier were houses, some of them half buried and collapsed from the lava and ash that had covered them.

I followed a path that lead to the face of the wall of rock and picked my way through a maze of stones to the upper surface of the lava field. It was tricky, but the jumble of rocks had plenty of places I could grab with my hands for support. I just had to be careful where I put my feet. Once I got to the top, I was rewarded with a nice view over the rooftops of the little town.

As I picked my way through the field of lava stones, it was incredible to imagine that the cold, black stone I was walking on had once been red-hot molten lava threatening to destroy the town.

Here and there small plaques on the stones marked the locations of the houses and buildings buried deep underneath.

15 meters below this stone the house of the Kiwannis Club Helgafell was situated. It was the first house belonging to a Kiwannis Club in Europe. The house was built in the year 1924 and was buried under a lava flow on March 27th, 1973.

There was something unsettling about these plaques and stones and the thought of a town buried fifteen meters beneath my feet. It was like walking over a graveyard, even though no one had actually died there. Their homes had died, though, I suppose. And somehow that was very sad.

I shivered and suddenly felt very uneasy up there on the lava with the harsh wind howling across the stones. Imagining the sound of footsteps behind me, I glanced quickly over my shoulder, terrified that I would find Erík standing there with his strong hands reaching out to grab me.

"What if Erík and Halldóra decide to go for a walk through the lava field?" the little voice in my head asked, starting to panic. "If he sees you here, he'll know you're onto him."

This was a stupid thing to think, I know. I mean, why would they decide to go for a walk in the lava field? And even *if* Erík happened to see me up here, he certainly wasn't going to jump to the conclusion that I had been following him all day and that I knew his secrets. He would just think I was out here sightseeing for the day.

Right?

"I better climb down off of here and go home," I whispered, startling myself with the sound of my own voice. I suddenly had a very strong urge to get back to my plane and off this godforsaken island.

Okay, it isn't a godforsaken island. That isn't fair. It is a lovely, charming, and beautiful place.

And it was an amazing day with the sun was shining brightly and the wind chasing clouds across the bright blue sky. But with my imagination running wild and me expecting to see Erík at every turn, I was only going to feel better once I put even more distance between him and me.

Only when I was airborne, and on my way back to Reykjavík, would I feel completely safe.

Chapter Twenty-Three
A Beautiful Sea Of Paper Airplanes

Walking back into town, looking over my shoulder nervously as I went, I soon found myself behind the controls of my trusty De Havilland Beaver. Waving goodbye to the grizzled and weather-beaten harbormaster, I taxied out into the harbor and powered up for takeoff.

Racing across the water, I picked up speed and was soon airborne. I can't tell you what a relief it was to feel the pontoons of my plane break free of the water and climb slowly and steadily into the sky. With every passing second, I felt lighter and more relaxed.

I banked my plane past the cliffs at the north end of the island and glanced back to see Heimaey's twin volcanic peaks diminishing in the distance. As I turned my head forward again, I saw something that seemed so impossible that it made me do a double take. Crouched in the grass at the edge of a cliff jutting out hundreds of feet over the ocean was a man with a long pole. The pole was at least three times taller than he was and had a small net fixed on the end of it.

"What in the world is he doing?!?" I asked as I continued my slow turn around the tip of the island.

As I looked on in utter astonishment, a small flock of puffins came sailing around the corner of the cliffs, riding the wind as they went, and in one quick fluid motion the man sprang into life, standing up and leaning out over the edge of the cliff with his pole.

"Oh, my god!" I cried out. He was so close to the edge that I was sure he would tumble head over heels and plunge to his death on the rocks and waves hundreds of feet below. Instead, he planted his feet firmly on the ground, swung his pole outward, and skillfully netted one of the puffins in mid-flight.

My jaw dropped open and I blinked hard. I couldn't believe what I had just seen.

"Did he just catch that puffin in mid-air with that stupid pole?" I asked as I continued my turn and the man disappeared out of sight on the other side of the cliffs behind me.

I played the whole sequence over in my mind again and again. If I hadn't seen it with my own two eyes, I am not sure that I would ever believe it. The man had been hiding in the grass on the top of a cliff so that he could catch himself a puffin.

"Why would he do that?!?" I wondered. "Why would he risk his life to catch a puffin?"

"He must be some kind of puffin scientist or something," the little voice in my head suggested. "Why else would he do something so crazy?"

But I knew that wasn't it. He was catching it for food. I remembered Konrad mentioning at dinner the other day that in Iceland, puffin was considered a delicacy.

"How can anyone eat such a cute little bird," I wondered as I leveled off and set course for Reykjavík.

Switching on some music, I sang along to a few songs. Before I knew it, I had passed over the coastline of the main island and was making a long, slow turn back toward the harbor at Reykjavík, bucking high winds as I went and coming in for a rather bumpy landing. I taxied my plane toward the dock and shut down the engine, letting my forward momentum carry me the rest of the way into my parking spot. Popping open the door of the cockpit, I climbed down onto the pontoons and tied up securely.

Glancing at my watch, I saw that it was a bit later than I'd expected, and I had to be sure not to forget my appointment to meet Albert at his lab. I decided to take a nice slow walk along the water, taking the scenic route to the university so that I would end up there right on time.

I took my iPod out of my backpack and put my headphones in as I strolled along the walking path at the edge of the bay. I came to a sculpture facing out toward the water that looked like the skeleton of a Viking ship, and decided to sit there for a while. The sculpture was called The Sun Voyager according to a sign posted nearby.

Today feels like a Coldplay day, I decided and scrolled through my iPod to C and pressed play. As the music filled my ears, I leaned back and let myself blissfully detach from the rest of the world, thinking whatever thoughts came into my head.

As my gaze traveled along the water's edge, I realized that I must be near the spot where the Vikings first landed in Iceland. Konrad had mentioned a few days earlier that the Vikings followed their custom of bringing with them a pair of wooden seat pillars from Norway to throw into the water when they came to land. They would watch to see where the pillars washed ashore, and that was where they would land and make their settlement. I realized that it was entirely possible that I was sitting at the exact spot where those wooden pillars had washed ashore more than a thousand years earlier at a place that the Vikings had called the Bay of Smoke, so named because of the wisps of geothermal steam they could see rising up from the ground.

"Iceland is a very unique place," Konrad had said. "Unlike Canada and the rest of the Americas, it is a place where the arriving Europeans did not have to conquer and subjugate any indigenous peoples already living there. When the Vikings arrived, there was no one here except maybe a few Irish monks along the southern coast.

"It is also a unique place because it is a country with no history before the arrival of the Europeans. And because the Vikings who first arrived here could read and write, Iceland is unlike almost every other place on Earth in that it is a nation without a pre-historic period of human habitation. It is a country without a past."

I liked the sound of that somehow—a country without a past. And sitting there at the edge of the water, with the majestic curving lines of the Sun Voyager rising up into the sky, I felt as though I understood exactly what that meant.

I sat there for a very long time with my eyes closed, feeling the sun and wind on my face as I leaned back and dreamed the afternoon away.

It was so beautiful and calming at the edge of the water that it was difficult to stand up again and leave it behind. But I had to force myself to get up so I wouldn't be late for my appointment with Albert.

Stuffing my iPod into my backpack, I started out across the city toward the university. It was a fairly short walk, and following the map that Albert's assistant had given me, I soon found myself in a remote outbuilding on the university campus where Albert's lab was located.

As I approached the open door, I checked my map one last time to make sure I was in the right place, and then I knocked tentatively.

"Albert?" I called out, pushing the door all the way open and stepping into the darkened lab. I was a bit early, and he might not have arrived yet. "Albert? Are you here?"

There was no answer.

When my eyes adjusted to the darkness, I saw that the only illumination in the large open space of the lab was a lamp on a desk at the opposite end of the room.

As I crept through the lab, I saw something that was so amazing and beautiful that it actually made me gasp. Sitting on shelves and tables, hanging from invisible wires from the ceiling, and even cluttered on the floor were hundreds of blue paper airplanes. They came in every conceivable shape and design and were made from the same royal blue paper that Albert had been using the night before when he'd folded a plane for me.

I looked around in astonishment at the beautiful sea of blue paper airplanes all around me. Some were incredibly tiny—a thimble-sized origami glider perched on a nearby shelf. Others were huge—a sleek, bullet-shaped plane more than a meter long sat on the floor on the other side of the room.

Some were simple in design—standard, pointy, and triangular shaped, like the kind that everyone knows how to fold. Others were vastly more complex, such as military fighter planes and graceful gliders that seemed almost alive and defied the possibility that they were merely folded bits of paper.

As I made my way down the length of the room, I was amazed and astounded at the dazzling array of shapes and designs that surrounded me. I couldn't believe that Albert had folded all of them. I reminded myself to ask him whether I could take some photographs of them when he arrived, not to mention that he had to show me how to fold one of my own. I wanted to make one of the complicated ones, I decided.

I tried to choose a design that I could ask him to teach me, but there were so many beautiful ones that it was difficult to choose.

I approached the desk and saw that there was another plane sitting there that Albert was apparently in the middle of folding. It was half-finished, with detached pontoons sitting off to one side, and the fuselage and wings were not yet connected, but it was obvious what kind of plane it was meant to be. Albert was folding me a De Havilland Beaver seaplane.

"Oh my god, that is amazing," I whispered, approaching the desk with tears welling in my eyes. "I can't believe it."

The plane was perfect. Even in its unassembled and half-finished form, it was absolutely beautiful. I walked over to get a better look at it.

"Oh, my god," I whispered again, but when I walked behind the desk, I saw something that made the expression on my face go from an ear-to-ear smile to a look of confusion and horror. I first saw a pair of shoes and legs, and then the rest of the body of a man lying motionless on the floor. It was Albert, and he was collapsed in a jumbled heap face down on the floor, lying in a large pool of dark red blood. "Oh, my god! Albert!" I shrieked, kneeling down onto the floor next to him.

At that moment, I caught some movement out of the corner of my eye and looked up just in time to see a large, fat man in a dark suit emerge from the shadows. He was lumbering toward me with his hands outstretched, and he tried to grab me.

I reacted completely on instinct; my mind and my body instantly remembered the self-defense classes that I'd taken in high school. I was crouched next to Albert's lifeless body, so I swiveled my weight onto my right foot and pulled my arm back. In one fluid motion, I made a fist and catapulted all my weight forward, punching the fat man straight in the crotch as hard as I could just as he was about to grab me.

The fat man stopped dead in his tracks, and with a low guttural groan, he doubled over in pain. With the benefit of hindsight, I now realize that this would have been the appropriate moment for me to make a run for it, but I was too stunned and shocked to move, and by the time I recovered from my temporary paralysis, it was too late.

The fat man in the suit looked up at me in anger, and before I could duck out of the way, his enormous fist flew out and hit me squarely on the left side of my face. This was the first time I'd ever been punched in such a way, so what followed next was a new and terrifying experience. The whole world flashed instantly bright white, and every bone in my head shuddered from the blow. My body went barreling backward, and I remember hitting the floor—hard. After that, everything went completely black.

Chapter Twenty-Four

The Tofino High School Stare-down Champion

A s I slowly regained consciousness, the first thing I became aware of was that I was in a vehicle of some kind, driving along the road. I could feel the familiar vibration of spinning tires and the rumble and bounce of shock absorbers riding over small bumps in the pavement.

My head gradually began to clear, and the second thing I became aware of was that the left side of my face was in excruciating pain—hot, swollen, and pressed up against a cold, hard surface.

What happened? I asked myself, my head swirling in confusion. *Where am I?*

I was lying face down in darkness with my face hurting and my hands tied behind my back. For a moment, I thought I was back in Alaska, sharing a tent with Charlie and Will as we climbed the Chilkoot Pass. But that couldn't be right, could it?

I opened my eyes and blinked hard several times to try to clear my vision. It was dark and my eyes were swimming in and out of focus, so I couldn't make out any of my surroundings. I closed my eyes again, and after a very long moment, the fog in my head cleared enough that I could remember what had happened back in Albert's lab—the paper airplanes, the fat guy in the suit, and Albert lying dead on the floor.

"Oh, my god, Albert," I whispered. "Who did this to you?"

I opened my eyes again, and this time my vision was much clearer. Even in the dim light, I was able to make out a bit more of my surroundings. I was lying in the back of some kind of canvas-covered industrial truck that felt like it was going very fast down the highway, judging from the general smoothness of the ride.

Straining with my bound hands, I tried to sit up so I could have a better look around.

"Here, let me help you," I heard a voice say from directly behind me, scaring the crap out of me and causing me to nearly pull my shoulder out of its socket as I kicked and flopped like a fish in an attempt to push myself over to the opposite side of the truck.

In the dim light, I saw two men sitting directly behind me. The man on the right was the fat man who had punched me in Albert's lab. Wearing a dark suit that seemed two sizes too small, his considerable bulk was barely contained within the fabric. The man on the left was much smaller relative to his companion, although he was of normal height and build. He was also dressed in a dark suit with a crimson tie, and with his close-cropped dark hair and angular features, he was probably what some people would consider handsome. He looked over at me with a sympathetic and pleasant smile on his face.

"Let me help you," he said as he stood up and reached over to help me onto the bench directly across from them.

Confident that I wouldn't slide down onto the floor again—a real possibility with my hands bound behind my back—the dark-haired man sat down again and looked me in the eyes.

"I must apologize for my colleague," he said, smiling pleasantly as though we were having a friendly business meeting instead of me being tied-up, battered, and bruised. "You surprised him with your...uh..."

He paused for a moment, as if trying to find the right words.

My what? I thought, still feeling a bit stunned and confused, but also growing increasingly frightened and angry.

"Your feistiness," he continued, shifting uncomfortably. "He didn't expect you to hit him...in the place where you did."

"Yeah, well, I didn't expect him to come sneaking out of the shadows to grab me," I heard myself say in a voice that sounded a lot braver than I felt.

"You are right," the man replied, nodding sympathetically. "And I apologize for that as well."

"What did you do to Albert?" I cried viciously, my voice rising in volume and intensity as I leaned aggressively toward him. "Why did you kill him?"

Surprised by my outburst, the man pulled back with a startled and confused expression on his face. He leaned over to his fat partner to murmur something in a strange foreign language before turning back to face me again.

"We dealt with Dr. Ørsted," he said, regaining his composure, "because he refused to cooperate with us."

For a few moments, the three of us simply sat there, staring silently at one another across the back of the truck. The smaller man's expression was a perfect poker face, revealing no emotion, while his super-sized compatriot retained the same blank expression that he'd had throughout the entire discussion thus far. I stared back at them with a look that I hoped was one of sheer defiance.

I can do this all day, I thought to myself, staring the two of them down with as much intensity as I could muster. *I was the Tofino High School stare-down champion.*

But of course this wasn't a game that we were playing. These guys were deadly serious, and I would be lucky to get out of this alive. The best way for me to figure a way out of this would be to stay calm and cool— and angry. If I broke down in tears and panic, I was finished.

As the truck rumbled down the highway, our stare-down continued until the smaller man finally blinked and lowered his eyes. *One small victory for me,* I gloated.

He looked up again with the same sympathetic pleasant smile on his face.

"It doesn't have to be as difficult as this," he said with a sigh.

"Oh, yah?" I replied brazenly, unable to think of a better comeback.

He sighed again, put has hands on his knees, and leaned back casually, still smiling...always smiling.

"As you well know," he continued, his voice smooth and reassuring, "Dr. Ørsted...Albert...was working on something that is extremely valuable to those of us in the aluminum business."

I blinked, struggling to remember what Albert had been working on.

The man leaned toward me, his elbows on his knees in his attempt to appear reasonable. "And there are many people," he said, "who would do just about anything to get their hands on the discovery that Albert has made."

"Like killing him?" I hissed cynically. I swallowed hard, suppressing the urge to spit in his face. I had to keep a lid on my emotions and stay calm until I saw my opportunity to get out of this mess.

The man lowered his eyes. "Yes, there are many people who would kill to have it," he replied slowly, staring at the floor of the truck.

"Aluminum smelting," I said aloud, finally remembering one of the things that Albert had been working on.

The man looked up at me, confused.

"Aluminum smelting," I repeated, staring him down. "Albert was working on a more efficient smelting process."

The man stared at me, sizing me up, before answering.

"Exactly," he said.

Albert's remarks from the previous evening were coming back to me now. "Not only a more environmentally-friendly smelting process, but one that required less energy."

The man nodded again.

"More profitable," I concluded, continuing my stare-down of the men in suits sitting across from me.

"Exactly," the smaller man replied. "Vastly more profitable."

I nodded in disgust. Such greed—it was the Yukon gold rush all over again, and games like these were played over and over again, every single day in every corner of the world.

"Vastly more profitable," I said. "But now that Albert's dead, you'll never know the secret."

"Au contraire," the man replied, smiling that pleasant smile again that made me want to punch him in the face. "That's where you come in."

I didn't understand. What did I know about aluminum smelting?

"Because now that he's gone," the man said coolly. "It's up to you to tell us everything."

The man leaned back against the side of the truck again, reaching into his jacket as he did so to pull out a long, black automatic pistol.

"And I trust that you will be more cooperative than your friend Albert was," he said, gripping the pistol tightly and laying the barrel across his knee.

I looked down at the gun in his hand and felt my anger and defiance disappearing rapidly, quickly being replaced with cold, sweating fear and a heavy weight in the pit of my stomach. I could talk tough as much as I wanted to, but that was still a real gun, and these guys were killers. I didn't know much about aluminum companies, but obviously they were multi-million dollar operations with plenty of muscle to back them up, legal or otherwise. Whatever it was that Albert had discovered, it was obviously something that such a powerful corporation would kill for.

The only problem was that I had no idea what they were talking about.

"And what if I decide to *not* be cooperative?" I asked, desperately trying to maintain my brave façade.

The man smiled and chuckled as he fingered the safety on his pistol. "You will be, Ms. Parker," he said simply. "Trust me."

Ms. Parker? I said to myself, wrinkling my forehead in intense bewilderment. *Who the hell is Ms. Parker?*

Chapter Twenty-Five

All In Good Time, Ms. Parker

Parker... Parker... why does that name seem so familiar? I asked myself as we continued our late-night drive to god-knows-where. Wherever we were going, it was obviously somewhere far out of the city, judging from how long we'd been driving fast and straight with no stops or turns. But where were we, and more importantly, where were we going?

The smaller man leaned over to his fat-faced partner, and the two of them had a short discussion in a foreign language, speaking low with both of them glancing over at me periodically. They were talking about me, I supposed—maybe about what to do with me, a thought that sent chills down my spine.

When they finished their discussion, the smaller man looked over at me, examining me with a look of what appeared to be concern. He put his gun inside his suit jacket and leaned toward me.

"Your face is bruised," he observed, straining to get a better look in the dim light.

"No kidding," I replied, still trying to sound tough despite the growing feeling of shivering panic that was running through my entire body like an electric current.

He sat up straight and crossed his arms in front of his chest. "You know, in my country we have this...ointment," he said, pausing and struggling to find the right words. "I don't know the English name for it, but I am sorry that I don't have any here with me. It would help you."

"Thanks," I replied, not knowing what else to say to that.

He sighed heavily, apparently bothered about something.

"In my country, it is not right for a man to strike a woman like this," he said, his constant smile fading a bit as he glanced over at his fat partner.

"I don't think it's acceptable behavior anywhere, actually," I replied sarcastically, wiggling around on the bench to find a more comfortable sitting position.

He nodded. "For this I am sorry," he said. "I would like for you to know this."

"What I would like," I replied, looking directly at him and keeping my voice as level as possible, "is for you to stop this truck right now, untie me, and let me go."

He laughed a cold, cynical-sounding laugh that made me feel uncomfortable.

"All in good time, Ms. Parker. All in good time."

There was that Ms. Parker again.

Who is Ms. Parker? I asked myself again. *And why does the name sound so familiar?*

"Someone to do with Albert, maybe?" the little voice in my head suggested.

That was it. That was exactly right. Avery Parker was the name of Albert's assistant who I'd spoken to the night before.

They think I'm her? Why do they think I'm her?!? I asked myself, mystified.

I tried to picture what Avery looked like, based on my very brief encounter with her. She was the same build but much shorter than me, and she wore glasses. I couldn't imagine that we we looked so much alike that someone would confuse the two of us.

"The red hair," the little voice in my head said.

Of course, that was it. Both Avery and I had dark red hair. To someone who didn't know either of us very well, our hair color was probably the only thing they saw.

"So that solves it," the little voice in my head said. "Just tell these guys they have the wrong person, and they'll let you go."

That's completely crazy, I thought. *If I tell them that, they'll realize that they don't need me after all, and god knows what they'll do to me then. Besides, if Avery is the one they're really after, then as long as I am here, she is still safe. If they figure out that they have the wrong girl, I'm liable to end up in a ditch somewhere, and they'll turn around and go grab her instead.*

"Of course, you're right," the little voice agreed.

I have to figure a way to get away from these guys and get back to Reykjavík before they do, I continued, thinking things through in my head. *I have to warn Avery and the police that these two are after her.*

"These three, you mean," the little voice said, "or maybe more."

Of course, there were more than just two of them. Someone was driving the truck, after all.

Whatever I do, I thought, *for now I have to make these guys think I am exactly who they think I am—until I find the right moment to get the hell out of here.*

Wherever '*here*' was, of course.

"Please don't hurt me," I said to them, putting on my best scared-and-willing-to-cooperate act, which wasn't difficult considering that I was completely terrified.

I remembered what we'd learned in Mrs. Kowalchuk's high school drama class about how actors can cry real tears when they need to by thinking about some personal trauma they have experienced, or by thinking about something that would bring tears to their eyes if they did experience it. Considering my situation, I am sure you won't be surprised to know that I had plenty of personal trauma to call upon to make me cry.

"Please, don't hurt me," I said again, the tears welling up heavily in my eyes. "I know all about the research that you want. I can give it to you. It's on a computer back at the university. You just need to take me there, and I will give it to you."

My plan was to make them take me back to Reykjavík. I figured that my chances of surviving and making a successful escape were exponentially better if I were in the middle of a crowded city instead of out in the deserted countryside.

"And then you can let me go," I continued, my voice wobbly and tears rolling down my cheeks. Maybe a bit of pity would help to lower their guard a bit.

The two men looked at each other for a second then back at me again, seemingly unaffected by my desperate tears.

"All in good time," the smaller man said, smiling that same creepy pleasant smile—the one that made me want to vomit. "We have to make a short stop first—a pre-existing appointment of ours—and then we will drive back and you will give us everything we want."

Chapter Twenty-Six

In My Country...

What kind of appointment could be this far outside of the city? I asked myself as I felt the truck begin to slow down, its gears grinding and moaning as it turned a corner.

At least I assumed we were out in the country. I still had no idea where we were, but the truck seemed to have been traveling on a highway for quite a long time, so this was the only logical conclusion I could think of.

Besides not knowing where we were, I also didn't know what time it was, how long I'd been unconscious before waking up in the back of the truck, or any other potentially useful information. I was completely in the dark, both literally and figuratively. I could guess that it was late at night, judging from how dark it was inside the back of the truck, but that was about all I knew.

After turning a corner, the truck accelerated again, but drove considerably slower than it had before the turn. The road seemed a bit bumpier as well. Were we finally approaching our destination?

On the bench opposite me, the fat guy in the suit continued to stare with his same blank expression—I don't think his face changed at all the entire time that we'd been sitting there. His partner was leaning back casually with his hands folded on his chest, glancing occasionally at his expensive-looking wristwatch, another indicator that wherever we were going, we might be almost there.

"So, what do we do now?" the little voice inside my head asked.

I'm not sure, I said to myself, completely clueless about what to do next. *But sometime between now and when we get back to the lab I have to make my escape before they figure out that I'm not Avery after all.*

The truck continued to rumble along the road, still driving slowly and shuddering as it hit the occasional pothole.

"Where are we going?" I asked timidly, still keeping up my scared and helpless act to gain their pity.

The smaller man looked over and smiled. "Somewhere that is the inspiration for many stories of this country's great literature," he replied ambiguously, his thoughts obviously elsewhere.

"Oh," I said. That wasn't really a helpful answer.

"In my country we also have a tradition of great literature," the smaller man continued, thinking aloud. "In fact, the greatest writer who ever lived was from my country. And he once wrote a story about a saintly man who was very trusting and pure in his heart. But people mocked this man for his kindness and innocence, and they considered him a fool. He did not fit into their corrupt and greedy society where everyone was only concerned with power and conquest. And in the end, this humble and compassionate man goes mad and ends up in a sanatorium."

I looked up at him, sitting there and stroking his chin thoughtfully as he pondered this seemingly random stream of thought.

"And?" I asked, my tone uncertain, not really sure what his point was. "Was this guy in the story really a fool?"

"He was a fool, no doubt about it," he replied, nodding. "But I was just thinking about what this story might say about our situation right now. And about which one of us is the fool."

I was pretty sure that I knew the answer to that question but wisely kept my mouth shut. The truck had begun to slow again, its gears rattling and complaining as we rounded another corner. This time the truck didn't accelerate again but instead pulled forward slowly for another few moments before coming to an abrupt halt, its brakes screeching harshly as it did. The rumbling of the engine fell silent, leaving only the sound of the howling of the wind as it swept harshly around the truck.

I waited to see what the men would do now. The smaller and more talkative one looked at his watch and turned to give his fat partner a curt nod. The fat one nodded, and then he got to his feet and lumbered awkwardly toward the back of the truck.

"We're a bit early," the smaller man explained as his partner unsnapped the canvas at the back of the truck and climbed over the tailgate.

As the fat man lowered his large body down to the ground, the flap blew open in the gusting wind and I could see that it was quite dark outside, but not completely pitch black. I could see a sliver of very dark blue sky through the flap before it blew closed again. In the more populated latitudes of the world, this kind of twilight would mean that it was either late in the evening or early in the morning. But as far north as we were, and with the long summer days approaching, it meant that it was some time deep in the dead of night.

Off to my left I heard the driver's door of the truck open and slam shut followed by the sound of footsteps on gravel walking around to the back of the truck.

I tried to look as innocent and stupid as possible while my brain raced to process all the sensory information it was receiving. Everything I was seeing and hearing might help me figure out where we were, what time it was, and most important of all, how to make my escape.

There wasn't much information to work from, but wherever we were, it was almost certainly somewhere very remote. That much I already knew from how long the drive had been. That meant that it was unlikely that there were any people or houses around. And even if there were, it was the middle of the night, and that meant that anyone nearby would probably be asleep anyway.

Over the sound of the howling wind tearing violently at the truck canvas, I could hear low voices talking indistinctly outside. There was the muffled snap of a cigarette lighter followed by the faint burning smell of a foul-smelling tobacco.

Across from me, the man in the suit shifted in his seat and reached into his jacket. My heart leapt into my throat for a moment as it looked like he was going for his gun again, but instead he pulled out a pack of cigarettes. He took out a fancy gold-plated lighter and lit his cigarette, filling the air with a dense, foul smoke that was much nastier smelling than the tobacco I was used to back in Canada.

He put the pack of cigarettes away and leaned back again, exhaling deeply and blowing a stream of smoke toward the ceiling.

"The Vikings came to my country too," he said, continuing to think aloud and make conversation, "at around the same time that they came to Iceland."

I couldn't decide if he was actually trying to be nice or playing some kind of good-cop-bad-cop game against me with his fat partner. Or, maybe he was just glad to have someone to talk to other than his silent, fat companion, who didn't seem to be the world's greatest conversationalist.

"When the Vikings came to my country," the man continued, smoking his cigarette casually, "they often burned and looted the villages they found. But when they came to Iceland, there was no one here, so they simply claimed whatever land caught their eye and set up farms and ranches."

I nodded and pretended to look interested in what he was saying, trying to play nice so that he and his sidekick might let their guard down a bit. But as I pretended to listen to him, I kept my eyes and ears finely tuned to what was going on around me, gathering information about my surroundings and looking for a chance to make a run for it.

"And while the rest of Europe was stumbling along in the midst of the Dark Ages," he said, staring thoughtfully off into the distance, "these so-called Icelandic barbarians had established a democracy—a Viking parliament. And they met here every summer—not more than a few hundred meters from where we're sitting—to vote on new laws, to settle disputes, and to have feasts and get drunk."

Wait a minute! I thought, my brain taking a sudden interest in what he was saying. *That sounds familiar.*

When I was planning my Icelandic sightseeing, Konrad had arranged for us to go somewhere that sounded a lot like what the man in the dark suit had just described—the place where the Vikings had established their first parliament. But unfortunately, as hard as I tried, the only thing I could remember about it was that it had a weird name, which was not really much help to me now.

The man took another deep drag on his cigarette and again blew the smoke up to the ceiling.

"Just over there was what they called the Law Rock," he said, pointing with his cigarette to some unseen location outside of the back of the truck. "And every year the man who had been elected the Law Speaker would stand up on the rock to recite the laws. He was elected to serve three years, and his job each year was to recite from memory one-third of the entire code of laws, so that by the end of his term he would have recited it all."

"Interesting," I said aloud, nodding. And I wasn't just pretending. I was hoping his casual chitchat would provide some useful information that would help me escape. Plus, I had to admit that it was actually kind of interesting.

The man in the suit smiled his pleasant smile. It was still creepy, but I forced myself to smile faintly in return.

"And while he was reciting the laws," he continued. "If he forgot one and no one spoke up to correct him, then the law was considered abolished."

I nodded again. "That's smart," I said.

And actually, it *was* pretty smart, considering how many crazy and outdated laws there are that are apparently still are on the books in many places. At least that's what the Internet told me on bored rainy afternoons when I randomly Googled all sorts of strange things.

The man took another long drag on his cigarette and stared vacantly into the distance. "I really admire the Vikings," he said. "They were so far ahead of their time in many ways. Did you know that even more than a thousand years ago women in Iceland could own land?"

I shook my head.

"It's true," he said, chuckling to himself. "Of course, the law stated that they could only own as much land as they were able to walk around from sunrise to sunset on a spring day while leading a two-year-old cow. But they could still own land."

He leaned forward on his elbows to look me in the eyes. I tried to restrain myself from pulling away in disgust.

Just be nice and friendly, I reminded myself as he leaned in closer.

"Do you have any idea how long it took for women to have rights like this in my country?" he asked, leaning close enough that I could smell his tobacco breath. He squinted his eyes and pointed his cigarette at me to emphasize the profound nature of the point he was making.

I shook my head. I had no idea how long it took. In fact, I had absolutely no idea what his country was.

He leaned back and took another long, slow drag on the cigarette, but then he stopped suddenly and cocked his head to one side as though he'd heard something.

I stopped breathing for a moment and listened as well, straining to hear over the howl of the wind. It was difficult, but I heard it too: the sound of a vehicle approaching, growing louder with every passing second.

Looking at me with raised eyebrows, he flicked the cigarette to the floor and squashed it under the heel of his expensive Italian shoes.

"Time's up," he said to me, rising to his feet and whistling loudly for his companions, nearly deafening me in the enclosed space in the back of the truck.

Time's up? I thought. *What the heck does that mean?*

Chapter Twenty-Seven
Charlie Would Have Tied My Wrists Much Better

I have to admit that I was quite worried when the man said "time's up." It sounded rather ominous, but apparently, he just meant that the time had arrived for whatever appointment it was that they'd been waiting for. After whistling for his partner, the familiar fat face appeared at the back flap of the truck and the oversized man climbed clumsily back onboard, causing the truck to wobble under his immense weight.

The smaller man had turned serious and cold, and was no longer smiling his pleasant but unnerving smile, but instead was tapping his fingers against his pant leg nervously. He nodded in my direction and the fat man plodded over and reached behind me to tie my wrists to one of the support poles holding the canvas to the truck bed. Clearly, they didn't want me going anywhere while they were doing whatever it was they were planning to do.

Tying off several layers of knots behind my back, the fat man stood up again and leaned over to grab a briefcase from underneath the bench on their side of the truck.

Let me guess; that's full of money, I mused wryly. It looked exactly like the kind of briefcase you always see on a television crime show filled with money.

The smaller man gave an approving nod and took the briefcase while the fat one climbed out of the truck, grunting with the effort involved.

After adjusting his blood-colored necktie, the smaller man turned to face me. "Don't bother screaming or doing anything stupid like that," he said. "Trust me when I say that the men we are meeting with will not care."

I hadn't even thought about it, actually, and I was surprised that the idea hadn't occurred to me.

The man finished fixing his tie and started to climb down off the back of the truck. "Or scream if you want to," he said graciously. "It doesn't matter. No one will care."

When he disappeared from view, somewhere behind me the sound of an approaching car was quite close, and I could hear its tires rolling across the gravel. After a few seconds, it came to a halt, and its engine was switched off. I heard a car door open and shut followed by faint footsteps and conversation in low voices, barely audible over the howl and moan of the wind.

I was now alone in the back of the truck, and for the second time in less than a year, I had been tied up and taken hostage.

Being tied to the pole was far more painful than just having my hands bound behind my back. My arms were now twisted up painfully, pulling the rope tighter so that it cut into my bare wrists. This nightmarish experience brought back unpleasant memories from the previous summer when I'd been taken captive out in the woods near Dyea, Alaska. The only difference was that this time around, my captors weren't going to turn out to be a group of benevolent outdoorsmen like Charlie and his brothers had been. These guys were frighteningly serious in their dark suits, despite the fake smile the smaller one kept on his face, and unlike what I had known about Charlie, I somehow knew that when these men talked about killing me, they might actually do it.

"Oh, God, how did I get into this mess?" I asked myself over and over again.

"I won't say, 'I told you so'," the little voice in my head advised me.

You do realize, I interrupted, *that whenever people say this, it is always followed by actually saying, "I told you so."*

"You're right," the little voice agreed. "But I did tell you so."

"Shut up," I muttered aloud. "You're not helping."

Although to be honest, I wasn't sure exactly what *would* have helped me in this situation. I only knew that I needed to think of something fast.

Tied up in the back of a truck is perhaps not the best situation to be in if you want to escape your evil kidnappers, but I suppose that things could have been much worse. At least I was finally alone.

But for how long? I wondered.

I looked around the inside of the back of the truck, straining against my bound wrists and squinting in the dim light.

The truck was one of those military transport trucks with canvas sides and a bench on either side of the truck bed for sitting on. As the wind gusted, the canvas flaps at the back of the truck occasionally flipped open, revealing a dim twilight world outside. I couldn't see much of anything, however. Everything looked pretty dark.

I could hear my captors talking nearby in some foreign language with whomever it was that had just arrived. It was difficult to make out over the wind, but it sounded like they were speaking Icelandic. And I can tell you that Icelandic is a language that is very strange and almost impossible to make any sense of if you're a native English speaker, but from what I could hear, the various tones and inflections sounded familiar somehow.

"You'd better hurry up," the little voice in my head reminded me. "We have no idea how long this 'appointment' of theirs is going to take."

I know, I know, I replied.

I was wondering if it was smart for me to make a run for it. Maybe I should wait until we got back into the city. What if there was nothing out there but endless countryside?

As soon as I had this thought, I realized how ridiculous it sounded. Endless countryside is a hell of a lot better than being tied up to a pole in the back of a truck. Not to mention that these guys might have absolutely no plan to take me back to Reykjavík in the first place. Out in the middle of endless countryside is also a perfect place to dispose of a body, after all.

I was far outside of the city and nowhere near anyone who could possibly give me some assistance. I was on my own with a group of dangerous killers. No matter what risks there might be outside, I had to get away from these guys as soon as possible, or my epic around-the-world flight (not to mention my young life) would be cut short after it had just started.

I was surprised at how calm I was. I didn't panic even though my mind was racing to think of a way out. I'd been on my own before. And if my experiences the previous summer had taught me anything, it was how to stay cool in desperate and frightening situations.

At the back of the truck, the wind gusted again, and when the canvas flap flew wide open, I caught a momentary glimpse of the sky. It wasn't completely black, but dark enough that I could see some stars. I quickly lowered my head to see if I could spot some constellations or maybe the polar star so I could orient myself if I set of into the woods, but the flap blew closed again before I was able to see anything useful.

Those stars brought back memories of the previous summer and the night on the shores of Lake Tagish when Charlie told the story of his family and the curse of the Yukon gold.

I smiled at the memory, but my smile quickly faded as I reminded myself to focus on my current situation and the fact that my hands were bound behind my back, and my wrists throbbing, bruised, and rope-burned. But even that pain brought back memories from the previous summer and my trek up the Chilkoot Pass, and all the various ways I'd tried to twist and wiggle my arms to get free.

Leaning back against the pole I was tied to, I slowly and powerfully twisted my wrists back and forth, over and over again, in an attempt to work the bindings loose. It hurt like hell, but it was going to hurt a lot less than what those men might do to me after they came back from their little conference out in the darkness. And in case I'd forgotten what they were capable of, my bottom lip and left cheek were still hurting and swollen from where the fat one had punched me in Reykjavík.

"Don't forget that these guys aren't Charlie and his brothers," the little voice in my head reminded me. "They won't turn out to be a bunch of nice guys in the end. They are deadly serious, and they very well might kill you if you don't get out of here."

I gritted my teeth and continuing working my wrists back and forth. The knots in the rope were slowly but surely getting tighter and leaving a bit of slack in the loops that were wrapped around my wrists. Just a couple more twists and I would slip my right wrist completely out.

"Trust me, I know full well that these guys aren't Charlie and his brothers," I told the little voice in my head with a grin as I strained and finally pulled my hands free of the ropes. "Charlie would have tied my wrists much better than that."

Chapter Twenty-Eight

An Unexpected Bonus

"So now what?" the little voice in my head asked after I pulled my hands free and was rubbing my painfully chafed wrists.

"Now, we get out of here," I said, getting slowly to my feet and easing along the back of the truck so I could peek out the flap. I moved slowly to avoid making the truck creak or move on its shock absorbers. I didn't want to attract the attention of the men who were still talking in low voices nearby.

I reached the back of the truck and carefully sneaked a quick look out through the canvas flap so that I could assess my surroundings and plan my getaway.

It was a bit lighter outside than I had initially thought. The glowing sky was illuminating the surrounding countryside and distant mountains in a dim and dark blue light, and it was just enough to know the mountains were there, but not enough to make out the details of anything. It was a world of deep shadows, but it wasn't as dark as it had seemed from inside the truck.

The truck was parked on some kind of small deserted parking lot surrounded by low bushes and trees. A black luxury sedan was parked a short distance away—the car that had driven up to join us, presumably—and three men in dark suits were standing close to it, still discussing whatever it was they'd come out here to discuss. The fat guy who'd punched me was holding the briefcase I'd seen earlier. Next to him was his smaller partner who was the one doing all the talking from their side, of course. But I couldn't quite see the man they were talking to because the fat one was standing directly in my line of sight. He was also participating in their conversation, occasionally interjecting to make some comment and gesturing with his hands as he did so.

Luckily, the three of them were a fair distance away and totally focused on their conversation. That meant that I had a good chance to climb down off the back of the truck without them noticing. The only problem was the fourth man—presumably the driver of the truck who I'd not seen before—who was standing a short distance back from the others, approximately halfway between them and me. He was concentrating on the conversation too, but he could easily turn around at any moment and spot me making my escape.

I would have to risk it. There was no other way to get out of the back of the truck. I didn't have a knife, so I couldn't cut through the canvas sides and escape that way. Besides which, canvas is pretty tough, and I'd probably make enough noise and fuss in the process of cutting it that they'd notice me long before I was able to make a hole big enough to slip through.

"I'll have to risk it," I repeated to myself, not quite convinced.

I took a deep breath and carefully lifted my right leg up over the tailgate of the truck, slowly lowering it onto the rungs of the ladder welded to the outside. This part was scary, because climbing over like that, with my butt in the air and my back to the bad guys, I couldn't see whether they might suddenly turn around and spot me.

With my right foot solidly on the top rung of the ladder, I quickly but carefully lifted my other foot and pulled myself completely over the tailgate. I crouched down and slid the upper half of my body out from behind the canvas flap. I glanced quickly over at the group of men once my head was clear, terrified that I'd see them looking in my direction.

I breathed a sigh of relief to see that they were still deep in conversation and paying absolutely no attention to what was going on with the truck. But that didn't mean that they wouldn't turn around suddenly, so without stopping for even a microsecond, I reached over to a support pole and in one smooth, fluid motion, I swung my body around the far side of the truck where I was almost totally out of sight.

I wasn't finished yet, however. If they looked over now, they would see my hands, left leg, and the left side of my body, even in the dim light. But that was at least a lot less noticeable than hanging off the ladder at the back of the truck.

Using every ounce of strength I had, I pulled all of my weight up with my arms and gingerly took my foot off the ladder. My entire body was now supported by the strength of my arms—a strength that I knew wouldn't last for very long—and I began slowly lowering myself down the pole, one painful grip after another, stretching my toes as far as I could to feel for the ground.

Where the hell is the ground? I thought, panicking as my toes continued to swing free after lowering myself for what seemed like an eternity. My biceps were burning in excruciating pain from supporting my weight for so long, but I couldn't jump because the sound of my feet on the gravel would bring the men in suits running over in an instant.

Finally, the toes of my boots hit solid ground, and I eased my weight off my arms and completely onto my feet again. I didn't have a second to lose. I was free and out of sight, but now I had to get as far away as possible before their little meeting ended and they came back to the truck and noticed I was missing.

Even in the dim light, I could see that the direction *away* from the men stretched out flat into the distance toward a lake, broken here and there by growths of scrub brush. I planned to go cross-country as fast as I could, using the scrub brush and occasional pockets of trees for cover as I went.

I wish there were more trees, I thought to myself as I planned my route over the barren landscape ahead of me. Iceland is a country with almost no trees. I'd noticed this not long after I first arrived. Konrad had explained that this was because the early Viking settlers had cut down most of the trees that were on the island when they first arrived.

Thanks a lot, Vikings, I thought as I tiptoed cautiously along the side of the truck, being careful not to make any sound on the gravel.

As I crept toward the front of the truck, I kept my ears open to make sure I could still hear the low voices of the men on the opposite side of the parking lot. As long as they were still talking, I could move relatively slowly and carefully, but the second I heard them stop and start walking back to the truck, I was going to bolt and make a run for it.

But I was lucky, and their conversation continued. In fact, it was even turning a bit more heated than it had been earlier. Their voices were rising in intensity, and it sounded as though they were on the verge of some kind of argument.

When I was near the front of the truck, I was finally close enough to the low fence surrounding the parking lot that, with a few more steps, I could hop over it and onto the soft grass beyond. The sound of my footsteps on grass wouldn't register with the men, not with this wind gusting in their ears, and once I was there, I would be able to start putting some serious distance between us. I could see a patch of low-lying bushes just beyond the fence. If I made it that far and took cover, I would keep the truck between me and the bad guys so they wouldn't see me making a run for it. Once I made it that far, I was planning to put the pedal to the metal to see if I could break the world record for a 500-yard dash over uneven terrain. I would just keep going until I simply couldn't run anymore, which should bring me somewhere in the vicinity of the Reykjavík city limits, I imagined, judging from how scared I was.

"Why don't you really put the pedal to the metal?" the little voice in my head asked. "Why don't you steal their truck?"

I stopped dead in my tracks. That might be worth considering.

Are the keys in the ignition? I wondered. I lifted myself onto my tiptoes and cupped my hands to the glass to look through the passenger window. The keys were there, hanging from the ignition, and the passenger door was unlocked.

Wait a minute; no, I can't do that, I thought. *They would know I was trying to escape the second I cranked the engine, and they would come after me immediately. They have another car, remember? If I go cross-country, then maybe I can be miles away before they finally finish whatever it is they are talking about over there, and by then they'll never find me.*

"Are you sure about that?" the little voice in my head responded. "All of them are going to come looking for you once they notice you're gone. Are you sure they won't be able to find you out there?"

Not if I'm smart about it, I replied. *Besides which, there's only four of them and a lot of open country out there to search in the darkness. I doubt they'd...*

My brain stopped in mid-thought and my heart jumped into my throat. Somewhere on the opposite side of the truck, the sound of voices in discussion had fallen silent, and I heard the sound of footsteps on gravel coming slowly back toward the truck.

I didn't have time to waste anymore. They were coming back. I decided what I had to do in an instant. I didn't have time to go cross-country anymore. I was taking the truck after all.

With that decision made, I immediately yanked open the passenger door and vaulted across the front seats to slide in behind the steering wheel. Glancing out of the rearview mirror, I could see my three captors making their way toward the back of the truck while the other man walked to his luxury car with the briefcase in his hand.

Never taking my eyes off them, I turned the ignition key and cranked the engine. The engine buzzed into life, and in the rearview mirror, I watched as looks of confusion, first disbelief, then anger, flashed across the faces of two of the smaller men walking back toward me. The fat guy's expression stayed blank as always, which almost made me laugh as I jerked the truck into drive and floored the gas pedal.

The rear wheels spun, spitting a shower of gravel over the three men, causing them to duck and cover their faces as I peeled away.

That was an unexpected bonus," I said as the truck gained traction. "Keep your heads down, guys. I'd hate for some flying gravel to knock your teeth out."

Glancing into the rearview mirror again, I watched the three of them continue to cover their faces from the deluge of rocks raining down upon them. But they were slowly regaining their senses and reaching into their suit jackets.

I knew what that meant—their guns were coming out—and I pushed the gas pedal as far down as it would go, sending an extra dose of gravel flying their way as I steered for the parking lot exit. The truck was starting to pick up speed by now, and in a second or two, I would hit the hard pavement and get the hell out of there.

Keeping my eyes focused both on the road ahead and the unfolding action in the rearview mirror I reached down and pulled the headlight switch to the ON position. Not only did I need to see where I was going, but I hoped that the taillights of the truck would blind them for a second or two and give me a bit more time before they started firing their guns at me.

The lights came on, and suddenly the scene in the rearview mirror was bathed in a harsh red glow. In what seemed like slow motion, I watched as all three of my captors pulled pistols from inside their jackets and began to level them at me before pulling the triggers.

It was scary—terrifying, really. I couldn't believe that in just a few short moments, three men with guns would begin to shoot at me—or more likely at the truck's tires or fuel tank—and there was a very real chance that I would be either recaptured or killed. And yet in that tiny instant, my attention was not on the three men with guns. It was on the fourth man who'd dropped his briefcase on the way back to his car and hit the deck to protect himself from flying gravel.

The briefcase had broken open when it hit the ground, and in true television crime show fashion, I could see several thick stacks of bank notes spilled out onto the ground.

How cliché, right? A briefcase full of money. But would you believe that even *that* wasn't what my attention was focused on in that instant before the guns started blazing at me.

What caught my attention in that too short instant was the man himself—the fourth man who'd driven out here in his fancy black luxury sedan, which I could now see was a Mercedes, so that he could meet up with these three suit-wearing thugs and take a briefcase full of money from them.

The man was someone I'd seen before.

He was the moderator of the town hall meeting I'd attended in Reykjavík with Kristín two days earlier.

His name was Tómas Finnsson. For some reason, I remembered this with perfect clarity, just as I also clearly remembered whom he worked for: the Icelandic Ministry of the Environment and Natural Resources.

Chapter Twenty-Nine
I Didn't Give You Enough Credit, Fat Boy

"What the hell is he doing here?" I asked myself, my head swirling in confusion. But there was no time to think about it because my three captors had almost finished raising their guns and would start shooting at any second.

Right at that moment, the rear tires of the truck hit the hard asphalt, and with a high-pitched bark of rubber on pavement, the truck shuddered and jumped suddenly forward, picking up speed fast as I kept the accelerator pinned to the floor.

And then the shooting started.

From behind me, I could hear the sharp firecracker-like reports of the pistols as the three men started firing. This was accompanied by the metallic thunks and whines as the bullets hit home or ricocheted off the body of the truck.

I ducked down in my seat for protection as I managed to continue steering, peeking up to look back in the rearview mirror every few seconds. I saw two of the men running after the truck, firing repeatedly as they went. The fat one wasn't running (no surprise there), but that didn't stop him from firing at me. In fact, I got the sense from the timing of the muzzle flashes from his pistol and the subsequent sound of impacts on the frame of the truck that he was the only one who was actually hitting me. The other two were firing too, of course, but I had the feeling that they weren't hitting anything with their shots. This wasn't surprising since the other two were holding and aiming their pistols sideways—'gangsta' style—which they probably thought made them look cool, but it didn't seem like the best way to aim a pistol.

I didn't give you enough credit, fat boy, I thought, watching the other two aiming their guns like they were bit-part actors in some modern gangster movie. *You're the only one who knows how to shoot properly.*

I could see up ahead that the parking lot access road ended in a T-intersection, and as long as my luck held and the tires or the truck didn't blow up, I was soon going to have to choose which way to turn.

"Left," I said, deciding in an instant. "Away from the lake. God knows whether the road to the right is a dead end or not."

I cranked the steering wheel left, pulled my foot off the gas for a second, and took the turn fast, the tires squealing and the truck shuddering violently as I fishtailed around the sharp corner. I floored the gas again and the truck roared straight ahead, the speedometer creeping blissfully higher as it went.

By this time, the shooting had stopped and I'd left all the men in suits far behind me in the dust. Thankfully, the tires were intact, the fuel tank hadn't exploded, and the engine was purring along nicely. I had the road to myself, and with every passing second, I was racing closer and closer to safety.

"But not for long," the little voice in my head reminded me. "Pretty soon you're gonna see some headlights in the rearview mirror as that black Mercedes comes cruising up behind you. And then you can be sure that the shooting is going to start all over again."

"I know," I replied. "Trust me, I know."

I kept my foot to the floor and my eyes on the road ahead, glancing back now and then for the flash of light that would tell me they were following me.

"How much time do you think you have?" the little voice in my head asked. "How long would it take them to recover themselves and jump into that Mercedes?"

I shook my head. I had no idea. But I figured they would be on my tail soon, so I kept the gas pedal to the floor even though I was approaching a dangerously high speed for such a small, dark road out in the middle of nowhere.

"Don't kill yourself trying to escape," I muttered, but somehow I couldn't bring myself to ease up on the gas, not even a little bit. "I'd rather die in a horrible car crash than end up in the grip of those three again."

Just then, a burst of headlights flashed in my rearview mirrors and my stomach turned cold. They were on the road and coming up fast behind me, but I didn't have long to dwell on this fact as I spotted another T-intersection coming up ahead of me, fast.

"Which way now?" I asked myself. "Left again, or right?"

Right, I decided for no particular reason, lifting my foot off the gas pedal again and hitting the brakes lightly to take the corner at quiveringly high speed, almost losing control of the truck as my back tires skated back and forth across the pavement.

Counter-steering against the skid, I soon recovered and had my foot all the way down again, accelerating up another long stretch of road.

As I gained speed, I watched the headlights continue up the side road perpendicular behind me, and I wondered which vehicle had a higher top speed—my stolen truck or the black Mercedes.

"Don't be stupid," the little voice in my head told me. "Of course the Mercedes is faster. And it will also handle a lot better than your big, clunky truck, which means it can take that corner back there at a much higher speed."

"That's very reassuring; thanks a lot," I muttered sarcastically.

So, like the tortoise and the hare, if I wanted to win this particular race, I would have to be incredibly smart about it. The only problem was that I had absolutely no idea how to do that. A lifetime of watching television shows and movies had taught me that, when it came to high-speed car chases, if the other car caught up with you, all you had to do was weave back and forth and smash your car into the sides of the other car until you finally ran it off the road in one of those spectacular Hollywood ramp-up-and-flip-over-in-the-air type of stunt crashes.

The only question was whether that actually worked in real life. I was willing to bet that it probably didn't. I was also willing to bet that when Mercedes caught up with me, the fat guy would calmly pull out his pistol, lean out of the car's window, and with that same blank expression on his face, pick off my tires one by one, causing me to fishtail all over the road and forcing me to pull over and stop or do a ramp-up-and-flip-over-in-the-air type of crash of my own.

Neither of those alternatives sounded particularly appealing, but I knew one thing for sure—I was getting pretty pissed off at these men and their dark designer suits, expensive gold watches, and Italian shoes. If it came down to it and there was no way to escape, then there was no way in hell that I planned to just nicely pull over and stop for them. If they took me down, then I would do my best to take them down with me.

Chapter Thirty
Am I Seeing What I Think I'm Seeing?

I t didn't take them long to catch up with me. Before I knew it, we were driving together in a bizarre convoy toward the distant low-lying mountains and across a rugged alien landscape that was made surreal by the light of the brightening sky and deep shadows. I kept my head down and eased off the gas pedal a little. There was no point in trying to outrun them, and barreling down the highway at a ridiculously dangerous speed could get me killed. I watched both mirrors anxiously to see what they would do, expecting at any second for them to start firing. It was difficult to make anything out in the half-light, half-dark shadow world of early morning twilight, especially with their high-beam headlights reflecting in the mirrors and blinding me, but it seemed that all they were doing was just following along behind me. For the time being they didn't seem intent on pursuit and capture.

"Maybe they are trying to decide what to do next," the little voice in my head suggested. "Maybe they are having one of those discussions that evil villains always have in action movies where they reveal the whole plot right before they plan to kill the good guys."

I chuckled to myself, in spite of my precarious situation. "Too bad I'm not back there with them, then," I said to myself. "I would certainly be interested in knowing what they were meeting Tómas Finnsson about in the middle of the night, and why they were handing him a briefcase full of money."

"I think it's pretty obvious," the little voice in my head replied. "He was taking some kind of bribe. He works for the government, after all. Why else would he be talking to these guys?"

Taking a bribe for what? That was the question.

"I bet Erík would know," I muttered to myself, actually laughing out loud despite the fact that I was driving a stolen truck at high speed across the rough Icelandic landscape with a car full of dangerous murderers tailing me. The irony of it was incredible. Half a day earlier, I was trying to get as far away from Erík as possible, and now I actually wished he was there with me. He was a big, tough-looking guy who was probably good to have around in dangerous situations, and he would also probably know exactly why it was that some flashy-suited corporate thugs from some foreign aluminum company were delivering a bribe to someone from the Icelandic Ministry of the Environment and Natural Resources.

"Can you believe it, Erík?" I said aloud, still keeping my head ducked down as far as I could while keeping an eye on the road ahead. "I actually wish you were here right now."

The little voice in my head wasn't convinced, and scoffed at the idea. "What can Erík do that you can't? He's not bulletproof any more than you are."

It would at least be something, I thought wistfully as I kept an eye on the black Mercedes.

But what were they doing back there? In movies, didn't they normally drive up close behind you and start bumping into the back of your car with theirs? These guys weren't doing anything like that. They were just following along behind me, keeping a few car lengths' distance between us. And although this was obviously better than having them shoot at me, I found it incredibly unnerving. What awful plan did they have up their sleeves?

As it turned out, the only plan they apparently had was the one I'd already expected. From somewhere behind me, I heard the *thunk* of a bullet hitting metal and the distant report of a pistol shot in the distance. Looking over at the side-view mirror, I saw the dark silhouette of a man leaning out of the front passenger window of the Mercedes with a gun in his hand, leveled right at the truck.

"Dammit!" I shouted, cranking the wheel of the truck to the left, then back to the right, swerving back and forth across the road to make myself a more difficult target. This had been my plan all along when I first saw them aiming to take a shot at me, but somehow I'd completely missed seeing the figure leaning out of the car window in the first place. I had to stop being so stupid or I was going to pay for it with my life.

I continued to weave back and forth across the road, hitting the accelerator as I did so and doing everything I could to make myself as unpredictable a target as possible. But still the shots came—slowly, deliberately, and methodically hitting the frame of the truck and ricocheting off the sides in a slow and deadly rhythm.

Are they just toying with me? I wondered. *Surely it can't be that difficult to blow out the tires on this thing.*

I spun the wheel over to the left again, screeching across to the side of the road then back. What was I going to do? I couldn't keep this up all night. Eventually they were going to get me.

"What do I do? What do I do?" I screamed, panicking as the bullets riddled the truck. A bullet punched a hole in the side-view mirror right next to me, and I screamed in terror as glass exploded all across the window inches away. Now I could only see what they were doing from the much more distant mirror on the passenger side of the truck.

"I have to think of something—and fast," I told myself as I gripped the wheel and barreled on.

And then I looked up at the road ahead and suddenly saw the oddest thing I'd ever seen in my entire life. I blinked my eyes hard and tried to focus. Was I actually seeing what I thought I was seeing?

I couldn't believe it. Directly in front of me, a half-naked was man standing barefoot in the middle of the road, waving his arms over his head with a frightening and deranged expression on his face. He looked pale and grey standing there with bony arms and legs sticking out of his underwear in the stark white light of the truck's headlamps.

"What the hell...?" I cried, cranking the steering wheel to the right, watching the truck swerve past him and missing him by mere inches.

I swiveled my body to get a second look as I drove by, watching him flash past the driver side window and disappear behind me, still waving his arms maniacally over his head, and now he was silhouetted against the blinding glare of the oncoming headlights of the Mercedes.

I watched in utter disbelief as the man stood there waving his arms as the black sedan bore down on him. At the last moment, the car swerved left, then right, then left again, trying to avoid him. The car skidded off the side of the road and rolled onto its side before coming to a stop upside down. It wasn't exactly the Hollywood stunt crash that I had imagined earlier, but it was spectacular all the same, and I enjoyed watching as the car skidded several feet before crashing against the jagged rocks on the side of the road.

The whole scene was so absolutely unbelievable and surreal that for an instant I forgot that I had to keep driving the truck or the exact same thing was likely to happen to me as well.

I turned my eyes forward again to see the nose of the truck already veering dangerously off the left side of the road and toward the ditch.

Twisting the wheel hard to the right, I desperately tried to correct the steering back onto the highway again, but it was already too late.

Chapter Thirty-One

Back To Plan A

Slamming down on the brake pedal with both feet, I gripped the steering wheel tightly as I lost control and the truck skidded off the road. Everything seemed to happen all at once, and I felt myself being thrown to the left, right, and upside down simultaneously. Tiny glass fragments exploded from the windows and were tossed around inside the cab of the truck along with my body as though we were trapped inside some crazy demonic washing machine.

The truck settled down on its roof and slid and shuddered a short distance in the ditch, spitting dirt and rocks and grass in the passenger compartment as it went, filling my mouth and nostrils with earthy grit as I lay like a crumpled marionette up against the truck's frame.

Then suddenly, everything was quiet. It was like someone had turned everything off. In an instant, the cacophony of destruction fell silent, and all that was left was the ever-present howling of the wind.

Oh, my god... oh, my god, I thought, twisting my body so that I could lie flat on the upturned ceiling of the passenger cabin. A miniature avalanche of rocks and glass slid off my jacket and sprinkled down onto the metal roof.

Spitting and snorting the glass and dirt out of my mouth and nose, I grabbed the frame of the window and tried to pull myself up and out into the open air. My biceps, still strained from my escape from the back of the truck, groaned and complained as I pulled and pushed myself through the window. But I was able to do it, and in a few seconds, I had dragged myself to safety.

I ran my hands all over my body, pressing and squeezing to find where I was hurt, but somehow it appeared that I had survived the crash without any serious injuries. Unable to believe that this was possible, I checked myself again for gushing blood or broken bones, but aside from various cuts and scrapes, I could find no evidence of serious injury.

My hands were shaking and my brain felt like I had just ridden a wild rollercoaster twenty times in a row, but I could stand and walk and move normally.

I looked around to survey the wrecked truck. It had slid off the highway, crashing into some rock and spinning around before coming to rest upside down in the ditch. I was lucky to be alive, and even luckier to be more or less unhurt. Or maybe the crash just looked worse than it actually was?

Remembering the half-naked man who had caused the accident in the first place, I dragged myself onto the asphalt surface of the highway and scanned up and down the road in both directions. I couldn't see him anywhere—just the dark black and blue sky above me and the rocky landscape all around with its thousands of jagged cracks and shadows.

I just stood there for a few moments, right in the middle of the highway, scratching my head and looking all around, trying to figure out what the heck had just happened.

"What was a half-naked man doing in the middle of the road out here so far from anything?" I asked aloud. "And why was he half-naked? And why was he waving his arms like that? Was he trying to warn me about something? Was there some danger up ahead?"

I turned to look in the direction I'd been heading before my crash, but there was nothing but open road as far as my eyes could see in this dim light.

Was that naked guy even real? I wondered. *I mean, why would there be a half-naked man out here?!? It's completely insane.*

I was frustrated by the complete absurdity of the situation. I'd just run off the road and had an automobile accident where I could have been killed, all because some half-naked idiot was standing in the middle of the road waving at me.

"Maybe he wasn't waving at *you*," the little voice in my head suggested.

Suddenly I remembered the black Mercedes full of men in suits. *How could I have forgotten? My head must be more jumbled up than I thought*, I mused dazedly.

I spun around on my heels and strained my eyes to look down the highway to see where their wrecked car had ended up after their spectacular Hollywood crash.

I took a few steps along the centerline until I could make out the crumpled shell of the Mercedes jammed up on its side against the rocky edge of the ditch on the opposite side of the road. My breath caught in my throat as I heard the faint sound of tinkling glass and groaning floating on the wind toward me.

Oh, my god, I thought. *They are still alive.*

"Um, it's great that you seem to be miraculously okay after your sensational car crash," the little voice in my head observed. "But if you survived intact, then doesn't that mean that they might also be miraculously okay as well?"

I took a step back and continued moving slowly away from the dark shadow of the wrecked Mercedes, but then I caught a glimpse of movement from inside it.

Oh, my god, I thought again, forgetting all about the half-naked man. *I have to get out of here.*

I turned and tried to pull myself into a run. All I could think was that I needed to put some distance between them and me as quickly as possible. Struggling painfully, I was acutely aware that I hadn't escaped the crash as injury-free as I'd thought. My body ached and creaked as I tried to sustain a decent running pace up the middle of the hard asphalt.

I had to stop for a minute. I doubled over, out of breath and hurting. I was going to have to take it a bit slower.

I took a moment to catch my breath I leaned forward with my hands on my knees, and as I did so, I heard a high-pitched whine shatter the air.

What the hell was that? I thought, standing bolt upright.

I looked over my shoulder in the direction of the wrecked Mercedes. I couldn't hear or see any signs of life back there, but I knew exactly what the sound I just heard was. Someone had just fired a gun at me.

In a panic, I stumbled and fell into the closest ditch. Staying low and scrambling down the side, I poked my head up for an instant to see if the coast was clear. I still couldn't see a thing, but that didn't mean it was safe.

"Back to Plan A," I told myself, taking one last quick look behind me before dashing across the ditch and quickly up the rocky ledge on the other side. "I'm going cross-country."

Peering over the ledge to the rocky landscape beyond, I could see that it was rough and full of places to hide and take cover—exactly what I needed. I poked my head up one last time to look up the road to where the shot had come from before pulling myself up and heading out across the open countryside.

Chapter Thirty-Two
Down The Dark Rabbit Hole

K eeping my head low, I half ran and half stumbled across the rough and jagged landscape. In some places, there were large patches of flat earth and grass where the going was much easier. But these open areas offered no cover from anyone who might be shooting at me from behind, so I crossed them nervously in the closest thing to a full-out sprint that I could manage, bracing against the pain with every footfall. In other places, the blocky volcanic rocks poked up out of the ground in a random, messy jumble that gave me perfect cover as long as I stayed low and scrambled over and through them like a mountain goat.

I constantly looked over my shoulder toward the direction of the road. I didn't see any sign of anyone following me, but I hadn't seen anyone on the road either, yet someone had most definitely taken a shot at me. Each time I turned around I expected to see some dark figures in a business suits lumbering up behind me, but there was no one to be seen anywhere. That was supposed to be a good thing, I knew, but I couldn't decide if I'd just rather know where they were instead of wondering whether they were following me at all.

"Nothing you can do about it," the little voice in my head said. "Just keep moving."

As I continued my scramble cross-country, the sky above me became lighter with each passing minute. You would think that having *more* light would make it easier, but actually, it was making it a lot more difficult. The increasing light made the dark shadows between the stones even blacker, and it was difficult to distinguish black volcanic rock from black empty shadows.

Every time I raised my eyes to look behind me or ahead toward the horizon, my eyes had to adjust to the brightness, which made it almost impossible to see anything when I looked back down to where I was putting my feet.

"This sucks!" I complained to no one in particular, stopping for a moment to catch my breath, annoyed and frustrated by how difficult it was to move over this terrain under these conditions. "I'm going to break my leg doing this!"

And of course, if I broke my leg, I was completely screwed.

"Just take it easy," the little voice in my head cautioned. "Go fast, but go slow."

"That's great advice, thanks," I said to myself as I peered over the edge of the boulder I was hiding behind to check out the situation behind me. "Go fast, but go slow."

But there was no other way to do it, so I pulled myself up again and continued on.

I came to a long low ridge of stone blocking the path in front of me. It wasn't very tall, and if I weren't running for my life, I probably would have thought nothing of it. Climbing over it would be easy and would take just a few seconds. But in my current situation, it looked as high as Mount Everest, and I glanced nervously back and forth along the length of it for a way to get to the other side where I wouldn't be completely exposed and in full view on the rock face. But there was nothing. I had no choice but to go straight over it.

Not wanting to waste a single second debating with myself, I dashed over the open space and immediately started climbing, terrified of spending even a millisecond more than I had to out in the open.

I'm going to make it! I thought as I put my hand up on the last boulder before scaling the top of the ridge. Famous last words, I suppose, because just then, I heard the hum and whine of a bullet close to my right ear, and I saw the surface of the stone not two inches from my hand explode in a shower of sparks and rock chips. A sliver of rock flew and cut me above the eye, and I heard the distant crack of a pistol somewhere behind me.

With a superhuman spurt of strength, I pulled myself up over the top of the rocky ridge and let myself fall down the other side, rolling as I went and catching a glimpse of my pursuer. He was a few hundred feet behind me, standing on top of a protruding rock and taking aim at me for a second shot. It was the smaller man who'd sat in the back of the truck with me—the talkative one. His face looked bloodstained, and his fancy business suit was torn and dirty.

"How the hell did he catch up with me so fast?" I shrieked to myself, dropping out of view down the other side of the ridge. He didn't appear to be in very good shape, but apparently, he was having no trouble keeping up with me. At least there was no sign of any of his companions.

I tried to calculate how long it would take him to reach the ridge and climb up to the top of it: thirty seconds...a minute...two minutes, maybe.

Whatever the answer was, that was how much time I had during which there would be this wonderful bulletproof ridge of rock between him and me, and I had to use that time to cover as much ground as possible. Jumping to my feet, I took off in a run, leaping from the top of one boulder to the next.

"Go fast, but go slow," I scoffed, panting as I ran. "Forget that. Now's the time to not only go fast but go faster!"

The faces of the boulders were uneven, and I found myself skidding occasionally before catching my balance again with my hands. But I was making good time, hurdling over the boulders and running flat out in the flat grassy spaces in between.

How long has it been? I wondered, looking back over my shoulder toward the top of the ridge. There was still no sign of him back there, so I just kept running.

"You're going to have to slow down and take cover pretty soon," the little voice in my head reminded me. "He's going to come over the top of the ridge any second now."

"I know, I know," I muttered as I prepared to skip across the tops of four boulders in a nice fast and fluid sequence: One boulder, then two, then three, and four. I made it!

I was almost having fun, jumping from boulder to boulder. I imagined myself looking super cool like the people in those crazy YouTube videos who jump and flip their way through various obstacle courses.

What is that called again? I wondered. I knew it had a French name. *Parcour, I think.*

But of course, the reality of my situation was more like watching some half-crippled teenager with wobbly balance jumping awkwardly from one rock to another, not to mention that she was doing so without a single backflip or cool move of any kind.

I reached the end of a string of boulders and prepared to jump down onto the next flat grassy bit. I looked back over my shoulder toward the ridge. The coast was still clear, but I decided not to push my luck. Once I was down on the low ground again, I was going to stay there and keep going, making my way through the maze of rocks and staying under the cover they provided.

It's probably a good thing that no one's videotaping me, I thought, well aware that I almost certainly looked like a complete dork frolicking over rocks for fun.

"But just watch this move," I said aloud.

Dropping down off the face of the boulder, I braced myself for a solid two-footed landing. The jump wasn't very far—barely five or six feet—but when I hit bottom, the earth seemed to give way, and I went straight through, dropping down into the black inky nothingness beyond.

Before my mind could even process what had just happened, my feet hit bottom, and my body fell sideways, cracking my head violently against a hard surface. Everything flashed white and then red, and for the second time that night, my world went completely black.

Chapter Thirty-Three
You Can Call Me Finn

R egaining consciousness was starting to become a familiar feeling. The second time that night that the mental fog began to lift, the first thing I became aware of was the sound of the wind—that endless howling and moaning that had played over and over like a soundtrack to my entire painful and terrifying adventure since being grabbed by the men in the dark suits at Albert's lab.

For a moment, I didn't know where I was, and thought I was in the back of the truck again, riding along bound and captive while the talkative man and his fat partner watched over me. But my hands weren't tied, and there was no sound of the truck's engine, not to mention that it wasn't dark enough to be the back of the truck.

I opened my eyes and realized that instead of darkness, there was a bright light coming from somewhere above me.

Blinking rapidly against the blinding light, I tried to force my eyes to adjust as I lifted my head up.

"Oh god," I groaned as I raised my head a few inches off the hard surface I was lying on. My head felt like it was splitting open with pain, so I put it back down, resting my forehead on the cold surface once again.

I raised my hands up and cradled my face in them. I checked for any blood or gaping open wounds, but there was nothing. Again I was lucky, it seemed. But then I felt the back of my head and discovered a very large and painful bump that felt about the size of a baseball. (It wasn't, of course, but it sure felt that way.)

That's when it started to come back to me. I was in a car crash and had been running cross-country away from the man in the torn and dirty suit who was shooting at me. I'd jumped from the last boulder and gone straight down into the underworld.

Raising my head again and opening my eyes for a second time, I forced myself to sit up, but I had to lean forward with my forehead in my hands to get my bearings and let my eyes adjust to the blinding bright light.

"Ohhhhhhh, my head," I groaned again, the act of moaning and whining making me feel marginally better.

It felt like the entire world was spinning around in crazy circles, like when you ride a merry-go-round for too long and then try to stand or walk or otherwise function normally back in the non-spinning world.

Everything just swims and spirals for a while until your brain finally figures out that you're not spinning anymore.

I lifted my head and tried to figure out where I was and what had happened. I appeared to be inside some kind of underground cavern with sloping sides that curved up toward the ceiling. The sun was shining in through a large jagged hole about a meter across, presumably where I had fallen through.

A million questions ran through my head all at once. If the sun was so high in the sky, then I must have been unconscious for hours. What happened to the man who was chasing me? Was he still up there somewhere stumbling around looking for me? Or, had he seen me fall through and left me for dead? Was he planning to come back again with the rest of his gang? Or, worst of all, what if he was waiting up there, just at the top of the hole, sitting on a rock with his pistol in his hand waiting for me to pop my head out so he could shoot me?

I looked at the sloping sides of the cavern and chuckled cynically. If my last scenario were true, he would be waiting a long time since I couldn't imagine how I would be able to climb out of this hole in the ground. The surface of the rock was still fairly rough and weathered, as opposed to perfectly smooth and polished, but there were very few handholds sticking out that would make climbing possible. Besides, even if I could somehow scale up the walls, I would still have to climb horizontally over to the hole in the ceiling, and to do that would require me to be Spiderman.

"So if you're waiting up there, buddy," I said, "you'll be waiting for a really long time."

Of course that thought hardly made me feel any better. How was I supposed to get out of this?

I pulled myself to my feet, wobbling dizzily as I did so. I closed my eyes until the feeling passed and I felt secure on my feet again.

I shuffled over to one side of the cavern. It was about twenty feet across and was shaped like a teardrop or a bubble. In fact, that's exactly what it looked like—a bubble—or, another way to describe it would be a section of an underground tube with collapsed walls at either end.

I didn't know much about geology, and I could barely remember anything from what we'd learned about volcanoes in school, but was there something in my memory about lava forming large gas bubbles and leaving round smooth chambers like this as it cooled? The idea sort of made sense, but unfortunately, all I could remember from school was building a homemade volcano and making it erupt using vinegar and baking soda.

That was exactly it, though, wasn't it? The bubbles of vinegar and baking soda represent the bubbles of molten lava. Maybe that's exactly what this cavern was? And the top of the bubble had thinned out as it cooled until it was just a few inches thick at the surface. It sat there for millions of years with the top growing weaker with rain and snow, until one day a stupid girl came along and jumped on it.

"And then, bam!" I said aloud, clapping my hands together and sending clouds of tiny dust particles into the air, floating dreamily in the bright shaft of light. "I fall down here, smack myself on the head and die of starvation because no one ever finds me ever again."

I laughed. A crazy insane type of laugh of the exact type that you would expect from someone trapped in an ancient underground volcanic prison, one that they could never expect to escape from because it was a mile out in the middle of nowhere from a road that was already itself out in the middle of nowhere and no one had any idea she was here except a bunch of suit-wearing criminals who actually thought she was a completely different person than she actually was.

Oh no, I thought. *What about Avery? Once they give up on me, they will surely realize that I wasn't who they thought I was, and then they'll go grab her and hurt her—or worse.*

I could feel the tears welling up in my eyes, and in desperation, I just let my legs go, and my body crumpled onto the floor. Somehow, I felt responsible for all this.

God only knows what they will do to poor Avery once they find her, I thought.

"Poor Avery?" the little voice in my head asked. "What about you? What about poor Kitty Hawk?"

"Her too," I agreed, speaking aloud. "Poor Kitty Hawk will never get out of this stupid hole in the ground."

"I can help you out," I heard a voice say directly above me. A shadow moved across the shaft of light streaming into the underground chamber, and I slid across the floor in a panic. The little guy in the suit was up there, and he was going to shoot me.

"Don't shoot!" I screamed, blocking the light with the palms of my hands and squinting to make out the figure silhouetted against the tiny square of open sky.

"Shoot?" the voice asked, sounding confused. "Why would I shoot you? I just said I could help you."

The voice didn't sound right. It was nothing like the guy in the suit at all. It was much younger and kinder, and it was singing as it spoke somehow, like a beautiful melody.

It was difficult to focus my eyes in the blinding light, but I squinted up at the hole and saw a teenage boy about the same age as me with a face that was every bit as kind and beautiful as his voice. He had light blonde hair that was almost white, and it blew across his forehead in the wind. Strands of hair blew into his big blue eyes as he leaned over the edge of the hole and peered down at me.

I don't know if it was the bump on my head or the crying or panic or the crazy rollercoaster of events that I'd been on for the past days—maybe it was just his beautiful, kind, big blue eyes—but I was completely speechless. I had absolutely no idea what to say.

"I'm Finnur," he said. "But you can call me Finn."

Chapter Thirty-Four
A Smell Worse Than Whalebreath

What a crazy week I was having. And just when I thought it couldn't get any crazier, some beautiful boy sticks his head into the hole in the ground where I am trapped and offers to help me get out.

"What's your name?" he asked in that strange and beautifully melodic voice of his.

"Kitty," I stuttered. "Kitty Hawk."

He grinned. "I like that," he said. "And what do your friends call you?"

"My friends?" I asked, still struggling to keep up with the latest crazy turn of events.

"You have friends, don't you?" he asked.

"Kit," I said. "My friends call me Kit."

He grinned again and stuck his head farther into the hole to take a look inside the cavern.

"Good to meet you, Kit," he said. "What do you say we try and figure out how to get you out of there?"

I couldn't imagine anything that I wanted more, but I suddenly remembered the reason that I was down in this underground cave in the first place.

"Are you by yourself, Finn?" I asked nervously.

He looked down at me, cocking his head to one side as he pondered why I would ask.

"Yes. It's just me," he said.

"And no one else?" I asked. "Are you sure?"

He pointed a finger at me, still grinning. "You're worried about the man in the ripped-up suit," he said.

My heart caught in my throat. That was exactly who I was worried about. Him and his friends.

I nodded.

"He left a couple hours ago," Finn said simply.

"A couple hours ago?" I repeated.

Finn nodded. "I was sitting up the hill," he said, nodding his head toward some unseen location up on the surface, "and watching him look all around for something. He looked for hours, but he didn't find anything, so eventually he left."

"He left," I said, breathing a sigh of relief.

"Something tells me it was you that he was looking for," Finn said.

I nodded.

"But he's gone now, right?" I asked. "You're sure?"

"Positive," Finn said. "Back to the highway where a car picked him up along with some other people, and they drove off in the direction of the city."

They drove back to Reykjavík? My heart caught in my throat again. Poor Avery; if they had figured out that they'd kidnapped the wrong girl, then she was in trouble.

"Finn?" I called up to him.

He looked down at me with his big blue eyes.

"You have to get me out of here," I said. "I have to get back to Reykjavík as soon as possible."

He nodded simply and disappeared from the hole without a word.

"Finn?" I called out, wondering what he was doing and getting nervous that he was out of sight. "Finn???"

He appeared at the hole again, leaning over the edge with his chin propped in his hands.

"Kit?" he said, grinning. "Don't worry, okay?"

I smiled. It was a thin and exhausted smile, but a genuine, heartfelt smile.

He disappeared from the edge again, and I waited nervously as the minutes ticked by.

What if those men in suits came back? I wondered, suppressing the urge to panic. *What if they grabbed Finn and are now holding him prisoner?*

"Don't be stupid," the little voice in my head told me. "Just breathe and be patient."

After climbing to my feet, I began to pace back and forth uneasily across the floor of the underground chamber, thinking about all the possible ways that the suit-wearing thugs might have already figured out that they'd grabbed the wrong redheaded girl. I knew that I had to get back to warn Avery as soon as possible.

After what seemed like an eternity of pacing, I heard the sound of movement above me. I opened my mouth to call out for Finn, but quickly closed it again instead.

What if that isn't Finn up there? I asked myself.

But it was, and I breathed another sigh of relief when I saw him poke his face out across the hole once more.

"Can you climb, Kit?" he asked, holding up a coiled length of rope in his left hand.

I nodded. My arms were aching and sore, as was the rest of my body, but no matter how much it hurt, I was getting out of this hole as fast as I could.

"Okay," he said, lowering one end of the rope down to me. "I am going to wrap my end around a boulder and brace it while you climb up, okay?"

I nodded, and within a few minutes, I grabbed the swinging end of the rope that Finn had lowered within my reach.

"Just take it slow, Kit," he said. "Once your weight puts pressure on the rope it's going to press against the sides of this hole here and the last thing we want is for a piece of the ceiling to break off and fall on you."

"Okay," I replied, gripping the rope tightly.

"Okay," he said, grinning. "See you soon, Kitty Hawk."

He slid back from the opening so he could secure the rope.

I soon felt the rope tightening, and saw it gain tension as it curved over the lip of the opening. Finn was right. I certainly didn't want a piece that rock breaking off and braining me on my way up. I'd had enough head injuries for one day, thank you very much.

"Okay," I heard Finn call out, his voice thin and distant and almost blending in with the sound of the wind. "Just take it slow."

I grabbed the rope and put my weight on it gradually, keeping a sharp eye on the edge of the opening above me. The rope tensed, creaking and groaning a bit as I put more and more weight on it, but it held, and so did the ceiling. Soon my entire weight was on it, and my feet were dangling above the floor.

Wrapping my legs and knees around the rope, I slowly eased my way up just like we'd learned to do in grade school. Who would have thought when we were fooling around in gym class back in Tofino trying to knock each other off the climbing ropes in the gymnasium of Wickaninnish Elementary School that this skill would actually come in handy one day.

It wasn't that far to the top, and climbing up to the opening actually took no time at all, which was a relief because my biceps were burning and throbbing from all the exertions of the past twenty-four hours.

As soon as I pulled my head up through the hole, I squinted my eyes in the blinding sunlight after the semi-darkness of the cavern. I looked over to see Finn gripping the rope tightly while he braced himself with his feet.

He smiled when he saw me and nodded in greeting. Up close and in proper light, I could see that his eyes were even bluer than they'd seemed from down in the underworld. And his face was even more beautiful.

"Okay," he said. "Now, nice and slowly, transfer your weight onto the edge of the opening, and hold yourself there until I can reach over to grab you, okay? But keep your knees locked around the rope in case it slips."

I nodded, doing as he said, slowly transferring my weight off the rope and onto my elbows, which were braced on the upper edge of the black volcanic rock. Once I was secure, Finn let go of the rope and spun around on his butt to face toward me. He propped his feet up against a narrow ridge in the rock surface and reached toward me with both hands.

"One hand at a time, Kit," he said, reaching out with his left hand.

Feeling nervous and scared, I slowly shifted my weight over to my left arm and reached out to grab his hand. It took me a couple tries, and I almost slipped each time because I was not able to reach far enough, but finally I did it, and the feeling of his rough callused hands locking around my wrists was the sweetest sensation I had felt for a very long time. His touch was reassuring—magical, almost. In the blink of an eye, my fear evaporated, and I felt calm and secure, somehow knowing that no matter what happened, he was not going to let me fall.

"Now the other hand," he said quietly, giving me another one of his reassuring smiles. "Nice and easy."

Reaching forward with his other hand, he pushed back against my weight with his left foot and strained his muscles to pull me forward. As he pulled, I felt an amazing surge of powerful energy flowing between us—from his strong hands into mine—giving me the strength to reach forward and latch onto him.

I strained forward with my left hand, trying to make myself as long as possible. Our fingertips touched, and slowly he pulled my hand into his until our fingers were curled into a tight grip.

"Okay," he said, then he locked his right hand onto my wrist and I grabbed onto his in return. "Now I am going to pull you up. Are you ready, Kit?"

I nodded. I was ready. I suddenly felt powerful and invincible, as if I could do anything.

"Here we go," he said, pulling me gradually out of the opening and onto the surface.

Everything went perfectly until the very last instant when I felt the earth shift beneath me and crumble away. The edge of the opening was collapsing, and for a moment, I thought I was going back down into the underworld again; but without hesitation, Finn calmly gripped my wrists tighter and pulled me smoothly the rest of the way as a chunk of rock plummeted into the darkness below, crashing onto the floor of the cavern.

The way he had pulled me up was almost graceful, just up and away from the edge of the hole, pushing with his feet and pulling me up on top of him in one clean, smooth motion.

Our faces were just inches apart—so close that his eyes looked bluer than the bluest blue I had ever seen, and the energy I had imagined flowing between us felt stronger than ever. He smiled and released his powerful grip on my wrists, and then he slid his hands into mine and held them between us.

It was one of those moments that you never forget, no matter how long you live. For that short instant, he and I felt absolutely and utterly at ease with each other, as if we'd know each other all our lives or even longer.

It was perfect. It was magical. I was lying there on top of this beautiful boy, my knight in shining armor, my hero, with his strong hands wrapped around mine.

This is probably the most romantic moment of my entire life, I thought, as I gazed deeply into the infinite depths of his eternal blue eyes. *Or at least it would be if his breath didn't smell so bad!*

Chapter Thirty-Five
People Eat Crazy Things, Apparently

I know how terrible that sounds. There I was, lying in the arms of this divinely beautiful boy who had just saved me from a certain agonizing death in the highlands of Iceland, and all I could think about was how bad his breath smelled.

What a terrible person I am. I mean, he was obviously not a city boy. Dressed in his big wool sweater that looked like it had seen better days, he obviously lived somewhere out in the country and was hardly expecting to run into anyone that morning, much less rescue a red-haired girl who proceeded to fall straight into his arms. How could I be so cruel as to even think about his bad breath?

I don't know. I don't like to think of myself as a cruel person, but you have to believe me that his breath smelled bad—really, really bad. You can judge me all you want, but trust me when I say that only something so atomic-bomb horrendously smelly could burst the magic bubble of that amazingly romantic moment.

At least I didn't let on that I'd noticed anything. I just smiled back at him until he slid out from under me and pulled me to my feet.

After letting go of my hands, he grinned and pointed across the countryside in the direction of the long ridge I had climbed over hours earlier.

"The highway is over that way," he said, but he noticed the look of unease on my face as I glanced in that direction. "That's the closest road. But I have a feeling you'd rather go a different way, right?"

I nodded.

"Then we go this way," he said, pointing in almost the exact opposite direction, up toward a low ridge of hills in the distance. "There's another road over here. It's a bit farther, but not too much."

"Thank you," I said simply, grateful that we wouldn't have to head back to where the men in suits might be waiting for me.

"Don't worry; I understand," he said, shrugging his shoulders. "But I think we'd better get going. I also have a feeling you need to get back to the city as soon as possible."

I nodded again. "I do," I replied. "There's...there's someone in danger. I need to help her."

"Then we'd better not waste any time," he said simply, and we set off cross-country together, walking briskly, side by side.

As we picked our way through the boulders and rocks, I looked over at my unusual companion.

"How did you know I spoke English?" I asked. Back when I was still at the bottom of the hole, he had spoken English to me.

"I heard you talking to yourself in English," he replied. "And crying."

I blushed.

"After the man in the ripped-up suit left," Finn explained, "I wandered down to see if I could find what it was that he was looking so desperately for."

"And you did," I said, my voice low, almost a whisper. "Thank you."

He looked back at me, grinning.

"You're welcome," he said, and looked forward again.

We walked a little while in silence; the only sound (of course) was the wind wailing and gusting over the rocks and bushes.

My stomach growled—loudly.

"You're hungry," Finn said.

I blushed again and nodded. I was absolutely starving.

"I'm sorry," he said, patting the bulging pocket of his sweater. "The only thing I can offer you is some Hákarl, and you're not going to want that."

"Don't be so sure," I replied, my stomach growling loudly again. "Right now I could eat just about anything."

He didn't look convinced.

"This you won't like," he said. "You won't be able to eat it."

"What is it?" I asked.

"Shark," he replied.

That didn't sound too bad. And my knees were so weak that if I didn't get some food in me soon, I was probably going to faint and hit my head again.

I held out my hand. "I'm willing to try," I said. "How bad can it be?"

He shook his head. "Trust me on this one," he said. "You're not going to want this."

"Oh, come on!" I said, laughing and smacking him playfully on the arm. "Give me a taste. It can't be that bad!"

He stopped and looked me over for a long moment before reaching into his pocket and pulling out a paper package wrapped in string. He pulled off the string and held the folded paper bundle over toward me.

"Don't say I didn't tell you so," he said.

Give me a break, I thought.

But not wanting to sound sarcastic, yet wanting to appear confident, I said, "I've eaten some pretty nasty things in my life. How bad can shark be? Isn't shark fin soup a delicacy in China?"

Finn just smiled and held out the package. I took it from him and unwrapped it, and then I leaned forward cautiously to smell it.

I didn't have to lean very far. The smell hit me like a freight train before my nose got anywhere near it.

"OH, MY GODDDDDD!!!" I cried, dropping the package on the

ground and stumbling over to the nearest boulder, steadying myself with my hand as I doubled over and retched, dry vomiting over and over again.

Do you have any idea how many muscles your body uses when you vomit? It's a lot. And it uses muscles that you didn't even know you had. And when you've just spent the last day being beat up, tied up, crashing in cars, and falling into holes, your muscles are pretty sore to begin with. Now imagine having to dry-heave with those muscles, and you can imagine what an excruciatingly painful experience this was.

What you cannot imagine, however, was how bad this shark stuff smelled. I cannot even describe it. It was worse than an outhouse in the middle of summer. It was worse than a beached whale rotting on the sand. It was worse than falling into a fishing net full of fish. It was the worst thing I had ever smelled in my life.

"Do you EAT THIS?!??" I shrieked at Finn between bouts of heaving my guts out.

Of course he ate it. That's what I smelled on his breath right after he rescued me from the underworld.

He walked over, grabbed the paper package off the ground, and wrapped it up once again. He set it on a rock and came over to comfort me, putting his hand on the small of my back, as I stayed bent over.

Slowly I got a hold of myself and managed to stand up straight again, the urge to throw up having passed, finally.

"I thought you said it was shark?" I cried, half-crazed. "I've seen plenty of sharks in my life, and they didn't smell like that!!! Why does it smell so bad?!??"

He shrugged. "It's how we prepare it, I guess. The process makes it a bit smelly."

"What could you possibly do to it to make it smell so bad?" I asked, my nausea passing and a coughing fit starting to kick in. (And in case you don't know it already, coughing also uses a lot of muscles that you didn't know you had.)

"We dig a hole in the ground," he said, stating this perfectly calmly as if it was the most natural thing in the world. "And we bury the shark meat for a few months until it rots and all the poisons drain away. Then we dig it up and cut it into pieces, and then we hang them up and let them dry for a few more months."

I looked over at him in complete disbelief, my mouth hanging open.

"Yah, right," I said, laughing.

He nodded sincerely, a dead-serious look on his face. He wasn't kidding.

"It's true," he said.

I was speechless.

"Why would you do that?!??" I asked, starting to freak out a little. "I mean, why would anyone ever do something like that?"

He shrugged again.

"You have to do it," he said. "It's poisonous otherwise."

"What's wrong with boiling it?" I asked. "Or roasting it or barbecuing it?"

"Still poisonous," he replied. "You have to let it rot for a few months to get rid of the poison."

Why would anyone do this? How did anyone even figure this out in the first place? How did anyone get the idea that sticking a poisonous shark in a hole in the ground for a few months would make it safe to eat? Then, after digging it up and smelling how bad it smelled, why would they still decide to eat it?

Of all the things I'd heard in my life, this was, by far, the absolute craziest.

"If it's poisonous, then why eat it at all?!??" I asked.

Yet again, he shrugged.

"It's good," he said simply.

I still couldn't believe what I was hearing. But as I thought it over, it occurred to me that as disgusting as it might sound, and certainly as disgusting as it might *smell*, I was going to have to try this stuff. I mean, how could I not? How could I tell anyone about this and admit that I hadn't had the courage to actually taste this stuff?

"Okay," I said, standing up and sticking out my open hand toward him. "Hand it over. I want to try it."

"Are you sure?" he asked, raising one eyebrow skeptically.

"I'm positive," I replied. "Hand it over."

He looked me up and down suspiciously, and then he gave me a crooked grin before handing me the wrapped paper package of rotted shark meat. I held it at arm's length, unwrapping it carefully until I saw the small chunks of crusty brown flesh inside.

"Hold this," I said, gesturing for him to hold the package. He took it from me, and while I held my nose with one hand, I picked up one of the squishy brown chunks with my other hand and quickly put it in my mouth before I could change my mind.

Making awful contorted faces and using every ounce of willpower to keep from spitting or vomiting it out, I chewed hastily four or five times and then swallowed it, feeling nauseous as it slid, tepid and slippery, down my throat. My stomach heaved—once, twice, but I didn't throw it back up.

I took several deep breaths, making sure that it wasn't coming back up again. It tasted like pee. Not that I had any idea what pee tasted like, but I imagined that if you took a sponge, peed on it, then buried it in the ground for three months, then hung it up to dry, and then ate it, it would taste exactly like that rotted shark meat.

Why would the Icelanders bury a shark in the ground then dig it up later so they could eat it? People do crazy things, apparently.

I looked over at Finn, defiant and proud. I'd done it. I'd eaten Icelandic Hákarl.

He smiled at me and tied the string around the package again before putting it back in his pocket. As he did so, a feigned and theatrical look of surprise came over his face, and he pulled another package out of his sweater.

"I can't believe it," he said, grinning mischievously. "I didn't just have Hákarl after all. I also have a few pieces of buttered Harðfiskur."

"Oh, god," I said, unable to imagine what horrific Icelandic delicacy he was expecting me to try now. "And what's that?"

"Nothing really," he shrugged. "It's just plain dried fish."

Chapter Thirty-Six
Feeling The Earth Move

"You did that on purpose!" I cried, stuffing the dried fish into my mouth and chewing greedily. I was absolutely starving, and unlike the rotted shark I'd just eaten, this stuff was actually pretty tasty—simple, but tasty. It was dried white fish, hammered out flat, and with some butter spread on it like you would butter a piece of toast. The concept was a bit strange to me—buttering fish instead of bread—but the result was very pleasant and satisfying. (Although, compared to the rotted shark, just about anything would taste good.)

Finn kept walking, looking down at the ground, but grinning as he went.

"How could I let you visit Iceland," he asked, "and go back to your family and friends without trying some traditional Icelandic food?"

I laughed. He was right. I was here to experience a different culture, and part of that included eating things that the people of that culture eat, even if those things turned my wimpy Canadian stomach on its head.

"Besides," Finn said. "Shark isn't the only food that we bury in the ground."

"Oh god, what else?" I asked, unable to imagine any other similar Icelandic delicacies.

"No, no, not like the Hákarl," Finn replied, laughing. "We have this kind of dark bread that is baked by burying it in places where the volcanic activity makes the ground hot."

"Don't you see how that makes much more sense?" I said, teasing. "Cooking food makes sense. Letting it rot does not."

The two of us walked for a while in silence across the rough terrain as it gradually sloped upward toward the summit of a low, rocky hill.

"What were you doing all the way out here, anyway?" I asked, breaking the silence.

"I live out here," Finn replied, looking over at me. "I live with my parents on a farm a short distance from here."

I looked around at the remote landscape surrounding us. "It's hard to believe that anyone lives out here," I said.

"We live a simple life," Finn replied, shrugging. "We raise sheep, grow what we can, and sell or trade what we don't need."

"It's hard to believe that anything can grow here," I commented, pulling the collar of my jacket up around my neck against the wind. As we made our way higher up the side of the hill, the gusts were becoming colder and more abrasive.

"You'd be surprised what can grow here," Finn said. "Right now, approaching the summer, the days are getting longer and the plants love all the sunlight."

"I hadn't thought about that," I replied. It made sense. The summers might be short here, but the days were longer with lots of sunlight.

"And because of the climate, we also don't have very many insects here," Finn continued. "So we don't have to use so many artificial substances to keep them from destroying the crops."

"My mom would love that," I said, laughing. "She's into all those organically grown vegetables and stuff. But I can't imagine her living out here. I think she likes her modern house with all its modern conveniences a bit too much."

Finn shrugged. "Everyone needs to find a balance between living their life and doing what they think is right."

We continued walking in silence again for a little while longer. The thought of my mother made me suddenly very homesick. God knows how worried my parents were right now.

Or are they worried? I asked myself. *For that matter, has anyone even noticed that I am gone?*

"Of course!" the little voice in my head replied. "You missed dinner with Konrad and Kristín last night. Surely, they must have told someone. And what about Albert? Someone must have discovered his body by now—probably Avery—and called the police. Surely they put two and two together and figured out that what happened to him had something to do with your sudden disappearance."

The thought of Avery reminded me, yet again, that in addition to all the other reasons I needed to get back to Reykjavík, I needed to warn her about those men and tell the police what happened to me.

"How much farther is..." I started to ask but stopped in mid-sentence as I felt a strange uneasiness in my stomach and an unusual sensation when I put foot down. It was a bit like when you're walking down a flight of stairs and you think you've reached the last step, but there's still one more to go. When you put your foot down, there's that instant where you expect your foot to touch solid ground but it just keeps on going.

I looked at my feet. I was standing firmly on solid ground, and yet something didn't feel right.

"It's an earthquake," Finn said, standing with his hands held flat out away from his sides as though he were trying to feel the vibrations in the air. "A very small one."

Standing there with my feet braced apart and my arms spread out for balance, my brain tried to make sense out of what my body was experiencing. I'd never been in an earthquake before, and the feeling was quite strange, as if the whole world around me suddenly became fluid and was in motion. There was no sound at all (except the wind, of course), but I could feel the earth moving ever so slightly beneath my feet, the sensation traveling up my legs and throughout the rest of my body.

After a few seconds, the tremor faded and the world felt solid and normal once again. I looked at Finn with an enormous grin on my face.

"That was so cool!" I said. "I can't believe it!"

Finn smiled. "It's all a part of life here, I suppose," he said, pausing thoughtfully for a moment. "We're used to living with the different whims of nature. Maybe that's why we feel so much more connected with the earth."

I looked down at my feet again, waiting and hoping that the ground would start to shake again, but there was nothing.

"And to answer your question," Finn said, climbing the last few steps to the top of the hill and pointing with his finger down the other side of the slope, "the road back to the city is just down there."

I scrambled up to join him. The view from the top revealed a low, rolling grassland stretching away into the distance that was dotted here and there with trees and farmhouses. Cutting across this view at the bottom of the long slope of the hill was a road running left to right.

I breathed a sigh of relief. A road has to be one of the surest signs of civilization there is, and I was so glad to see it.

"You'll be able to catch a lift back to the city, no problem," Finn said. "There're cars along here all the time."

I looked over at him, confused.

"Aren't you coming down there with me?" I asked.

He shook his head.

"I need to get back to my parents," he said. "They'll be expecting me."

I felt a pang of disappointment and sadness as I realized that he and I would now have to say goodbye. My head must have been a bit muddled after being banged around because somehow I'd expected that he would ride back to Reykjavík with me.

"I'm not sure..." I said, feeling uncertain about what I should do.

"Didn't you say that you needed to get back to the city?" Finn asked, taking a few steps toward me. "And that someone was in danger?"

I nodded.

"Avery," I replied, biting my lip. "I have to warn her."

Finn smiled—a warm, amazing smile.

"Then get going," he said. "And don't worry. Everything will be fine."

I smiled back at him, gradually recovering from my uncertainty and knowing what I had to do. I had to get back to Reykjavík to help Avery.

"Thank you, Finn," I said, wrapping my arms around him to give him a hug. "Thank you for everything, and for saving me."

He put his arms around me in return, and for a long moment, we stood there just holding each other. He was warm and strong, and in his arms, I felt safe somehow.

"Take care of yourself, Kit," he said as we stepped back from each other and I took my first few steps down toward the road.

"I will," I replied, looking back over my shoulder at him and waving goodbye. "Thank you again."

He raised his arm to return my wave and watched as I continued down the hill away from him.

As I made my way down the hill, I suddenly had a thought and stopped dead in my tracks. I turned toward Finn and scrambled back up the hill toward him.

"What is it?" he asked in surprise.

Without a single word, I leaned forward to put a finger on his lips, and then I wrapped my hands around the back of his neck. I didn't care if his breath smelled bad. Mine probably smelled just as bad after eating that vile Hákarl, too. If this was going to be goodbye, then I was going to kiss him before I went.

And so I did. Right on the lips. And it was as perfect a kiss as can possibly be, warm and soft and close as we stood on top of that hill in the spring sunshine with the never-ending cold Icelandic wind whipping and swirling around us.

"Thank you, Finn," I said softly, looking into his big blue eyes one last time before heading back down the hill again toward the highway.

After a few steps, I turned to wave goodbye again, and he waved back. But when I continued down the hill a bit farther and looked back over my shoulder to wave one last time, I saw that he was already gone.

Chapter Thirty-Seven
I've Heard That One Before

S aying goodbye to Finn was sad, but I accepted that my trip around the world was going to be an adventure with many goodbyes along the way. Of course, if I had been thinking more clearly, I would have at least asked him for his e-mail address or something. (Although, I have a feeling that he probably didn't have Internet access on his farm in the middle of nowhere.) But I was mainly concerned with my need to catch a lift back to Reykjavík as soon as possible so that I could warn Avery that her life was in danger. I could only hope that it wasn't already too late.

I continued down the slope of the hill toward the highway and across a landscape that was far different from how it had looked further back. On this side of the hill there was grassland with horses and farmhouses—not *many* farmhouses, but some. This landscape was more familiar to me than the lava fields, but even so, it still had its own unique Icelandic qualities.

Here and there on my side of the highway, the grass gave way to areas of red and brown rock and mud. Wisps of steam rose from occasional tiny cracks in the earth, and as I walked across these barren areas, I could feel the heat rising from the ground. *This must be the kind of place that Finn had talked about. Where bread can be baked by burying it in the ground*, I mused.

Several cars passed by on the highway during the time it took me to climb down the hill. My plan was to continue straight down to the highway and then to flag a car down. If that didn't work, then I would hike up the road to the left, in the opposite direction of Reykjavík, but toward a group of buildings at the side of the road that I could see in the distance. Some cars and a small group of people stood close to the buildings, so if all else failed, I could convince someone up there to give me a ride.

As I came closer to the highway, I got a better look at the group of people standing in the distance. They were so far away that it was difficult to tell, but it looked as if they were all waiting for something.

What in the world can they be waiting for out here? I wondered.

A second or two later, I had my answer. In a flash of bright, white mist, a tower of water suddenly exploded out of the ground and rose dozens of meters into the air before it collapsed in on itself and crashed back down again. It was a geyser. In fact, for all I knew it might have been the one-and-only original geyser, since Konrad had told me that the English word itself comes from a specific spouting hot spring in Iceland called Geysír.

With all this activity from the ground—earthquakes, steam rising, and geysers erupting—I was reminded that the powerful elemental forces of nature were always close at hand in Iceland. They were constantly lurking just beneath the surface.

I hoped that the geyser might go off again, so I kept my gaze on the people as I covered the last few steps to the highway. In the distance, I could see a light grey sedan coming down the highway toward me.

Perfect timing, I thought. *All I have to do is wave it down and hope they will give me a ride.*

"What if they are axe murderers or something?" the little voice in my head asked.

Then I won't flag them down, I replied. *Duh!*

As the car drove closer, I stepped onto the side of the asphalt and waved my hands in the air as a signal for them to stop. When they slowed down and pulled over to the side of the road, I saw a middle-aged couple in the front seat, and a young teenaged girl, who I assumed was their daughter, in the back seat.

You see? I told myself. *It's a nice family—not axe murderers.*

"That's usually what axe murderers look like," the little voice in my head grumbled as the car pulled up next to me.

Seated on the passenger side was a woman about forty years old with shoulder length dark brown hair and wearing a pair of oversized sunglasses and a black turtleneck sweater. The driver was a man about forty-five, overweight, and balding with a beard that was grayer than its original black. He was wearing a zipped-up blue windbreaker. The girl in the back seat was about twelve or thirteen years old. She had dark brown hair, and was wearing a pair of jeans and a windbreaker that matched the man's.

"Oh, my Lord, what happened to you!" the woman screamed. She opened the door of the car before it came to a complete stop and was starting to get out. She had a look of absolute horror on her face, and for a moment, I didn't understand what she was talking about, but then I remembered. After the night that I'd had, I probably looked like a complete train wreck.

The man brought the car to a stop and pulled up the parking brake before he walked around the front of the car to join the woman.

"You look a mess," he said as he put on his glasses, which hung from a string around his neck. "It looks like you've been through the wringer and back."

"I...I'm okay," I stammered, overwhelmed by their reaction to my appearance. "I... I... was in a car accident."

"We need to get you to a hospital, honey," the woman said. She leaned closer to examine my face.

"Yes!" I cried. "That's exactly what I wanted to ask you. I need a ride back to Reykjavík. It's an emergency."

"Of course, child, of course," the man replied. He ushered me toward the backseat of the car and opened the door for me.

"Sasha, get in the front seat, will you?" the lady said to the girl peering out at us through the open car door. "I want to sit in back and see if I can get this poor thing cleaned up a little bit."

Sasha hopped out and got into the front passenger seat, and the woman and I climbed into the back. In no time at all, we were back on the road. We sped toward Reykjavík. The woman pulled out a first-aid kit from her shoulder bag and unwrapped a pair of surgical gloves and some alcohol wipes. She spread them on her knees in an orderly and professional manner.

"We're the Andersons," the woman said. She leaned close to clean some of the blood off my face. "We're from Eau Claire, Wisconsin. I'm Susan. Up there in the driver's seat is my husband Harold. And across from him is our daughter Sasha."

"It's good to meet all of you," I replied softly. "I'm Kitty from Canada."

Susan leaned closer to wipe the area around my eye where the sliver of rock had cut me. She looked me over carefully, and a stern frown grew on her face.

"Good to meet you, too, Kitty," she said, still frowning. She looked up toward the front seat and exchanged a meaningful look with her husband in the rearview mirror.

"What is it?" I asked, worried. "Is something wrong?"

Susan shared another look with her husband, and then she leaned back in her seat.

"I'm an emergency room nurse, Kitty," she said calmly. "And Harold up there is a policeman. And thanks to that we've both seen our share of people who've been in car accidents."

Susan leaned forward again, placed her fingertips gently under my chin, and turned my left cheek toward her.

"And I have never seen a car do that to a person," she said simply.

I glanced up to Harold and caught a glimpse of his eyes watching me in the rearview mirror.

"Someone hit me," I said quietly.

Susan nodded.

"I know," she said tenderly, and she smiled in pity. "I've heard that one before. And maybe they also threw you down the stairs—or maybe worse?"

They had completely the wrong idea.

"No, no!" I cried out. "It's not like that at all!"

Susan nodded again, still smiling kindly with pity in her eyes.

"I told you I was a nurse," Susan said. "And I've heard that one before, too."

"No, really," I replied, almost laughing at the absurdity of it all. "It's not what you think!"

"Why don't you explain it to us, then?" Harold said from the front seat. "And tell us what really happened."

I looked up at Harold's eyes in the mirror, across to Sasha, who was looking at me wordlessly, and then back to Susan again.

"Someone punched me," I began. "Then they shot at me. Then chased me and shot at me again. Then I fell into a hole in the lava field and hit my head."

Susan gave me a look of disbelief mixed with horror.

"It's true," I said. "Oh, and I was in a truck accident somewhere in there as well. I forgot about that for a second."

Chapter Thirty-Eight
The Shock Of My Life

A nd so, I told them the whole story of my crazy night while Susan continued to clean up my various cuts and bruises. I told them about visiting Albert's lab and finding his body lying in a pool of blood. About being punched and knocked unconscious by the fat guy in the suit who'd appeared out of the shadows. About waking up in the back of a dark truck with my hands tied behind my back because the men in dark suits mistook me for Albert's assistant Avery. About their clandestine meeting in the middle of the night with Tómas Finnsson from the energy ministry. About how I stole their truck and they'd chased after me. About the strange naked man in the middle of the road who caused us to crash both of our vehicles. About being shot at and deciding to make a run for it out across the countryside. About being chased cross-country and getting shot at again. About falling into the lava tube or bubble or whatever it was and being rescued by Finn. I even told them about the disgusting horrible rotted shark that Finn had given me.

As I told them the story of my crazy night and Susan continued to clean up my various cuts and bruises, I watched their eyebrows rose higher and higher in disbelief, particularly at the part about the naked man in the middle of the road. I wasn't sure that even *I* would believe that if I hadn't seen it with my own two eyes.

"And that," I said, "is how I came to meet the three of you, who so kindly pulled over to help me."

For a moment no one spoke.

"That is unbelievable," Harold said in a hushed voice.

"I believe her," Sasha said with a grin. Before I'd started talking, she had been very bashful and quiet, but as the story unfolded, she became very interested, smiling and laughing along with me as I described some of the crazier parts of the adventure.

"Of course we believe her, too, Sasha," Harold said, and he turned around to give me a quick smile. "But it's quite a remarkable and incredible chain of events."

Susan hadn't said anything yet. She had a look of concentration on her face as though she was thinking about something important.

"You see, Harold?" she said, swatting him on the shoulder with the palm of her hand. "I told you we should have brought the cell phone with us on this trip. There're no payphones out here, and we could have used

143

it to call someone right now if we'd brought it."

"We're on vacation here!" Harold protested. "I didn't want your sister calling us every ten minutes."

I laughed and leaned forward to give Harold's shoulder a friendly nudge.

"Don't worry," I said. "I don't know Avery's telephone number anyway, or even where she lives. So we couldn't call her even if you had your phone. I just need to get to the university and find someone there who can get in touch with her."

Susan glanced at me with a surprised look on her face.

"I wasn't thinking of calling Avery," Susan said. "You need to call the police, dear. Kidnapping? Assault? Murder? These are very serious crimes."

Call the police? I thought. I hadn't even thought that far ahead yet. I was too focused on getting to Avery and making sure that she was safe.

"We can kill two birds with one stone," I said. "You can take me to Albert's lab at the university. Someone there will know where to find Avery, and by now it must also be full of police as well."

Harold nodded.

"It's probably the most expeditious solution," he agreed. "And we're almost at the outskirts of the city now, so it won't be long before we reach the university."

I looked out of the window to take in the sight of the city coming into view. We had returned to civilization, but as we wound our way through the traffic circles and streets of Reykjavík, I started to grow more anxious. Was I too late to warn Avery?

I knew that I would find out soon enough, and I leaned forward between the seats to give Harold directions through the last series of roads leading to the university and to the parking lot next to the building where Albert's lab was located.

When we turned the last corner and into the parking lot, I could see that I had been right—the police had arrived, and several patrol cars were lined up next to the building. Harold pulled into an empty space and switched off the engine.

In my anxiousness, I had already opened the car door and had one foot outside when Harold twisted his body around to speak to us in the back seat.

"I'll go in with her in case they need us to make a statement or something," Harold said to Susan. "You and Sasha stay here."

"I'm so sorry," I said to Sasha and Susan. "I am being so rude. But I'll be back to say goodbye once we know what's going on."

"Go, go!" Susan said, waving me out the door with her hand. "Don't be silly."

Harold and I walked the short distance along the sidewalk to the open side door that led to Albert's lab. It seemed like a lifetime ago since I'd been there, but not even twenty-four hours had passed.

When I stepped tentatively into the lab with Harold, I could see various groups of police and other official-looking people standing around. Above their heads were the marvelous blue paper airplanes that I'd seen the night before. With the lights switched on, they were an even more amazing sight.

"Oh, my god, it's Kitty!" I heard a familiar voice say, and I turned to see Konrad rushing over. "What in the world happened? We were looking all over for you! We were worried sick!"

I wrapped my arms around Konrad and hugged him close. A flood of emotions washed over me. It felt so good to feel safe again that I couldn't keep from bursting into tears.

"I'm okay," I said, sniffling and wiping the tears from my eyes. "I just had a very rough night."

"I can tell," Konrad replied. He bent down to get a better look at my battered and bruised face. "What in the world happened to you? How did you get so banged up?"

"It's a long story," I said, shaking my head anxiously. "And I have to tell it to you and to the police, but first I need to find Avery. She's in a lot of danger."

"Avery?" Konrad replied. "Who's Avery?"

"Kitty?" I heard a voice from behind Konrad say. We both turned to see a red-haired girl in glasses walking toward us with a confused look on her face. It was Avery.

"Thank god, Avery, you're okay!" I cried as I walked toward her quickly.

"Of course I am okay." She looked incredibly confused as I wrapped my arms around her in a giant hug. "Why wouldn't I be?" she asked.

I couldn't blame Avery for being confused. I would be confused too if I was in her position

"It's a long story," I said, with tears of relief streaming down my face.

"Uh, okay," she replied, and she patted me on the back in a tentative effort to comfort me.

I hugged Avery for a few more moments. I took a step back to explain to everyone why I was acting so crazy, but before I had a chance to say another word, I looked over Avery's shoulder toward the corner of the room and had the shock of my life when I saw who was standing there talking to a pair of police officers.

Chapter Thirty-Nine

The Greatest Writer That Ever Lived

"Albert?!??" I cried in amazement. I couldn't believe my eyes. It was Albert standing there alive and well with a large bandage wrapped around his head. He wasn't dead after all.

"Everyone has been worried sick about you," he said as he limped over toward me.

"Worried about *me*?" I replied as I took a few steps in his direction, still unable to believe my eyes. "I thought... I thought..."

Albert raised his palms and shrugged apologetically. "I know, I know, but don't worry about me. It's just a bump and a cut on my head; nothing too serious."

"Thank god," I said.

"What about you?" Albert continued. "Are you all right? You look like you've been to hell and back."

I nodded.

"I've had quite an incredible night," I admitted, "and I'm glad that the police are here because they'll want to hear what happened to me as well."

At that moment, Harold walked toward us with a tall man who looked like a police officer. The tall man put out his hand to shake mine.

"Hello, Kitty," he said, smiling kindly. "I am Inspector Galdur Valdason of the Metropolitan Police. Your friend Harold has been explaining to us how his family found you this afternoon, and he tells us that you have quite a story to tell."

I looked around at all the worried faces encircling me: Konrad, Avery, Albert, Harold, Inspector Galdur, and a couple other police officers as well. I had been so focused on Avery and Albert that it hadn't even occurred to me that I would suddenly become the center of attention and worry.

I took a deep breath and told them about coming to meet Albert in his lab and finding him on the floor, and all the crazy events that unfolded as a result. Inspector Galdur took notes as I spoke, and I occasionally became a bit emotional; my voice shook and tears welled in my eyes. Somehow, I got through the whole story, and when I finished, the whole group just looked at me in silent astonishment.

Inspector Galdur continued writing on his notepad for a few more seconds. "And you have no idea who these men who kidnapped you were?" he asked, glancing up for a moment. "You've never seen them anywhere before?"

I shook my head. "Never," I replied.

"They must be working for some aluminum corporation," Konrad said, thinking aloud as he looked around at the group.

"And they're obviously the ones who broke in here last night," Albert said, "looking for my smelting research."

"Do you have any idea which of the aluminum companies might be interested in such research?" Inspector Galdur asked.

Konrad and Albert both laughed.

"All of them," Konrad replied.

"If we ever get it to work, it will be worth millions," Albert said.

"*If* we get it to work," Avery added.

The group of them continued to talk as they tried to figure out some clue as to the identity of the men who had grabbed me. I listened to them for a few moments, but then did some thinking of my own, and reflected on everything I'd seen and heard the previous night that could provide a clue.

I closed my eyes and replayed everything from the moment I'd regained consciousness in the back of the truck to my dramatic escape. I tried to picture what each of the men had been wearing. I definitely remembered seeing expensive Italian suits and shoes. Maybe the men were Italians? I pictured the expensive watch that the smaller and more talkative man had been wearing. I was sure it was Swiss. Could they be from Switzerland?

That's not it, I told myself. *Lots of men with money—or who pretend to have money—wear Italian suits and Swiss watches.*

There had to be something else. I strained to remember any other details that might solve the mystery. Perhaps the fancy gold-plated lighter the man had used to light his cigarette—or even the cigarettes themselves. Judging from the smell, those weren't expensive cigarettes. But I wasn't sure because I couldn't see the label on the pack when he took it out of his suit pocket. It was too dark.

There must be something, I thought to myself, still struggling to think of anything that could help.

Then it came to me.

"Who is the greatest writer that ever lived?" I asked, waving my hands excitedly to interrupt the animated discussion and get everyone's attention.

Everyone stared at me blankly for a few seconds.

"The greatest what?" Konrad asked.

"The greatest writer," I repeated. "Who is the greatest writer that ever lived?"

Everyone looked confused.

"Hemingway?" Konrad suggested.

"Shakespeare?" Harold asked.

"J. K. Rowling," Albert said.

Everyone laughed and looked over at Albert, certain that he was joking, but his straight face told them otherwise.

"Halldór Laxness," one of the police officers said, and Inspector Galdur nodded enthusiastically in agreement.

"Who?" Harold asked.

"Philip K. Dick," Konrad suggested.

"Who?" Inspector Galdur asked.

"Oscar Wilde," another officer suggested.

"Dostoyevsky?" Konrad said.

"And what are the biggest aluminum companies in the world?" I asked. "What countries do they come from?"

"Alcoa, of course," Konrad said. "They're based in the United States."

"Rio Tinto Alcan," Albert said. "They're from Canada. They're the ones supporting my research."

"There's Chalco, based in China," Konrad said, "and Rusal from Russia."

"That's it!" I cried out. "Russia!"

Everyone stared at me.

"They were Russians," I said. "The men who grabbed me were Russians."

Inspector Galdur looked at me skeptically. "How do you know?" he asked.

"There was this one little guy who couldn't stop talking," I explained. "He kept saying 'In my country this' and 'In my country that'. He said that the greatest writer who ever lived was from his country."

Everyone continued to stare at me.

"Dostoyevsky," I said. "They were Russians. They just have to be!"

No one looked very convinced.

"She's right," we heard a voice say behind us. We turned to look and saw a pair of men walking toward us. The taller of the two was wearing a long tan overcoat and looked like a typical television police detective, which was probably the case since the man with him was a uniformed police officer.

Inspector Galdur stepped to the side and made room for the new arrivals. "This is Inspector Óðinn of the National Police," he explained, introducing the man in the overcoat.

Inspector Óðinn nodded in greeting.

"You are right," Inspector Óðinn said, turning to address me directly. "Those men are Russians, and I've been following their activities with great interest for several months now."

"That's fantastic!" I said enthusiastically. "Now you can arrest them for kidnapping me and trying to kill Albert!"

Everyone looked at me in confusion.

"Trying to kill me?" Albert asked. "When did they try to kill me?"

I looked at him, perplexed, not sure of what I was hearing.

I pointed to the bandage wrapped around his head. "Last night I found you lying here in a pool of blood. Isn't that why your head is bandaged?"

Albert raised his hand up to his forehead and touched the bandage gingerly.

"I didn't see any men in suits here last night," he said.

I was confused. Had they attacked him from behind so that he couldn't see their faces?

"They're the ones who did that to your head," I explained patiently. "Right before they grabbed me."

Albert shook his head.

"They didn't do this to me," he said, touching his bandage-covered forehead gingerly. "Erík Grettirsson did this."

Chapter Forty
BBC Breaking News

"Erík did that?!?" I asked, completely bewildered by this new piece of information in the already confusing jigsaw puzzle of events. "What does he have to do with any of this?"

"He and I got into a bit of a shouting match last night," Albert explained. "There was some pushing and shoving, and I fell and hit the corner of my desk with my forehead. I was knocked unconscious, and there was a lot of blood, but otherwise I was okay. It was an accident, and Erík ran to get help for me."

"A shouting match about what?" I asked. "How do you even know Erík?"

Albert chuckled. "Everyone knows Erík," he said, and everyone laughed. "And what else would we be arguing about other than Erík's favorite subject—saving the environment."

I looked around for a place to sit down. This was getting to be too much, and my head was beginning to spin.

"We should get Kitty to a hospital and have her checked out," Konrad said, and he walked over and put his arm around me. "We can talk about all of this later."

Everyone nodded in agreement, and the group disbursed. Konrad and Inspector Óðinn walked with me to the parking lot. Harold gave his business card to Inspector Óðinn in case the police needed any additional information. He handed one to me as well, and patted me on the shoulder as he told me to let them know how things turned out. I assured him that I would, and then I walked over to the Anderson's car to say goodbye to Susan and Sasha. I thanked them very much for helping me.

With all the goodbyes finished, I followed Konrad back to his Land Rover, and he drove me the short distance to the hospital where a pair of nurses and a wheelchair were already waiting for me.

The nurses wheeled me away to a treatment room where I changed into a hospital gown. They cleaned my wounds and bandaged them before a female doctor arrived to do some tests and take measurements of the kind that doctors in emergency rooms all over the world take.

"You are a very lucky girl," the doctor said after she had looked me over thoroughly and made a final check of my vision and reflexes. "You look like a truck ran over you, but I don't see any sign of serious injury or concussion."

"I know," I replied. My body ached and felt broken all over, but it was good to hear that it was nothing that a nice long rest couldn't fix. I planned to get started on my recuperation as soon as I got back to Kristín's apartment. Stinky geothermal water or not, I couldn't wait to get into a hot bath and climb into bed.

"I'd still like to keep you overnight, however, and check in on you again in the morning to see if we need to run a CT scan or not."

So much for my hot bath, I thought wearily.

"Okay," I said. "Whatever you think is best."

The doctor nodded and left the nurse to wheel me to the elevator and up to a hospital room where Konrad and Inspector Óðinn were waiting for me. The nurse helped me into bed, and then she gave Inspector Óðinn a stern look.

"Ten minutes," she said, tapping her watch for emphasis. "Then out so she can sleep."

Inspector Óðinn nodded, and the nurse left us alone.

"The Inspector just has a few questions," Konrad said as Inspector Óðinn pulled a stack of photographs out of his shoulder bag and spread them on the wheeled table, which he rolled in front of me so that I could sit up in bed and look at them.

"We've been watching these Russians for some time because of suspicions about their company's involvement with different members of the Icelandic government," Inspector Óðinn explained as he organized the photographs for me. "But so far we haven't been able to prove anything."

They were standard surveillance photos—candid shots taken from a distance using a telephoto lens that showed men getting in and out of cars, eating in cafés, or standing around smoking cigarettes.

"Do you recognize anyone here?" Inspector Óðinn asked.

I put my finger down hard on a photo of a man walking out of the door of what looked like an office building. It was the small talkative one who had ridden with me in the back of the truck.

"Him!" I cried enthusiastically. "He was one of them."

"You're sure?" Inspector Óðinn asked.

I nodded. "One hundred percent sure," I replied as I scanned the faces on the photos in front of me and put my finger down on a photo of the fat one. "And him, too. He's the one who punched me. I would know him anywhere."

"Anyone else?" Inspector Óðinn asked hopefully.

I continued to scan for any face that looked like the third guy from their little group, the one who was driving the truck, but the problem was that I hadn't seen him very well. I wasn't sure I would recognize him if I saw him again.

I shook my head slowly. "I don't think so," I said. "I didn't really see the other one very well."

Inspector Óðinn glanced over at Konrad, who nodded his head that it was okay to continue. "Just take your time and tell me if you recognize anyone else in these pictures."

I shook my head again. "Sorry, I only recognize those two guys," I said, picking their photographs along with a third one of Tómas Finnsson. "And of course this one is Tómas Finnsson from the environment ministry, or whatever it is. He's the guy they gave a suitcase full of money to."

Inspector Óðinn leaned toward me and looked me in the eye with a deadly serious expression on his face.

"And you're absolutely sure about that?" he asked.

I nodded. "Absolutely," I replied, and Inspector Óðinn seemed satisfied.

"Okay, Kitty," he said, smiling as he pushed his chair back. "Then I won't bother you any further this evening."

"What will you do now?" I asked.

Inspector Óðinn put the photos away and closed his shoulder bag. "We'll have to make some arrests and see where things go from there," he said. "We already found two torched wrecks out on a back road in the highlands—one industrial-sized truck and one car belonging to the Ministry of Environment and Natural Resources that was reported stolen this morning by Deputy Minister Tómas Finnsson. That's solid confirmation of your story, but I want you to know that I will try to keep you out of this as much as possible. I want to build a case against these people that doesn't rely on your having to testify at a trial."

I was surprised. "I can testify," I said. "I don't mind."

Inspector Óðinn smiled a thin smile. "I know, and I am thankful for that. But this is a serious and dangerous business, as you know better than anyone, and if I can do it, I am going to keep your name out of this completely for your safety."

"Fair enough," I replied. "Thank you."

Inspector Óðinn pulled his bag over his shoulder, and he and Konrad got to their feet to leave.

"Get some sleep, Kitty," Konrad said, and he patted me on the feet through the hospital blanket. "I'll be back to see you first thing in the morning."

"I will." I said tiredly, finding it hard to keep the weariness out of my voice.

"Take care of yourself," Inspector Óðinn said, and they both headed for the door. He smiled and glanced up at the television hanging from the ceiling in the corner of the room. "You picked a good time to visit," he said, pointing to the television. "Not many people who come to Iceland get to see a volcano erupting."

I looked over at the television screen. The sound was off, but the pictures flashing across it were worth a thousand words. Across the rugged landscape of the Icelandic highlands, enormous clouds of smoke and ash were billowing high into the air.

BBC BREAKING NEWS, the caption read. ICELAND VOLCANO.

Chapter Forty-One
The Entrance To Hell

After Konrad and Inspector Óðinn left, I picked up the television remote from the table next to the hospital bed and switched on the sound. Against a backdrop of images showing snow-covered mountains and black volcanic mounds spewing fountains of lava, the BBC reporter described the scene.

"Scenes like this, while not commonplace in Iceland, are also nothing out of the ordinary either. Situated atop a volcanically active ridge between the North American and European tectonic plates, Icelanders have coexisted with powerful forces of nature such as those seen here for hundreds of years. In fact, in medieval times, the residents of Iceland believed that volcanoes were entrances into hell, and it is from this belief that the English expression 'What the heck?' originates—Hekla being the name of one of Iceland's ancient volcanoes.

"The eruption here today near Askja in northeast Iceland began late this afternoon in an area that volcano experts have had their eye on for some time as a possible location for Iceland's next big eruption. The mountaintop crater lakes here have been thawing much earlier than usual in recent years, leading to speculation that some form of volcanic activity beneath the surface was warming the lake water and causing the early thaws. Such speculation now appears to have been confirmed as the volcano spews lava, smoke, and volcanic ash high into the sky.

"The area around the volcano is desolate and uninhabited, visited by only a few scientists and extreme tourists every year. But farther down the river valleys to the north, authorities have evacuated local residents and workers due to concerns that the volcanic activity here may trigger another eruption in one of the volcanoes farther to the south underneath the enormous Vatnajökull ice cap. That ice cap covers eight percent of Iceland's land area, and is the largest ice field in Europe. An eruption there could trigger catastrophic flash flooding due to the sudden melting of the glacier ice, so the authorities here are, of course, monitoring the situation carefully.

"On a more global scale, aviation authorities in Europe and North America are also watching the situation, and are hopeful that there will not be a repeat of the extensive shutdown of European airspace that took place a few years ago during the eruption of Iceland's Eyjafjallajökull volcano. Ash clouds from that eruption brought flights in Europe to a standstill for weeks and cost the airline industry hundreds of millions of dollars.

"Thankfully, while the ash cloud from today's eruption has caused a closure of Icelandic airspace to the east of the country, this has thus far only affected flights between Iceland and the European continent. Flights within Europe, or between North America and Europe, are expected to continue unless the situation worsens.

"For the time being, the situation seems stable, but the authorities will continue to keep a close eye on the volcano and take whatever action is necessary should the volcanic eruption intensify.

"Patricia Weald, BBC News."

The images accompanying this news story were absolutely incredible. Fountains of lava streamed into the sky. Steaming dark rocks spitting fire and chunky red-black lava flowed lazily downhill while helicopters chattered overhead and loomed dangerously close to the hellish scenes.

No wonder the ancient Icelanders considered volcanoes to be the entrances to hell, I thought. *That's exactly what it looks like.*

I muted the television again and leaned over to grab my backpack from the chair where Konrad had placed it for me. I'd left my bag on the floor by the door of Albert's lab the night before, and after all the excitement, I thought that maybe I'd lost it, but Konrad had retrieved it and kept it safe for me.

I pulled out my iPhone and checked for any missed calls or messages. I had twelve messages and several missed calls from my parents in Canada.

Taking a deep breath to prepare myself, I dialed my parents. My mother answered on the second ring and was relieved to hear my voice. Konrad had already updated her on my situation while I was being treated by the nurses, but she was anxious to hear the news from me directly. She put me on speakerphone while I told her and my dad the entire story of the last twenty-four hours. I gave them the slightly shorter and sanitized version so my mother wouldn't worry so much.

"But don't worry," I said as I ended my story and tried to downplay the situation. "I am totally fine—just some little cuts and bruises here and there."

"I don't know how you get yourself into these things, Kit," my mother said, taking me off speakerphone. "Just wait a second. Your father wants to talk to you."

I could hear some rustling at the other end of the line, and after a few seconds, my father came on the phone.

"Hey, Kit," my father said, sounding as cheerful as always. "I'm glad to hear that you're okay."

"I am, Dad!" I tried to sound convincing. "Everything here is fine."

"I know it, Kit," my father replied. "Your mother wants the phone again. We'll talk soon, and I'll try to convince your mother that she doesn't need to fly off to Iceland to take care of you."

I laughed, and after a few seconds, my mother came back on the telephone again.

"Listen, Kit," she said, and her voice sounded more serious this time. "I will be on the next plane if you just say the word. I am not kidding."

"I know you're not kidding, Mom," I replied. "But you have to trust me that everything is okay, and you don't need to drop everything and fly over here."

There was silence at the other end of the line for a long moment, and then my mother spoke again.

"Okay, Kit," she said. "I trust you—of course I do."

"I just need some sleep right now," I said.

"Okay, Kit," my mother said again. "Then get some sleep, and we'll talk soon."

"I promise," I replied, and we said goodbye and ended the call.

I switched off the television then slowly lowered myself out of the bed and shuffled over to the bathroom. I looked in the mirror and was shocked by my reflection. It was the first time I'd seen myself since the Russians had grabbed me the night before. I looked absolutely awful. It was much worse than I could possibly have imagined, and I was surprised that people had managed to act even remotely normally around me when they saw me again after my ordeal.

The left side of my face was one enormous, ugly, purplish-red bruise from where the fat Russian had punched me. Underneath and above my right eye were long cuts from where slivers of rock had hit me. All over my face were smaller cuts and bruises from exploding glass and being thrown around the cab of the truck after I'd lost control and swerved off the highway. Last but not least was the large bump on the back of my head, which I thought must be clearly visible, despite my hair covering it. I turned the vanity mirror and twisted my body to get a look at the back of my head. I couldn't see anything, but the bump felt so big under my fingers that I was still convinced that everyone could see it.

After taking a deep breath, I shuffled back to the bed and called for the nurse to help me flatten it so that I could go to sleep. She arrived seconds later and worked the bed controls until the mattress lay flat.

"Call me if you need anything," she said, and she switched the lights out and walked toward the door.

"I will," I replied. "Thank you."

Even with the lights out, it was only half-dark in the room. Through the window, I could see that it was still light outside despite the late hour, and the florescent glare from the hallway leaked in underneath the hospital door. But I didn't care. I would have no problem falling asleep. I was beyond exhausted.

I eased onto my left side and placed my left cheek gently onto the pillow.

It hurts to lie on this side, I thought. *I should flip over the other way. Do I have enough energy? I don't know. I should probably flip over. There are bruises on that side, too, though, but not as many. I don't know. What should I do?*

And so the discussion went inside my head until I just fell asleep on my bruised left side.

Chapter Forty-Two
People Always Forget That I Have A Plane

A different nurse came in to check on me the next morning. Konrad was with her, and they found me already awake and watching the television news coverage about the ongoing volcanic eruption in the northeastern region of Iceland. The doctor who'd seen me the night before arrived soon after, and she examined me thoroughly once again before giving me the okay to go home.

"If you have any symptoms such as dizziness, headaches, nausea, or problems with your vision, then you come back and see me, okay?" the doctor told me.

"I will; don't worry," I replied. "But I really feel fine."

The doctor left us alone, and I shuffled to the bathroom to change into my street clothes so that Konrad could drive me home. I was still dreaming of the hot bath I would finally get to have when I returned to Kristín's apartment, followed by crawling into bed with a good book and spending the entire day napping and reading.

On our way out of the hospital, we met Inspector Óðinn at the front doors. He looked tired and rumpled, and had a grave expression on his face.

"I'm glad I caught you before you left," he said, walking up to us and shaking hands.

"What is it?" Konrad asked. "Has something happened?"

Inspector Óðinn shook his head. "There's nothing to worry about. I just wanted to update you on the situation. Last night we went out to see Tómas Finnsson and bring him in for questioning. We found him with some cuts and bruises consistent with having been in a car accident, but he says that he got hurt falling down the stairs at his home. We're still holding him for further questioning today, so we'll see if he feels like being a little more cooperative when he gets tired of being at the police station."

Inspector Óðinn took a deep breath and looked from me to Konrad then back at me again.

"The news about the Russians, on the other hand, is not as good," he said. "We've been trying to find them since last night, including searching their apartments and those of any known accomplices, but without any luck so far. The bad news is that a private jet belonging to the Russian Aluminum Corporation was allowed to fly out of Keflavík this morning to

New York before we could stop it and conduct a search. We're in contact with the FBI, and hope to have them intercept the plane once it reaches the United States, but their legal search options might be limited, and I'm afraid that our Russian friends might have managed to escape."

Konrad looked over at me with concern. "Does Kitty need to be worried about anything?" he asked the Inspector.

Inspector Óðinn shook his head.

"No, no," he said confidently. "Kitty's name hasn't been connected to this at all, and don't forget that they still have no idea that it was her they grabbed. They probably still think they grabbed Avery Parker, and we'll keep a close eye on her as well. It's just unfortunate that they have almost certainly managed to escape prosecution. Unless they come back to Iceland and risk being arrested here, there's very little that we can do."

Konrad and I nodded silently, and stood there for a few moments absorbing the news. We thanked Inspector Óðinn for coming by to tell us, and he promised to keep us up to date on any further developments in the case. We shook hands again and said goodbye, and walked to Konrad's Land Rover parked nearby in the patient pick-up lane.

We didn't talk much on the short drive to Kristín's apartment. I was trying to sort out my confused feelings about the Russians escaping and dreaming of the hot bath that I hoped to find myself enjoying soon.

Maybe I'll go swimming at the geothermal pool this afternoon, I mused.

It sounded like a good idea, but the thought of facing the world with my battered and bruised face and body seemed like more than I would have the energy to deal with for at least a couple of days, although it might scare the shower attendant into letting me keep my bathing suit on during the showering process.

"Kristín has late classes today," Konrad said as we pulled onto Kristín's street. "We should be in time to catch her and have a coffee before she leaves for school."

Coffee sounded like a perfect idea to me, and Kristín always had a good supply of various Nespresso capsules to choose from, including the latest special edition blends.

Konrad expertly backed his Land Rover into the first available parking spot, and I pulled open the door to step down onto the sidewalk. We stopped quickly at the café across the street to buy a few pieces of skúffukaka then continued up to Kristín's apartment.

I unlocked the door with my borrowed key and pushed it open, holding it for Konrad as he followed me inside.

"Hello?" I called out to the quiet apartment. "Kristín?"

There was no answer.

I continued down the hallway past the bathroom and spare room where I was staying, and down to the main bedroom. The door was half-open, so I knocked quietly. The door swung open as I did so.

"Kristín?" I called out again. "Are you here?"

There was no sign of her anywhere.

"I guess she left for school already," I said as I headed back to the kitchen. I checked the bathroom along the way to make sure she wasn't in there.

When I came around the corner of the hallway and walked into the kitchen, I saw that Konrad had a slightly worried and confused expression on his face. He pointed wordlessly to an envelope propped against a bottle of olive oil in the middle of the kitchen table leaning against a bottle of olive oil.

Wrinkling my forehead, I walked around the table to look at the envelope more closely and saw that it was meant for me. My name was scrawled in handwriting on the outside.

"What's this?" I asked as I picked the envelope up and flipped it open.

Konrad shook his head and watched as I pulled out a handwritten letter.

dear kitty,

i am so sorry for what has happened to you. and i hope that you are okay but i suppose this is what happens when we surrender our freedoms and allow corrupt government officials and their corporate taskmasters to dictate environmental policy in our country. i apologize that our country is not better than this and that you had to pay the price for our stupidity. but rest assured that by the time you read this i will be on my way to make things right again. the highlands around the construction site for the dam have been evacuated because of the volcano and erik and i are going there to put an end to the destruction of our country's pristine nature once and for all. erik is right. if we let them build even one more dam they will never stop until our entire country is completely and irreparably "dammed" (ha ha). and if we let them do that there is no going back. not ever! but let's see them build a dam once we blow their unnatural machines into a million pieces.

i am sorry that they did this to you, kitty.

love,

kristin

p.s.—please don't tell my father.

"I can't believe it!" I said, starting again at the beginning of the note to read it a second time.

"What?" Konrad asked in concern. "What is it?"

I finished my second reading of the note and handed it to Konrad. I watched as his eyes darted back and forth across the page. His face reddened the more he read the letter.

"Dammit!" he shouted as he finished the letter for a third time. "How can you be so naïve, Kristín? There are better ways to fight for what you believe in than this."

Konrad pulled out his phone, and I watched over his shoulder as he quickly dialed Kristín's number. When he raised the phone up to his ear, I could hear it go straight to voice mail. Her phone was switched off.

Konrad pounded his hands on the kitchen counter in frustration, and then he stood for a moment taking deep breaths to calm himself and think things through.

"We have to stop her, I said, "before she does something she might regret later."

Konrad shook his head. "I don't see how we can. The construction site is more than a six-hour drive from here, and they obviously have a significant head start. If we do make the drive, by the time we get there, they will have done whatever stupid thing they're planning to do."

It's funny. People always forget that I have a plane, don't they?

Chapter Forty-Three
That Idiot Erík

"What if you could be there in just forty-five minutes?" I asked. "Instead of six hours?"

Konrad looked at me. It took him a few moments to clue in to what I was suggesting.

"Is it safe to fly?" he asked uncertainly. "Didn't the volcano shut down the airspace around Iceland?"

"That was the south and east of the country," I replied. "Those areas are downwind from the volcano. We will be flying around the northern region—upwind of the volcano where the airspace is still open."

Konrad nodded. "Yes, that's right," he said. "You're right."

"Plus, I'm pretty sure the ash cloud would only affect high-altitude aircraft," I said. "I saw plenty of footage of helicopters on the news flying right up close to the lava fountains yesterday. If they can fly, then so can we. Besides, we won't be going anywhere near the volcano anyway."

Konrad grabbed me by the elbow.

"Let's go," he said. "We don't have any time to waste. I can make some calls on the way to the airport to make sure it's okay to fly."

The two of us rushed out of the apartment, and before I knew it, we were back in the Land Rover and racing down to the harbor where my trusty De Havilland Beaver was waiting.

Konrad made several phone calls as he drove quickly and parked near the harbor. He spoke in Icelandic to each person, and I only caught fragments of words that sounded slightly familiar to me after my brief stay in this country.

"It's okay; we can fly," he said as he hung up the phone, and we walked briskly down the dock toward my plane. "I've confirmed that the construction site has been completely evacuated, so there's no one up there who can do anything to stop them. But I talked to a friend of a friend who is an air traffic controller, and he confirmed that the airspace to the north is still open and that the ash cloud is right now only affecting much higher altitudes of fifteen thousand feet or more."

"Okay," I replied as we reached my plane and I started my exterior pre-flight inspection.

"I also called Ásta and explained the situation to her," Konrad continued. "And I also called Magnús, who lives near Akureyri. He will meet us there to find a place to park your plane in the harbor. He'll also lend me one of the company Land Rovers so I can drive up to the highlands. Akureyri is closer than Húsavík anyway, so that will save us some time. That won't be a problem, will it?

"No problem at all," I replied as I crawled on my knees to inspect the underside of my plane, pulling on trusses and wires to make sure their connections were secure.

Satisfied that everything was okay, I pulled open the pilot's side door and let Konrad climb in before me so he could crawl over to the passenger seat. As soon as he was settled, I pulled off the mooring ropes and used my foot to push the plane into the water, jumping aboard the pontoons as I did so.

I climbed up into the pilot's seat and closed the door behind me. I did a quick pre-flight check of everything inside the cockpit and then began my start-up procedures. I reached up to push the fuel mixture lever all the way forward with my right hand, and then I leaned down to pump the engine primer with my left—one, two, three, four, five—until I felt pressure in the lines.

"Okay," I said, looking over at Konrad. I flipped the master power on and pumped the throttle a few times before I hit the starter switch. The prop began to spin and the engine farted and grumbled a bit before I hit the mags, causing the engine to spark into life. It idled roughly, and I pulled us slowly away from the dock to let the engine warm up.

As we taxied into the harbor, I kept an eye on everything around the plane while I pulled my GPS out of my backpack and plotted a course for Akureyri. I showed it to Konrad on the map to make sure I was heading for the right place, and he nodded in confirmation.

"Take this," I shouted to Konrad over the sound of the engine, and I handed him a headset and pulled my own over my head as well.

"Thank you," I heard his tinny voice say through the headset.

"Is everything cool?" I asked, noticing the worried expression on his face. "I mean, are we ready to go?"

He nodded, and following my example, he pulled the seatbelt harness across his chest and locked himself in.

"Here we go," I said, cranking the flaps down and taking one last look all around to make sure everything was clear. We were good to go, so I pushed up the throttle and listened to the engine grumble faster and faster until it settled into a nice, throaty roar—one of the most beautiful sounds in the world to my ears.

We sped across the water and bounced over the waves until the plane pulled into the air and headed northeast.

"It's gusty out here today," I observed as some nasty crosswinds pushed and pulled at us as we climbed into the air. "Does the wind ever stop blowing here?"

Konrad looked over at me and tried to smile. "Not usually," he said. "It's windy here all year round. We're on a tiny island in the middle of the ocean. But it's much worse in winter when the temperatures drop."

I shivered. "I can imagine," I replied.

"People never believe it, but we actually have quite mild winters here," Konrad said. "Thanks to the Gulf Stream bringing warm water from the Gulf of Mexico, it generally doesn't get too far below freezing here on the coast, even in the dead of winter. But the wind-chill factor makes it feel as though we're living at the North Pole."

"I'll bet," I replied, shivering again at the thought of it.

We continued our climb, and I put us on a heading to the northeast that would take us almost straight to Akureyri.

"I'm glad we're not flying over there," I said to Konrad, nodding toward the east where some dark and ugly storm clouds had begun to form. I double-checked our course to make sure we didn't get anywhere near the bad weather.

"That's the volcano," Konrad said with a tinge of awe in his voice. I turned to see what he was talking about and realized that what I'd thought was bad weather was actually clouds of smoke and ash from the erupting volcano.

"Oh, my god," I breathed, mesmerized by the sight of the dark, boiling clouds of smoke rising into the sky and painting the entire eastern horizon in shades of dark, ominous gray.

Konrad and I watched in amazement as the angry column of smoke and ash grew increasingly larger until it filled our view to the right of the aircraft.

"Is that lava?!?" I asked in astonishment as we drew closer, and we were able to make out tiny hints of glowing red and orange along the mountaintop. It was the source of the dark tower of smoke.

Konrad nodded reverently. "It is," he said. "Just imagine what it must be like up close if we can see it from this distance."

"I know exactly what it must be like," I said as I banked left and started my descent toward the harbor at Akureyri. "It must be like the entrance to hell itself." Just like the Icelanders had once believed, and I could see why.

Konrad looked over at me with a worried expression on his face.

"And somewhere down in that hell is Kristín," he said, "with that idiot Erík."

Chapter Forty-Four

A Towering Inferno Of Smoke And Ash

I brought us in for a nice landing through a long inlet on Iceland's north coast where the town of Akureyri is located. Mountains with small patches of bright white snow lined the sides of the inlet. They curved into rolling, grassy foothills that led down to the colorful houses of the town.

As we taxied over to the docks in the harbor, I saw the familiar face of Konrad's colleague Magnús—the man I'd met on the trips out to the construction site a week or so earlier. He waved his arms to get our attention and guided us into a berth at the dock where we could tie up.

I shut down the engine and the two of us climbed onto the pontoons to guide the plane in. I grabbed a mooring line, jumped across to the dock, and braced my feet on the edge to pull the plane into position before I tied the lines off and secured the plane.

"It's good to see you, Magnús." Konrad shook his hand, and then the three of us walked up the dock. "We just saw the situation from the air. But please tell me that things aren't that bad on the ground."

Magnús shook his head. "Don't worry," he said. "I saw the situation up at the site on the webcams when I was at the office not five minutes ago. There's still no sign of Kristín or Erík, but things up there are okay. The volcano is much farther inland, and the wind is carrying the smoke and ash in the opposite direction."

Konrad breathed a sigh of relief. "Thank you, Magnús."

Magnús nodded curtly and pulled a set of car keys from his pocket. "I brought you one of the Rovers." He pointed to a black Land Rover that was identical to the one Konrad drove. Apparently, Konrad's company had quite a few of them. "If you drop me at the office on your way out of town," Magnús said, "I can monitor the situation for you from here and keep you updated."

"Good idea," Konrad said, pushing the unlock button on the key remote. The lights of the vehicle blinked and we heard the *thunk* of the door locks disengaging.

Konrad slid in behind the wheel, and I pulled myself into the front passenger seat beside him.

"Okay, let's go," Konrad said after Magnús had climbed into the back seat behind me. With a spray of gravel, he peeled out of the parking lot and sped through the streets of Akureyri. The town was much larger than

I'd expected, but in Iceland, large is a relative term. We left the city behind in just a few minutes.

After driving a short distance, Konrad stopped at a collection of mobile offices on the outskirts of town, and Magnús jumped out of the back seat.

"Keep your phone on," Magnús called out as he waved his cell phone at us and jogged toward one of the mobile offices.

Konrad looked over at me expectantly as I sat in the passenger seat next to him.

"Let's go," I said, unsure of why he wasn't driving off already.

"You need to stay here with Magnús," Konrad said. "You can't come with me up to the site. It's too dangerous."

I laughed a loud, hearty, and completely disobedient kind of laugh that startled Konrad with its intensity.

"You'd better start driving right now," I said, my voice cold and deadly serious. "You're just wasting time, and you'll waste even more trying to get me out of this car, Konrad. I am not going anywhere but up there with you. Kristín is my friend."

Konrad frowned sternly and opened his mouth to say something more, but the defiant and stubborn look on my face made him change his mind. He closed his mouth and put the car into drive, and sped off down the highway.

Smart move, Konrad, I thought to myself proudly as we raced down the deserted highway toward the east.

"He probably just felt sorry for you," the little voice in my head teased. "All those bruises and cuts on your face made you look pitiful more than menacing."

No, I told myself. *He knows I'm not kidding around.*

I looked over at Konrad, who stared intently through the windshield at the road ahead. He was worried about Kristín and angry, too, but more worried than anything else.

I reached over to put my hand on his shoulder.

"Don't worry," I said, and he looked over at me and smiled thinly.

He reached into the pocket of his jacket and pulled out his cell phone. "Can you hit re-dial on Kristín's number?" He handed the phone over to me.

I hit redial and held the phone up to my ear.

The same as before, it went straight to voice mail. I looked over at Konrad and shook my head. He frowned some more and turned us south onto a rough and bumpy back road. Ahead of us in the distance, a gigantic tower of dark smoke poured into the sky. This towering inferno of volcanic smoke and ash looked as if it was belching forth from the depths of hell itself, and we were driving straight toward it.

Chapter Forty-Five

Thirty More Seconds And We're There

With the massive column of smoke billowing in front of us, we continued up the rugged back road in the Land Rover. The sky seemed to grow darker with every passing second as the volcanic smoke blackened out the sun and filled our view.

I leaned forward to look at the sky, worrying that it was darkening so quickly, and for the first time, I began having second thoughts about that I'd been so insistent about coming along. The forces of nature were as powerful as they were unpredictable, and what we were seeing in front of us in the distance was nature's power and fury at its most intense.

"Someone's been down this road very recently," Konrad said, pointing to a set of tire tracks in the mud leading up the road ahead. "We can't be too far behind them."

I leaned forward to get a better view.

"How far ahead of us do you think they are?" I asked.

Konrad shook his head. "I have no idea."

Just then, Konrad's cell phone rang and vibrated in my hands, scaring the crap out of me. I was so startled by the sudden vibration that I actually jerked my hands up and the phone flew off and bounced into the back seat.

"Sorry, sorry!" I cried as I unbuckled my seatbelt and leaned back to retrieve the phone.

"Put it on speakerphone," Konrad said as he twisted the steering wheel left and right to avoid potholes while driving as fast as realistically possible.

I picked up the phone and slid back down into the front seat, pressing the speakerphone button as I went.

"Konrad?" we heard a thin voice say from the other end of the line. It was Magnús.

"Go ahead, Magnús," Konrad replied loudly to be heard above the noise of the Land Rover as it rumbled and bounced along.

"A truck just pulled up at the site," Magnús said. "It's Erík."

"And Kristín?" Konrad asked. "Is she with him?"

Magnús paused for a moment. "Yes," he said. "I'm sorry, Konrad."

Konrad shook his head at the news. "Don't worry, Magnús. Just tell me what they're doing."

"They parked out by the explosives shed." Magnús then gave us a play-by-play account of what Erík and Kristín were doing. "They got it open somehow. I don't know how they managed it. They must have had a key or something."

Kristín must have stolen a key for the explosives shed, I thought, and I glanced over at Konrad, who gave me another worried look.

"What are they doing now, Magnús?" Konrad asked.

"I'm not... sure..." Magnús said slowly as he watched the video feed from the construction site. "I can't really see what they're doing, but I guess they must be grabbing some explosives."

Konrad pounded the steering wheel with his fist. "Doesn't she know how dangerous this is?" he asked no one in particular. "Doesn't *he* know how dangerous it is?"

"Okay, wait," Magnús said. "I see them again. They were grabbing some explosives, yes. Erík is carrying a big crate of explosive packs, and Kristín has a few reels of wire."

"What are they wiring, Magnús?" Konrad asked. "Where are they placing the explosives?"

"Um," Magnús replied, watching the video feed and describing what they were doing as they did it. "It looks like they're placing explosives everywhere, Konrad. This Erík seems to know what he's doing, and he's working very fast. It looks like they're trying to blow up everything—the offices, the machines, even the Port-a-Potties."

"The Port-a-Potties?" I asked.

Magnús was bewildered. "Why would they want to blow up the outhouses? This is crazy."

"Tell me about it," Konrad replied. "What are they doing now?"

Magnús was quiet again for a few more moments.

"They've gone back to the explosives shed again and grabbed another big box of packs, and now this Erík kid is climbing down the front face of the rock pile. I think he's planning to blow the foundation of the dam."

"He's crazy," Konrad said. "Not even the entire shed full of explosives would put a dent in that."

"How far away are you?" Magnús asked. "Are you almost at the site?"

Konrad looked at the instrument panel of the Land Rover for a second then glanced at his watch. "Not much longer," he said, "but long enough, unfortunately. We might not get there before they decide to blow everything."

"I think Erík gave up on the idea of blowing the dam face," Magnús said. "He just wired up the crate and threw the whole thing down the rock pile."

"What's Kristín doing this whole time?" Konrad asked nervously.

"She's wrapping wire around everything," Magnús replied, "and running lead wires from every explosive pack to one of the large bulldozers."

"She'd be safer carrying the explosives instead of placing all the detonators," Konrad said angrily. "Why is Erík making her do those?"

"Are you almost there, Konrad?" Magnús asked. "I hope so, because they're almost finished. Erík is back with Kristín at the big bulldozer now, and they're wiring everything to the triggers. Five more minutes and they'll be finished, Konrad."

"I'll be there in three," Konrad said, jerking the steering wheel to the right and taking another side road. "I just passed the ridge, and I'm heading into the gorge now; two more minutes."

We bounced and shuddered over potholes as we raced into the river valley. Ahead of us, the construction site came into view, and we saw what Magnús had been describing over the phone.

Parked at the center of the site was a large bulldozer with two figures perched at the top. The smaller of the two was Kristín, with her long black hair flowing in the wind as she scrambled up and down the ladder and spooled out wire as she went. The other figure was unmistakably Erík; his bright red hair was visible from a mile away.

"I think they've spotted you coming down the access road," Magnús said slowly. "Yes, they've spotted you. They're taking cover in the cab of the big bulldozer, Konrad."

"Thank you, Magnús," Konrad said. "We can see them now. Thirty more seconds and we're there."

"Okay," Magnús replied. "I will continue to monitor things from here. Call me if you need anything."

"Thank you, Magnús; we will."

I reached down to press the End Call button on the phone.

"Be careful," Magnús said before I hung up. "It looks like they've finished wiring all the detonators to the triggers."

Chapter Forty-Six
Apparently A Yokelfloop Means Bad News

Konrad put the Land Rover in low gear and brought us to a slow crawl for the last hundred meters of road that led to the construction site.

"Nice and easy," he muttered to himself as he kept an eye on the big bulldozer. We saw no sign of them as we approached and parked the Land Rover at the edge of the site. We were close to where Erík had parked his beat-up old truck.

Konrad switched off the engine, and the seconds ticked by as we watched the bulldozer in silence. The seconds turned into minutes, but there was still no sign of Kristín or Erík.

"What do we do now?" I asked after we'd sat there for three or four minutes.

"I think we get out and talk to them," Konrad said hesitantly. "I was hoping that they would show themselves first."

Konrad waited another minute or two before pulling on the door handle and opening his door. I followed suit, and stepped out into the cold wind.

In the distance, I could hear the roar of the river as it crashed and flowed down the gorge. High above us in the distance, the smoke and ash cloud from the volcano boiled into the sky continuously. The sun was tinted a deep blood red, which gave the landscape a surreal and infernal glow. I am not sure if it was the cold of the wind or the creepiness of the setting that made me shiver, but I instinctively pulled the collar of my jacket tighter around my neck.

"Kristín!" Konrad shouted over to the bulldozer as he walked slowly toward it. I stayed a few steps behind him. "Kristín, honey—it's your father."

We heard a noise from the cab of the bulldozer and saw Kristín raise her head up over the side.

"Dad?" she called out. "What are you doing here?"

Konrad continued to approach the bulldozer carefully and cautiously, as though it was a wild animal.

"I came to help you," Konrad said soothingly, "and to stop you from doing something you'll regret later."

"Don't come any closer!" Kristín yelled. "We have this entire place rigged with explosives."

Konrad slowed his pace but continued to inch closer to the bulldozer.

From behind the protection barrier next to Kristín, we saw Erík get to his feet and turn to face us.

"You can't stop us!" he bellowed. "We won't let you stop us! We cannot stand idly by and let you and your corporate masters destroy our country!"

"Erík!" Konrad snapped, his voice sounding very angry now. "Shut up! I'm not talking to you. I am talking to my daughter."

Erík looked like he wanted to say something else, but wisely kept his mouth shut.

"He's right, Dad," Kristín said. She peeked a little farther out from behind the barrier. "We can't just stand by and do nothing while these foreign companies come in and ruin everything that makes Iceland beautiful."

"But there are better ways to do this." Konrad said, his voice now soft and non-threatening again.

"Like how?" Kristín mocked. "By doing what you do? Working with these evil companies and the corrupt government officials they buy off?"

Konrad nodded understandingly. "I know you haven't always agreed with how I've chosen to protect our environment," Konrad said. "But you know that I believe that I can do more good for the environment by working from the inside than otherwise. I just hope that I don't become corrupted myself."

"Your way doesn't work!" Kristín screamed, her voice cracking with emotion.

"Maybe it does and maybe it doesn't," Konrad replied. "But that's not for either of us to decide. We can only make decisions for ourselves. That's the path I've chosen, and at least it doesn't involve violence. What *you* have to decide is what your own path will be, and how *you* will work for what you believe in—and I hope you don't hurt anyone in the process, including you."

"I *have* chosen," Kristín said. She rose to her feet and crossed her arms defiantly. "We're going to blow up all these machines of yours and end this entire dam-building project."

"And when they bring out new machines?" Konrad asked.

"Then we'll blow those up, too," Kristín replied.

"You will go to jail," Konrad said.

"Probably," she replied, "but people will hear about what we've done and join the fight on our side."

Konrad took a deep breath and paused for a moment to think.

"You have to choose your own way in life," Konrad agreed with her. "And if this is what you've chosen, then there's nothing I can do to change that."

"Exactly," Kristín said firmly.

"Even if I strongly disagree with you," Konrad continued, "you are my daughter, and even if it hurts me, I have to allow you to make your own mistakes and decisions."

"Exactly," Kristín said again, but her voice sounded a bit less convinced than it had the first time.

Konrad stepped closer to the bulldozer and looked up at his daughter. "If this is what you need to do, then I will let you do it."

"Thank you," Kristín said, but her voice sounded more uncertain and emotional now that her father seemed to be giving in so easily.

"But you do have to do one thing for me," Konrad said. "You have to ask yourself why you are doing this."

"You know why I am doing..." Kristín interrupted, but Konrad kept speaking.

"You have to ask yourself why you are doing this," Konrad repeated, "and decide whether you are doing this for you and for the environment, or whether you are doing this for him." Konrad pointed to Erík, who stood defiantly nearby.

"I am doing this for me, *and* for the environment, *and* for him." Kristín shuffled over to her left to wrap her arm around Erík's elbow. "I love him and he loves me."

I was surprised to hear this, and it made me chuckle when I remembered what I'd seen that day on the island between Erík and Halldóra.

"You might want to tell his other girlfriend that," I muttered under my breath.

"His what?" Konrad asked in surprise, turning to face me.

Kristín frowned and looked over at me. "What did you say?" she asked accusingly.

I looked back and forth between the two of them.

"His other girlfriend," I said, wondering what they didn't understand about such a simple statement. "You know, Halldóra—the Elf Lady."

"Halldóra is married," Kristín said, but she turned to Erík for an explanation.

"She's a housewife, right," I replied. "But married or not, the two of them were pretty friendly the last time I saw them out on the Westman Islands."

Kristín let go of his elbow and took a step backward in shock, but Erík just stared at me with a smoldering look of anger.

"What were you doing out on the Westman Islands?" Erík asked.

"What does that matter to you?" I snapped back at him. "I was sightseeing, but I saw you and Halldóra there... together... *intimately* together."

"Is this true?!?" Kristín asked angrily. her voice ice cold as she took another step away from Erík. "You told me that there was nothing going on between you and her."

Erík glared down at me before he reached out his hand to Kristín, but she slapped it away.

"It's not true," Erík said reassuringly. "They're just telling you this to turn you against me."

I snorted through my nostrils.

"It's true," I said with a cynical laugh.

"I can't believe this!" Kristín screamed at Erík. She shook her head furiously. "I can't believe I risked everything for you and your stupid plans. They will kick me out of school! I will go to jail!"

Konrad had remained silent through all this, not sure what to make of it, but now he spoke. "Kristín, honey, it's not too late to change your mind."

"I feel like such a fool!" Kristín shrieked as she slapped away Erík's hand again. "I can't believe that I ever listened to *anything* you ever told me!"

Kristín burst into tears and continued screaming insults at Erík. I listened for a few moments but was distracted by a vibration in the pocket of my jeans. It was Konrad's phone ringing again.

I took the phone out and checked the caller ID. It was Magnús again.

"Hello?" I said, and then I pushed the speakerphone button and held the phone close to my ear while I walked a short distance away so that I could hear him over all the shouting. I couldn't make out what he was saying.

"I'm sorry, Magnús, can you say that again? I can hardly hear you."

Magnús spoke again, but I still couldn't understand him. I simply couldn't hear him properly with Kristín and Erík fighting so loudly.

"Shhhhhhhhhhhhhhhhhhhh!!!!!!" I hissed at them, which startled everyone silent. "It's Magnús on the phone, and I can't hear what he's saying. He's trying to tell us about a yokelfloop or something like that."

Upon hearing that word, Konrad, Kristín and Erík turned simultaneously to look upriver with an expression of intense fear on their faces. I had no clue what a yokelfloop was, but apparently, it was not good news.

Chapter Forty-Seven
Just Trying To Save His Country

"Konrad! You have to listen to me!" Magnús shouted over the speakerphone. "The eruption has spread under the ice cap, and there's a Jökulhlaup coming right for you!"

Konrad looked upriver then back up at Kristín with a desperate look on his face. "Kristín?" he said. "This is serious. We have to get out of here. Now!"

Kristín nodded grimly, and without another word, she rushed over to the side of the bulldozer and climbed down the ladder toward us.

"Erík?" Konrad said, calling up to him as he helped Kristín down the last few steps. "You too. We have to get out of here."

Erík stood on top of the bulldozer and stared thoughtfully upriver. "No," he said after a few moments.

"Erík, this is serious," Konrad pleaded. His voice conveyed a very real sense of deep, uneasy fear. "You know what a Jökulhlaup means."

Erík might know what a Jökulhlaup meant, and so did the other two, obviously, but I was in the dark.

What the hell is a yokelfloop? I thought. *And why are they so scared of it?*

"No," Erík said again, standing up tall. "I'm staying right here."

"Erík, don't be stupid!" Kristín screamed up at him. "It doesn't matter anymore."

"She's right," Konrad said calmly. "Everything in this valley is going to be washed away completely when the flood hits. It will all be destroyed."

I was starting to get an idea of what a yokelfloop might be, judging from how everyone kept looking nervously upriver, and discussing how everything was going to be washed away. It must be the Icelandic word for a flash flood of some kind, probably caused by the volcanic eruptions happening under the ice cap. As I knew well from my time in Alaska, glaciers were huge, mighty rivers of ice, and I could only imagine the power that would be unleashed if a volcano erupted underneath one and quickly melted all that ice into water.

"Then I will get washed away with it!" Erík bellowed, putting his hands on his hips and standing proudly on top of the bulldozer.

"Don't be a hero!" Konrad shouted. "It's pointless now! You win! All these machines are going to be swept downriver, and the whole construction site will be destroyed!"

Erík shook his head defiantly. "And then you will just bring new machines and start all over again," he said, still shaking his head. "No! This ends now, and I want everyone in Iceland to know about it so that it never happens again!"

From upriver and around the bend in the canyon I could hear a low rumbling sound that was getting louder with every passing second. The clear water of the river had turned a dark and dirty gray colour.

"Erík!" Konrad yelled angrily. "Don't be a fool!"

Kristín was tugging on the sleeve of her father's jacket and looking nervously at the growing swell of water approaching us. "Forget it, Dad," she said. "He's too stubborn. Trust me."

"We can't just leave him!" Konrad shouted.

"We have to!" Kristín replied, still looking anxiously upriver. "There's no time!"

Konrad hesitated for a moment. He put one foot on the ladder to climb up to the top of the bulldozer, but then he looked over at the swirling maelstrom of mud and water barreling toward us. Stepping off the ladder again, he grabbed Kristín and me by the hands and pulled us along as he made a run for the Land Rover.

I looked up the canyon and saw the river turning darker and surging down toward us. The roar of the water grew louder, and I began to get very frightened. I had known that a flash flood would be dangerous, but this was quickly becoming more powerful than I could have imagined. Konrad was right. The floodwaters would wash away everything in its path, including the entire construction site and Erík along with it.

As we ran frantically for the Land Rover, river overflowed over its banks and tiny rivulets of water began to snake across the construction site.

We're not going to make it, I thought in a panic as we splashed through ankle deep water for the last few meters before reaching the Land Rover.

Kristín jumped into the front seat and I dove into the back as Konrad ran around the other side of the vehicle to get in the driver's seat. He started the engine before his door was even closed, and put the Land Rover in gear. Cranking the steering wheel over, he then hit the gas and spun around, heading straight for the access road that was the only way out of the gorge. If we could make it there, we would be able to drive up to higher ground out of harm's way.

The Land Rover rocked and bumped over the uneven ground, tires splashing and sending waves of water exploding off to either side of the vehicle. I looked out of the window and could see the dirty water rising higher and higher, almost reaching the Land Rover's running boards.

"Dad!" Kristín screamed as she looked out of the window at the swirling water climbing the sides of the vehicle. "Hurry, Dad!"

Konrad was focused intently on the road ahead of us. We were almost there. The access road was just a little bit farther. The Land Rover's front tires thumped heavily as it hit a deep pool of water, which sent high walls of water spraying out as we covered the last few meters of the construction site.

Back on dry land again, Konrad put the truck into a lower gear and began the steady climb up the access road, which carried us higher and farther away from the rising waters. The three of us breathed a sigh of relief. We were finally safe.

About halfway up, Konrad turned into a pullout where we could safely watch the raging river it swept through the gorge below us. We jumped out of the car and rushed over to the edge of the drop-off where we had a commanding view of the valley below.

The first thing I did was look for Erík, hoping that he'd come to his senses and made a run for his own truck. But he was still there on top of the bulldozer, standing firm and looking upriver.

"Oh, my god, Daddy," Kristín cried, wrapping her arms around Konrad and burying her face into his jacket. "What do we do?"

Konrad shook his head. There was nothing we could do for Erík now.

I heard the sound of an engine behind us, and turned around to see another truck driving down the access road toward us.

"Who the hell is that?" Konrad asked as the other truck came closer and pulled off the road next to us.

A man jumped out of the car and gave us a friendly wave before grabbing a big, professional-looking video camera out of the back of his truck. He was a news cameraman who had apparently come to shoot footage of the flooding river.

"Is that a person down there?" he asked me as he pulled his camera up onto his shoulder. He pointed down into the valley where Erík was still standing stubbornly at the top of the bulldozer.

I nodded.

"Is he crazy?" the cameraman asked, focusing his camera on Erík. "What does he think he's doing?"

"He thinks he's being heroic and clever," Kristín said tearfully and buried her face in her father's jacket again.

Down below us at the construction site the waters continued to rise higher and higher, steadily climbing the sides of the bulldozer where Erík was standing tall and proud. With his arms folded defiantly across his chest and the river rushing past him, he looked just like a Viking captain standing at the bow of his ship in a raging storm.

"Whoa! Look at that!" the cameraman said, turning to capture the shot with his camera. One of the temporary office trailers at the construction site had started to float away, swept along by the raging floodwaters. It floated slowly at first, stopping and starting as it hit bottom, but then in one sudden motion, the walls of the office crumbled in on themselves, and the entire building was washed away, spinning and swirling downstream.

Erík's truck and the smaller bulldozers were the next to go. They were much heavier, of course, and were slowly turned onto their sides before rolling an inch at a time downriver, carried gradually along in the angry current.

By this time, the waters had reached the top of Erík's bulldozer and were swirling around his feet. He climbed a bit higher, standing at the highest point on top of the enclosed cab.

"What are those things in his hands?" the cameraman asked.

"Explosive triggers," Konrad said calmly as explosions suddenly began to rock the river gorge beneath us. The first explosions blew the nearly submerged bulldozers and construction machines to pieces one by one, sending plumes of fire and water shooting into the air.

"Whoa!" the news cameraman said, struggling to capture all the action on video. "This guy is insane!"

After running out of explosives, Erík threw the triggers away and braced himself as the water rose up around his ankles and calves. Turning to meet the rising river head on, he raised his arms above his head and bellowed defiantly.

The waters continued to rise, and we watched in horror as they swept around Erík's knees. He was having difficulty keeping his balance in the force of the powerful flood, but somehow, he was still hanging on.

The water level rose more quickly, and soon he was submerged to his waist. He wouldn't be able to hold on much longer.

He raised his arms above his head and bellowed again like a wild animal. But the river was too much for him, and he fell backward into the swift current and was washed downstream, sputtering and bellowing loudly as he went.

We all watched as he was swept out of sight around the next bend in the river. Kristín put her hands over her face and cried desperately while her father tried to comfort her. I stared downstream, unable to process everything that I'd just experienced. It all seemed completely unreal.

"That was unbelievable," the news cameraman said in awe, lowering his camera and walking toward me. "What was that guy trying to do, anyway?"

I thought about that for a moment before answering.

"I think," I replied slowly, "that he was just trying to save his country."

Chapter Forty-Eight
A Place By The River

We spent most of the drive down from the highlands in silence. Kristín sat in the front seat staring vacantly out of the window and sobbing quietly. Konrad called his wife to tell her what had happened, and to reassure her that Kristín was safe. We decided that we'd had enough excitement for one day and would spend the night in their house in Húsavík before flying back the next day.

Konrad had arranged to rendezvous with Magnús at a highway intersection somewhere between Húsavík and Akureyri.

"I'm going to ride back with Magnús to the office," Konrad said as we pulled over to the side of the road where Magnús was already waiting. "I need to alert the company executives about what's happened and take care of some other business."

Kristín and I nodded.

"How long will you be?" Kristín asked.

Konrad leaned over the seat and gave her a hug. "Not more than a couple of hours," he said. "Are you okay to drive back to Húsavík? Or should Kitty drive and you show her the way?"

"I can do it," Kristín replied softly. "Don't worry."

Konrad gave her another hug and then opened the door to get out of the car. Kristín climbed over into the driver's seat and I climbed into her place up front on the passenger side.

"Just take it easy, honey," Konrad said. "I'll be home in a little while, and we can get pizza from Salka's or something, okay?"

Kristín nodded, and Konrad gave her one last hug before leaving us and walking over to where Magnús was waiting in yet another black Land Rover. (Whatever else might be said about these aluminum companies they certainly did not have a shortage of Land Rovers—a definite sign that they were doing just fine financially.)

Kristín put the car in gear and we both waved goodbye as she pulled a U-turn onto the highway and headed back in the direction of Húsavík. Neither of us said anything as she drove. I wanted to say something wise and helpful, but I couldn't think of anything that seemed adequate.

We came to an intersection in the road with a sign pointing left toward Húsavík, and I expected Kristín to slow down and make the turn, but she didn't.

She must be taking a back way into town, I thought as we continued past the intersection and went straight ahead instead.

Shortly after we came to another intersection, which had a road leading off to the right, instead of continuing straight, Kristín made the turn and headed in what seemed to be the complete opposite direction from Húsavík.

"Okay, something is definitely up," the little voice in my head said nervously. "She seems to be heading for the highlands again."

I know, I said to myself. *But why?*

Kristín drove for a while without a word. I gazed at the enormous column of smoke from the volcano towering high in the sky in the distance.

"Did you really see Erík and Halldóra together?" Kristín asked, finally speaking after we'd driven up the bumpy road for a while. "Or were you just saying that to convince me to get off the bulldozer and not blow up the construction site?"

I nodded. "Yes, I saw them together."

Kristín sniffled and took a long, deep breath.

"And they were together?" she asked, looking over at me desperately. "Like *together* together?"

I nodded again. "I'm sorry, Kristín."

Kristín looked forward again and used the sleeve of her jacket to wipe the tears from her eyes.

"I shouldn't have been so stupid," she said, but she didn't glance over again this time. Instead, she stared straight ahead with a steely expression as we continued up the rough back road. "I never should have let him talk me into all of this."

I reached over to put my hand on her shoulder. I tried to think of something profound to say that would make her feel better, but everything I could think to say seemed empty.

"I'm so sorry, Kristín," I finally said, looking up the road ahead nervously. "I can't imagine how much this must hurt you."

"I'm sorry, too," Kristín replied. "I'm sorry I dragged you into all of this."

She looked over at me, and I smiled at her.

"Don't worry," I said.

"I have to know what happened to Erík," Kristín said.

"I thought we knew that already," the little voice in my head commented. "I thought it was pretty clear after he got swept away in the raging floodwaters of the yokelfloop or whatever it was called."

I looked over at Kristín again, trying to read her eyes.

"Is that why we're in this direction?" I asked.

Kristín nodded and wiped away a tear that was rolling down her cheek.

"But where is it that we're driving to?" I asked. "And what are you hoping to find out?"

Kristín was quiet for a moment, staring blankly at the road ahead.

"There is a place by the river not far from here," she said finally. "It's where Erík and I would meet. If he survived, that's where he'll be."

I looked over at Kristín in pity.

"You don't really think he survived, do you?" I asked.

"I don't know," Kristín replied. "But if anyone could do it, Erík could."

I didn't know what to say. The power of the Jökulhlaup had been incredible. It had swept away trucks, offices, and bulldozers. I couldn't imagine how anyone could have survived that furious surge of water.

"Just let her go see whatever it is that she wants to see," the little voice in my head told me. "What harm is there in doing that?"

"Just do whatever you need to do," I told Kristín understandingly, but she wasn't listening to me. She was staring intently at the road and gripping the steering wheel so hard that her knuckles were white.

"You see?" she said, looking over at me with tears in her eyes. "I told you so."

I turned my head to see what she was talking about, and I couldn't believe my eyes. Just ahead of us was a large figure standing at the side of the road. It was Erík.

Chapter Forty-Nine
You Watch Too Many Movies

At least I think it's Erík, I thought to myself as Kristín pulled off to the side of the road. It could have been just about anyone; that's how utterly filthy the tall figure at the side of the road was. He was soaking wet and covered from head to toe in disgusting grey mud—volcanic ash, I assumed, from the Jökulhlaup. He looked completely monochromatic, like an old black and white photograph. Not even his distinctive red hair was red anymore, but was a dingy gray color instead.

Kristín rolled her window down.

"Get in, Erík," she yelled sternly, leaning out of the car window.

Erík smiled and walked over to her side of the Land Rover.

"I knew you would come," he said, smiling. Even his teeth were dirty, soiled with volcanic ash along with the rest of him, and I cringed at the thought of him swallowing that dirty river water. His eyes were the only color on his entire body—deep blue and bloodshot red.

"Just get in," Kristín said coldly. "You and I are over. We are never ever getting back together. But the last thing I'm willing to do for you is to give you a lift back into town."

Erík smiled cockily and pulled open the back door. "Whatever you say," he said, sliding into the back seat, his clothes making a horrible squishing sound.

Kristín rolled up her window again and cranked the steering wheel around to take us back in the direction of Húsavík.

"Well, this is awkward," the little voice in my head commented sarcastically as Kristín, Erík, and I drove back to Húsavík in uncomfortable silence.

Better this than the two of them fighting, I thought. *Or worse yet if Erík tries to talk to me and asks why I was spying on him.*

I didn't have anything to worry about from Erík. The only sound he made on the entire drive was an occasional squishy sound as he changed position in the back seat. It was like having a wet dog back there. He even smelled a bit like wet dog.

"I'll drop you off at the house," Kristín said as we reached the outskirts of the town and she began to navigate down the side streets. "Hopefully my dad isn't back yet."

"Okay," I replied simply. I wondered what she and Erík would do after that, but it was none of my business, so I didn't ask.

"Dammit," Kristín said as we turned into the driveway of the house and saw that her father's Land Rover was already there along with another car. She hit the brakes and seemed to consider backing up and making a run for it, but she continued hesitantly up the drive to where her father was waiting for us.

Standing with her father were two other men. One of them I recognized immediately—it was Inspector Óðinn—and I could only assume that the other man was also a police officer.

"Who are those men with my dad?" Kristín asked. I realized that she hadn't met Inspector Óðinn yet, so of course she didn't know who he was.

"Police," I replied quietly.

Kristín closed her eyes for a second and sighed deeply. "Stay down, Erík," she said as she pulled closer and switched the engine off.

"It's good to see you again, Ms. Kitty Hawk," Inspector Óðinn said, walking over and greeting me warmly after I had jumped out of the car. "How are you feeling? How's the head?"

"It has a giant bump on it still," I replied, reaching up to feel the back of my head. "But it's better than it was."

Inspector Óðinn smiled kindly. "I have some good news for you," he said. "It's about the Russians."

"I thought they escaped to New York," I replied.

Inspector Óðinn grinned and chuckled. "That's where their flight plan was set to take them, yes, but apparently they never had the slightest intention of going there and changed course in mid-flight to return to Russia."

"And then?" I asked, not understanding why Inspector Óðinn was grinning so much.

"And that took them right into the path of our little volcano here," he said, gesturing up at the towering cloud of smoke and ash on the horizon. "They tried to take a shortcut through the closed airspace that took them right into an invisible cloud of volcanic ash. The ash got into their engines and they began to fail. They had to turn around and make an emergency landing right here in Iceland."

Inspector Óðinn was still grinning.

"And you were able to arrest them?" I asked.

"Of course!" he replied, clapping me on the shoulder heartily. "Fate delivered them right back into our hands so we could prosecute them!"

"And they are going to leave your name out of it, Kitty," Konrad added, stepping forward. "The Inspector is confident that their case will be strong enough without you having to testify and thus endangering you further."

Inspector Óðinn nodded in agreement.

"What about Tómas Finnsson?" I asked.

"He will be dealt with by a separate court," Inspector Óðinn replied. "We have a special court for such government crimes here in Iceland."

I looked back and forth between Inspector Óðinn and Konrad for a moment.

"That is good news," I said. "But something tells me that you didn't drive all the way out here just to tell me this."

"We flew, actually," Inspector Óðinn said, glancing over at Kristín, "in a police helicopter. But you are right. We didn't come all the way out here to tell you this."

We all looked over at Kristín who was standing off to the side trying to be invisible. She looked terrified.

"So what now?" I asked, stepping protectively in front of her. "You slap some handcuffs on her and take her away at gunpoint?"

Inspector Óðinn laughed loudly.

"My dear, you watch too many movies," he said. "This is Iceland, not America. Police don't even carry guns here."

"Kristín, honey," Konrad said gently, taking a few steps toward her. "They aren't going to arrest you, but there will be a hearing in Reykjavík tomorrow afternoon, and you will be charged."

"Charged with what?" Kristín asked, looking very small and frightened.

Konrad walked over and put his arm around her. "With some minor offences," he said. "We will meet with a lawyer tomorrow morning who will explain it to us."

"But wait a minute," I said, turning toward Inspector Óðinn. "If you're not here to arrest her, then why *did* you fly all the way out here?"

Inspector Óðinn smiled thinly.

"To arrest him," he said simply, pointing toward the Land Rover.

Don't they think Erík's dead? How do they know he's in there? I asked myself as I turned to look back at the vehicle. The answer was obvious. On the outside of the rear passenger door was a mess of drying volcanic ash and large male handprints.

That same door opened slowly and Erík stepped out, squishing wetly as he did so. Everyone did a double take at his appearance. He was caked with a thick layer of dried mud and ash, but some had crumbled out of his most defining characteristic—his bright red hair.

"Hello Erík," Inspector Óðinn said, stepping toward him and gesturing for his colleague to do the same.

"Don't worry," Erík said. "I am not planning to run. I am not ashamed of what I did, nor would I ever deny having done it. I am proud of it, in fact."

Inspector Óðinn nodded. "I know," he said simply.

"But leave Kristín out of it," Erík continued. "She had nothing to do with any of this."

Inspector Óðinn chuckled. "You know that's not true, Erík," he said. "And besides, you know it's not up to me. The prosecutors and judges will decide on all of this tomorrow."

Chapter Fifty

Heroes And Villains

The public gallery of the courtroom was mostly empty when we arrived the following afternoon. After flying back together to Reykjavík early in the morning, Konrad and Kristín went to meet with her lawyer. A few hours later, Ásta left their son Pétur with a babysitter and came to pick me up to attend the hearing.

We sat off to the side of the gallery so that Konrad could translate everything for me. I was a bit excited to see what the hearing would be like, but I was also very worried about what would happen to Kristín.

I had expected the hearing to be something dramatic and interesting, like the courtroom dramas depicted on *Law & Order*, but for the most part, it was actually more like 'Law & More Law' with everyone droning on at great length about the various legal ramifications of Kristín and Erík's actions. The presiding judge explained the purpose of the hearing and the various charges being laid against Kristín and Erík, which Konrad had trouble translating into English, but which amounted to charges such as trespassing, destruction of property, and some kind of non-criminal mischief. It was nothing too serious, I hoped.

"What about Halldóra?" I whispered to Konrad at one point. "Will she not be charged with anything?"

Konrad shook his head. "At best she could be charged with some kind of fraud," he said, "but considering the circumstances and her unusual line of work, it would be rather difficult to prove. But she's destroyed her reputation as a psychic medium, to say the least."

After the very lengthy legal discussions, we finally got to the interesting part of the hearing. The presiding judge asked Kristín to stand.

"Kristín Ástasdóttir," the judge said, "you have heard the charges against you, and I now ask you to tell the court how you will plead."

Kristín hesitated for a moment and then spoke. "Guilty, Your Honor," she said.

The judge nodded and asked her to be seated.

"Erík Grettirsson," the judge said as Erík rose to his feet, "you have heard the charges against you, and I now ask you how you will plead."

"Guilty, Your Honor," Erík said in a loud clear voice. "I'm proud to say that I am guilty of these charges."

The judge cut him off.

"This is not the time for speeches," the judge said sternly. "You will have your chance to speak shortly. You may take your seat."

Erík nodded curtly and sat down again.

"Before I pronounce sentence on these charges," the judge said, his deep voice filling the nearly empty courtroom, "there are a number of matters that need to be put on the public record and on which I require additional information. Firstly is the issue of the University of Iceland researcher, Albert Ørsted, and the injuries he sustained as a result of an altercation with the defendant, Erík Grettirsson."

The judge looked at the prosecutors and addressed them directly.

"As I understand it, according to a statement given by Dr. Ørsted, the injuries were the result of an unintended confrontation between the two parties and were purely accidental. They were as much the fault of the wounded party as of the defendant. This argument stemmed from a disagreement between the two parties regarding the research that Dr. Ørsted was conducting into the development of low-resistance underwater cables that would allow the export of energy from Iceland to mainland Europe. The defendant's opposition to this research lies in his belief that it will result in the greatly expanded exploitation of energy resources in Iceland and the large-scale destruction of the environment."

The prosecutor nodded and half rose to his feet. "That is correct, Your Honor," he said, and then he took his seat again.

"I further understand that the defendant, Erík Grettirsson, immediately obtained medical assistance for Dr. Ørsted following the accident, and for these reasons, no charges have been laid."

The prosecutor half rose to his feet for a second time. "That is correct, Your Honor," he said again.

The judge nodded and shuffled some papers on his desk. He made a few notes before continuing.

"The second matter is perhaps somewhat peripheral, but as it may affect sentencing, I wish to put it in the public record. It has to do with the events in the northeastern region of Iceland at the construction site for the hydroelectric dam.

"Following preparations by the two defendants to destroy virtually all of the construction equipment at the site through the use of explosives, it is my understanding that nature intervened and that the machines were instead destroyed as the result of a flash flood that was caused by the volcanic activity in the highlands. A rather explicit video of this event and the defendant's participation in it was captured by news crews in the area, which has since become a so-called viral sensation on the Internet. As a result of this media exposure, the Icelandic public has expressed general dissatisfaction with the national energy policies. As a result of this outcry, the Icelandic energy company, Landsvirkjun, has cancelled the project to build the dam pending further consultations with the Icelandic people."

"That is correct, Your Honor," the prosecutor said. He did not bother to rise to his feet this time.

The judge looked sternly over the rims of his reading glasses at Erík. "That all being true, however, I have seen the video of the events, and I understand that as the floodwaters were threatening and ultimately destroyed the machinery at the site, the defendant still chose to detonate as many of the planted explosives as he was able to before he was swept away down river."

"Also correct, Your Honor," the prosecutor said.

"Hmmmff," the judge snorted, and he looked at his papers to gather his thoughts. Erík looked at the floor sheepishly, awaiting his sentence.

There was complete silence in the courtroom as the judge made some additional notes before continuing.

"There is one final matter I would like to address to the defendants themselves," the judge said, finally. "This has to do with events that took place before the catastrophic flash flood. I am referring to the repeated incidents of sabotage to the construction machinery on at least nine occasions prior to the final destruction of the site."

The judge looked up from his papers at Kristín and Erík.

"You have pled guilty to perpetrating these previous acts of sabotage, but what I am interested in knowing is how you were able to access the site undetected and disable the machinery on so many occasions despite the presence of on-site security guards and security cameras."

Kristín looked over at Erík, and he nodded for her to answer the question.

"Your Honor," Kristín said nervously as she rose to her feet to address the court. "Because I was familiar with the security measures at the site, I knew the placement of the various cameras as well as the fact that they do not operate very well at night. I also knew that the attention of the security guards at the site was directed away from the river due to the impossibility of anyone approaching from that side. They were focused only on any potential trespassers who might approach by land. Thanks to this, Erík was able to avoid being detected."

Kristín sat down again and put her face in her hands.

"I am not sure that I understand," the judge said. "Are you telling me that the two of you would access the construction site from the river?"

"Yes, Your Honor," Kristín replied. "Erík would do that, I mean—not me. I would drive him to a location upriver from the site, and with his clothes and shoes in a waterproof bag, he would swim across and downriver until he reached the site. He would then disable the machines and swim farther downriver to a prearranged meeting point where I would be waiting for him."

The judge looked at Kristín over his reading glasses for a moment, and then he looked across at Erík.

"He would swim across a fast-moving, glacial river?" the judge asked incredulously.

"Yes," Kristín replied.

"Through freezing cold whitewater?"

"Yes, Your Honor," Kristín replied.

The judge raised his eyebrows and took off his glasses.

"You appear to be aptly named, Erík Grettirsson, the judge said. "Although you would be better served with your father's name."

Everyone in the courtroom laughed while Erík sat silently.

"It's from one of the Icelandic sagas," Konrad explained quickly. He was struggling to keep up with translating what everyone was saying. "One of the outlaw heroes of the sagas was a man named Grettir who once swam across a river so cold that he emerged covered with ice."

"You have an appropriate physical appearance to match Grettir's as well," the judge continued. "Although I hope you are luckier than he was below the belt."

Everyone in the courtroom laughed once again, even Erík this time.

Konrad struggled to explain. "Let's just say that according to the sagas, Grettir wasn't as powerful in all departments as he might have appeared to be."

I stifled a laugh as the judge put on his glasses again and consulted the papers in front of him.

"I believe that I have sufficient information to pass sentence," the judge said finally. "Do either of the defendants have anything further to add before I do so?"

Kristín shook her head. "No, Your Honor," she said.

Erík rose to his feet. "I do, Your Honor." His powerful voice boomed through the courtroom.

"I had a feeling you might," the judge said. "But please keep it brief."

Erík nodded. "I am not known for keeping things brief, Your Honor, but in this case, I wish only to say a few simple words."

"Please proceed," the judge said, leaning back in his chair.

Erík took a deep breath. He spoke softly and forcefully instead of his normal tendency to bellow everything,

"We have seen many changes in our country in the past years. We have watched our banks collapse and take down the entire economy with them. We have seen protesters on the streets of Reykjavík where no protesters had ever been seen before. We have seen police shoot tear gas into crowds of peaceful protestors for the first time in half a century. We have seen enormous hydroelectric dams built and endless tracts of wilderness destroyed for the sake of cheap electricity for foreign corporations and their giant smelters that pollute our air and water.

"I know that most people think of me as some sort of environmental nut," Erík continued, "and they are probably right. I believe that Iceland is one of the last few truly pure places on this entire planet. But it is not simply the destruction of the environment that troubles me when I think about these changes to our country. Change is inevitable, and we must change and adapt if we hope to have a future, but I do not believe the changes we've seen are welcomed by a majority of our countrymen and women. If building these huge dams and geothermal plants and aluminum smelters is the will of the Icelandic people, I could accept them. I would argue against them to my last breath, of course, but I could accept them.

"But if our recent history has taught us anything, it is that these things are *not* the will of the Icelandic people. We have corrupt politicians who accept bribes and foreign corporations that grease the wheels with endless supplies of money, and the average Icelander seems powerless to stop them."

His voice rose to its familiar booming level. "We are sick of being powerless, and maybe the only way to fight these corrupt officials and greedy corporations is to meet them on their own terms—with lies and deception, and a few explosives."

Everyone in the courtroom laughed again.

"Iceland is a country of laws," Erík said, speaking softly once again, "and we have been for more than eleven hundred years. It was with laws that our land was built. Isn't that what it says on every police car in this entire nation? It is a quote from our sagas. But there is another half to that quote that we should not forget—that with lawlessness, our country shall be laid to waste and spoiled.

"If I have acted lawlessly," Erík concluded, "then I have only done so to protect our country from the lawlessness of others in the hope that our beautiful land will not be laid to waste and spoiled."

Erík lowered himself into his chair while the judge and prosecutor nodded thoughtfully at what he'd said.

"It's a quote from Njal's saga," Konrad explained, "and a quote that every single Icelander knows well."

I nodded. Apparently, I was going to have to read some of these sagas.

The judge spoke. "Very well said, Erík." the judge said respectfully. "Your point is very clearly taken."

The judge gathered his papers together and placed them off to the side.

"Will the defendants please rise for sentencing," the judge ordered.

Kristín and Erík rose to their feet. Erík looked as proud and defiant as he always did. Kristín glanced back at her mother and father nervously.

"Kristín Ástasdóttir," the judge said, addressing Kristín first. "You have broken the law, but you are young, and I can remember being young once myself. As much as the aluminum companies might wish to see you severely punished for your involvement in this deception, they are not the masters of this court. I doubt there is a single Icelander who would see you put in jail for what you've done. In fact, I would expect that a great many would applaud you.

"Defendant Kristín Ástasdóttir, I sentence you to six months' community service, and I will personally send a letter to the university administrator with my suggestion that you be allowed to finish your studies there. It is my heartfelt belief that having put this bit of youthful foolishness behind you, you will prove to be an immense asset to our country."

Ásta and Konrad let out a sigh of relief and put their arms around each other as Kristín sat down.

"Defendant Erík Grettirsson," the judge continued, "your crimes are of a more serious nature, but while I sincerely question your judgment, I do not for one moment question the depth of your beliefs. Whatever you have done, I fully understand that you believe that you have done it for the good of Iceland. As you have so wisely made your point to this court by quoting from the sagas, I would remind you that the sagas make clear to us that we have a long tradition of outlaws in our country, and we have often made them into heroes.

"But you are not a hero," the judge said, peering grimly down at Erík from the bench. "You are an outlaw, and as you have also rightly pointed out to this court, with lawlessness, our country shall be laid to waste. That same principle applies to your actions as well. I therefore sentence you to eighteen months of community service. I will write a recommendation to the supervising officer to suggest that your service be done *with* the energy and aluminum companies to bring a fair and balanced assessment of the benefits and impacts of energy development to the people of Iceland in all of the towns and cities that will be most affected."

The judge leaned forward and looked over his glasses at Erík.

"And when I say fair and balanced, I mean exactly that, or I will see you back in my courtroom again. Do I make myself clear?"

"Yes, sir," Erík stated firmly, and he sat down in his chair.

"It looks like you'll be seeing a lot more of Erík for the next eighteen months," Ásta whispered to Konrad.

"No kidding," Konrad replied. "I think the judge just sentenced *me* as well."

The judge cleared his throat loudly and gave Konrad and Ásta a stern look to silence their whispering and giggling.

"If there is no further business to conduct," the judge concluded, "then this court is now adjourned."

Chapter Fifty-One

There Are Plenty Of Strange Things Around

I am happy to report that the rest of my time in Iceland contained a lot less excitement than the first week did. I don't mean that it was boring. I just mean that no one hit me, kidnapped me, or shot at me, and that was exactly what I needed.

After the court hearing, Konrad and his family decided to drive out to their house in Húsavík and spend some time there. I stayed behind in Reykjavík at Kristín's apartment and spent the next couple of days in bed. I rested, read, wrote e-mails, talked to my parents on the phone, and just generally enjoyed being lazy.

To be honest, I was a little embarrassed to go outside because of the giant bruise on my face, which had gone from its original dark purple and red to varying shades of deep blue and yellow. Even the few times that I did have to go out to get some food, I was on the receiving end of well-meaning comments from some of the shopkeepers.

But of course, I couldn't stay inside forever, so I eventually ventured into the outside world to do some of the touristy things that I'd planned to do before I was sidetracked by my other set of adventures.

I didn't want to overdo it, so I started small and took a Reykjavík city tour on a bus full of other tourists. I was asked, "Oh dear, what happened to you?" more than once on that bus, I can tell you that.

I walked around the city a lot. I visited the Hallgrímskirkja, the strange white church at the heart of the city that I'd seen from the air when I first arrived. I went to the National Museum. I went for coffee at a dozen different cafés and tried a dozen different kinds of skúffukaka.

I did a lot of stuff—normal tourist kinds of things.

Konrad called to invite me out to Húsavík to spend some time with his family there. I hesitated at first, and said that I didn't want to impose on them so soon after all the excitement, but he assured me that everything was fine. Besides, the volcanic eruption had started to die down, so it would probably be my last chance to see it.

I packed some things and flew across the country, passing as close to the volcano as I dared along the way. Konrad was right—the eruption was definitely dying down. Compared to the hellish nightmare of smoke and ash that I'd seen previously, the volcano now looked almost tame by comparison.

I spent a few days in Húsavík with Konrad and his family. I rested and read some more, went on walks with Kristín, and definitely ate too much good home-cooked Icelandic food—lamb and fish mostly, but definitely no rotted shark.

When the time came to return to Reykjavík, Konrad and Kristín came with me in my plane, while Ásta (who is scared of flying) and Pétur drove back on their own. We took a leisurely route around the country and did some aerial sightseeing along the way. We passed endless fields of ice, soaring cliffs, and plunging waterfalls, with Konrad explaining everything we were seeing.

Back in Reykjavík, life went on as usual. Kristín went back to school, and after a couple days of sightseeing with me, Konrad went back to work, after which I made my final preparations to leave Iceland and continue my around-the-world flight. I wasn't looking forward to saying goodbye to Iceland and all the amazing people I'd met there, but I was excited about what new adventures awaited me elsewhere in the world.

As I made some final preparations one afternoon, the doorbell rang. It was Inspector Óðinn.

"I just wanted to check in with you and see how you were doing," he said after I pulled on some shoes and a jacket to come downstairs to meet him. "Should we get some coffee somewhere?"

"Coffee sounds perfect," I replied, and we walked across the street to the café where I'd sat and staked out Erík's apartment so many days before.

"How's your face?" Inspector Óðinn asked. "It looks much better."

"It doesn't hurt at all anymore," I replied. "Just a bit of color left from the bruise."

Inspector Óðinn smiled. "Good," he said as he stirred some cream into his coffee with a wooden stir-stick.

"How is the case with the Russians going?" I asked.

Inspector Óðinn smiled again. "Well, that's another reason why I stopped by to see you," he said. "But unfortunately there isn't much to report so far. The Russians have been charged and are still in custody. They've pled not guilty, so for the moment, we are just awaiting the trial, which could be months away."

"Do you know what I've been wondering?" I said. "Why they told me that they were the ones who killed Albert—I mean Dr. Ørsted."

"Pardon me?" Inspector Óðinn asked, looking up from his coffee.

"When I was in the back of the truck with the Russians," I said. "I confronted them about killing Albert, and they said they had."

"Did they actually say that?" Inspector Óðinn asked.

I thought about that for a second. I wrinkled my nose and forehead as I tried to remember. Maybe they hadn't actually *said* it, but they certainly didn't deny it.

"They certainly pretended that they did it," I said finally.

Inspector Óðinn laughed. "I think they were just taking advantage of the situation, and using the misunderstanding to frighten you into doing what they wanted."

"Oh," I replied. That made sense, I suppose.

"This one Russian guy," Inspector Óðinn continued, "the smooth-talking one—he tells me that in his country, there is a long tradition of using mock executions to scare people into cooperating."

"See? I told you so," I said with a laugh. "Everything with him was all about how things are done in his country."

Inspector Óðinn laughed along with me. "I am surprised that you can laugh about this!" he said.

Good point, I thought, but kept laughing anyway.

Inspector Óðinn called the waitress over to order a piece of skúffukaka.

"Do you want one as well?" he asked.

I hesitated, and he ordered a piece for me anyway.

"There are a few things about the case that I also wonder about," Inspector Óðinn said.

"Like what?" I asked.

"Like this teen boy you met after escaping from the car crash. Finn?" Inspector Óðinn said. "We talked with all the farmers who live near the crash, and none of them know of anyone matching his description or anyone named Finn in the entire area."

I looked across at Inspector Óðinn.

"What does that mean?" I asked. *Do they think I lied about that?* I wondered.

Inspector Óðinn shrugged. "It doesn't mean anything," he said. "But I'll tell you something else that I wonder about. Who was this half-naked man that you saw in the middle of the highway that caused your accident?"

I shook my head slowly. "I have no idea," I said. I was getting nervous. "But I saw him. I swear to god."

Inspector Óðinn laughed loudly. "Don't worry, Kitty, I absolutely believe that you saw him, and Finn, too. The Russians also saw this half-naked man. That's what caused them to run off the road as well. It's just so completely bizarre that I sometimes wonder about it."

The waitress arrived with two plates of skúffukaka, and we thanked her. Inspector Óðinn leaned across the table toward me and waited for the waitress to be out of earshot.

"I probably shouldn't tell you this," he said quietly, "but some of the farmers that we talked to out there had seen this half-naked man as well."

Inspector Óðinn leaned back in his chair and picked up his fork.

"What does that mean?" I asked, keeping my voice low.

Inspector Óðinn shrugged his shoulders. "Maybe it's some crazy old farmer who lives in the area and likes to make trouble," he replied. "Or maybe it's something else. I have no idea. But here in Iceland, there are plenty of strange things around that we will probably never understand."

"The hidden people," I whispered under my breath.

"The Huldufólk," Inspector Óðinn agreed with a nod. "But if you ever tell anyone that I suggested such a thing..."

He didn't finish his sentence, but merely smiled enigmatically as he leaned forward in his chair to take his first bite of skúffukaka.

Chapter Fifty-Two
It's Called Outside

I spent most of my last full day in Iceland floating around happily in the steamy warm waters of the world famous Blue Lagoon—a manmade spa where runoff water from a nearby geothermal energy plant forms a large shallow pool in the lava fields.

Konrad and Ásta lent me a car for the day—a Land Rover, big surprise—and I drove out to the Blue Lagoon.

These Land Rovers are pretty nice, I thought as I drove along the highway through endless stretches of dark lava. *I might have to get one of these when I'm back in Canada.*

"Good luck with that," the little voice in my head commented cynically. "You know how Mom and Dad feel about buying a car for you after already giving you your own plane."

The little voice was right. There was no way my parents were going to buy me a car. If I wanted a Land Rover, I'd have to buy it myself, and I had a funny feeling it would be a little bit outside of my price range.

Maybe I'll get a crappy beat-up old truck, I thought. *Better yet, a motorcycle! That's an even better idea!*

The little voice in my head laughed. "Now you're *really* dreaming!"

Reaching the turnoff for the Blue Lagoon, I left the highway and continued down to the remote spa out in the lava fields. I parked the car, paid my entrance, and headed for the pool. Thanks to my earlier experience with Icelandic pools, I was psychologically prepared for the mandatory no-bathing suit shower policy and the stern-faced shower attendants who enforced it.

Wrapping myself in a bathrobe after my shower, I proceeded down to the pool area where a helpful map showed me the water temperature at various points around the pool as well as some points of interest. Committing the map to memory, I stepped outside, hung up my bathrobe, and headed down the stairs.

The water was wonderfully warm—maybe even *too* warm, actually, but it was still perfect.

I continued down the stairs and was a bit surprised to discover that instead of a smooth floor, I was standing on raw lava stone with black sand and squishy white silica mud.

Oh, that's an interesting sensation, I thought. I made a face as the mud squished between my toes. I pushed off and swam over to the mud dispensing stations, and followed everyone's example and made a facial mask with the fine white mud.

Then I just floated.

I lay on my back, closed my thoughts and eyes to the world, and floated.

I thought about everything that had happened to me during my time in Iceland. I thought about everyone I'd met and the friendships I'd made. I thought about the times when I'd been terrified and frightened, and when I'd felt completely exhilarated and awed by this strange and beautiful land. I thought about my plans for the next day when I would leave Iceland and continue on my journey around the world.

But mostly, I didn't think about anything at all. I just floated.

I floated a bit too much, actually. Before I knew it, my skin was as wrinkled as a prune from having spent so much time in the water, and I needed to hurry back to the city to meet Konrad and his family for dinner. We'd arranged to meet at the same restaurant where they'd first welcomed me to their country.

"It seems like just yesterday when we first ate here," I said as the owner took my jacket and led us to the same private dining room we'd eaten dinner in when I'd first arrived in Iceland. I reached up to wipe some tears from my eyes, and Ásta and Kristín rushed over to give me a hug.

"We'll see each other again," Ásta said. She smiled brightly, but she also had tears in her eyes.

"I'd love to see Tofino sometime," Kristín said. "I will come and visit."

I nodded enthusiastically.

"Any time, please do," I said as I wiped another tear from my cheek.

Konrad shrugged. "It's probably pretty much the same as Alaska, right?" He grinned.

"That just shows how completely stupid you are," Ásta snapped at him. "And why you don't deserve to come from one of the most beautiful places on the planet."

Everyone laughed, and we took our seats around the table.

"You're probably right; I am completely stupid," Konrad said good-naturedly as he sat down. "But that probably means that you shouldn't have let me order for everyone in advance."

"Well, fortunately, when it comes to eating, you are a genius," Ásta replied, and everyone laughed loudly.

I am going to miss this so much, I thought to myself as I looked around at everyone's bright, smiling faces.

The meal started with an appetizer of smoked trout topped with berries followed by a steaming bowl of seafood soup. The main course was roasted lamb. They eat a lot of lamb in Iceland, and a lot of pickled herring, too.

"Leave room for the second main course," Konrad said as everyone dug into the lamb.

"The second main course?" all of us asked in surprise.

Konrad nodded earnestly and grinned.

"It's something typically Alaskan, and will make Kitty and me plenty homesick," he said.

I had some of the lamb, but saved plenty of room for the second main course, and was glad that I did because it was fresh cod with celery and bacon. Konrad was right; the taste of the fresh cod did remind me of home. He clearly wanted to make me cry as much as possible on our last evening together.

After all of us were finished and could not possibly eat another bite, the waitresses cleared the table and brought around coffee and tea.

"We have a saying in Iceland," Konrad said as he rose to his feet. "Without a book in his hands, a person is blind."

Across the table, Ásta nudged Pétur with her elbow, and he bashfully slid off his chair and ran around the table to hand me a beautifully wrapped present.

"Oh my god, you shouldn't have," I said, and I started crying yet again.

"Open it!" Kristín said excitedly.

I pulled off the wrapping paper and discovered inside a beautiful leather-bound book of Icelandic sagas. I held the book up to my nose and inhaled the wonderful leathery smell.

"I don't know what to say," I said quietly. I had to choke back tears.

"I think you'll like them," Konrad said. "Some of the tales in there speak of how the Icelanders came to North America hundreds of years before Columbus was even born and discovered America."

"I learned about that back in Newfoundland," I replied with a nod. "The Vikings had settlements there a thousand years ago."

"And just in case you needed further proof that Icelanders were far ahead of the rest of the world," Konrad continued, "I think you will also find the sagas surprisingly readable. Because while the rest of Europe thought the best way to tell stories was to write them in cryptic poetic verse, the Icelanders just came out and told it like it is."

I stared at Konrad blankly. I didn't understand what he was trying to say.

"It reads like a normal book, in other words," Konrad said in mock frustration. "Instead of 'to be or not to be, that is the question' type of writing."

Ásta smacked Konrad on the arm.

"Ignore him," Ásta said. "He's being stupid again."

"It's true," Konrad replied, and he took his seat again. "And don't forget that since the Icelandic language has changed so little in the past thousand years, any Icelandic child in school can pick up the sagas and read them in their original language without being bored to death! Imagine a kid in school back in Alaska being able to pick up Shakespeare in its original written form and not being bored to death because modern writing is so different."

Ásta smacked Konrad again, but by now, all of us were laughing.

"And now it's Kristín's turn," Ásta said. "She has a gift from all of us."

I turned to Kristín, who pulled a large box from under the table and handed it to me.

"Oh no," I said. "This is too much."

"Just open it," Kristín replied. "I think you will like it."

I pulled the string off the box and flipped open the lid. It was a beautiful black-hooded windbreaker that I had admired earlier when Kristín and I were walking through the city window-shopping. It was from an Icelandic company called 66° North whose ads were *everywhere* in Iceland, and all featured a stern-faced Icelander standing in front of a typically bleak Icelandic scene accompanied by amusing and sardonic captions, such as, *There is one place in Iceland where you must absolutely wear clothes from 66° North. It's called outside.*

"This is the best jacket you will ever own," Konrad said reassuringly, "and I should know. I was a fisherman."

I couldn't speak. I was too choked up. So I just walked around the table and hugged the jacket and everyone else along with it as I went.

"Thank you," I said when my voice finally returned. "Thank you so much. I will never forget this, nor any of you. Not ever."

I wore the jacket proudly home from the restaurant with my book of sagas tucked under my arm. We hugged and cried again as we all said goodbye for the last time. Konrad, Ásta, and Pétur would drive back to Húsavík early the next morning, so I wouldn't see them again before I left, and Kristín had early classes, so I would only see her briefly in the morning.

I stood with Kristín in front of her apartment and watched the rest of her family drive off in their Land Rover, waving as they went. It was almost impossible to believe it, but my adventures in Iceland were at an end.

Kristín and I stayed up and talked a bit longer, but eventually we said goodnight, and I brushed my teeth and changed into my pajamas before I crashed into bed.

I'd better post something on Twitter, I thought as I flipped open my laptop. *I haven't tweeted anything in a while.*

"Maybe because you hate the word tweet," the little voice in my head suggested helpfully.

"Yeah, maybe."

I grinned as I typed out a quick tweet before checking my e-mail.

Kitty Hawk @kittyhawkworld
Last night in Iceland. Tomorrow I continue around the world and I have the perfect jacket for it thanks to my new Icelandic family.

EPILOGUE – PART ONE

Bad News With Some Good News To Even It Out

From: Charlie Lewis <chlewis@alaska.net>
To: Kitty Hawk <kittyhawk@kittyhawkworld.com>
Subject: Bad news with some good news to even it out

Hi Kitty.

First off, I want to say how relieved I am to hear that you are all right after your horrible misadventures in Iceland. I can't believe all this has happened to you, and I have been thinking a lot about it lately, and I am sure I know the reason why. It's the money, Kitty. It's the curse! We've used that godforsaken gold to finance your around-the-world flight, and the curse has followed you along with it.

I know you will probably say that this is nonsense, but I don't see it that way. I am sorry, but I could not live with myself if anything happened to you, and I hope you would agree that your epic world flight is going to be tricky and dangerous enough as it is. You don't need to take any extra risks, even if they might possibly be nothing but my own crazy imagination.

As such, I cannot allow the money from the gold to continue to finance you. I am sorry, and I hope you can understand.

But please don't think that I would ever just let you down like this either. I have already made some arrangements that will pay for everything you need (and more) on your journey.

Please write me as soon as you can to let me know your feelings about this, because I have arranged for you to meet briefly with someone who can explain all the details to you before you fly out of Reykjavik tomorrow.

Write soon please.

Sincerely,
Charlie

EPILOGUE-PART TWO

Whatever You Think Is Best

From: Kitty Hawk <kittyhawk@kittyhawkworld.com>
To: Charlie Lewis <chlewis@alaska.net>
Subject: Don't worry, whatever you think is best is fine with me

Dear Charlie,

I will admit that your e-mail shocked me and scared me to death for a second. But after the shock wore off, I realised that you are not trying to mess with me, or anything like that. You are trying to help me, and I cannot thank you enough for that. I am eternally grateful, and although you are right, I do not think that the curse has anything to do with any of the things that have happened, but I respect that you think the opposite. You're also right, I don't want to risk anything on this long flight of mine, superstitious or not.

I guess what I am trying to say is that I agree with you. But don't worry about anything, please. Whatever arrangements you've made are fine with me. Just send me the details of what I should do tomorrow morning to meet with the people you mentioned, and everything will work out fine.

Charlie? Thank you again so much for helping me. Without you, none of this would have happened in the first place.

Talk to you soon.

k.

EPILOGUE – PART THREE
I Could Go For Some Sushi Right About Now

T he next morning was a complete blur. Both Kristín and I slept late, so we were only able to share a quick coffee together at her kitchen table, and then we were hugging and crying one last time before she dashed off to school.

When the door slammed behind her, I was left alone, but I was also in a rush to make my own appointment that morning—the meeting that Charlie had set up for me to explain the new financing arrangements he'd made.

I took a quick shower and packed all of my things together in my backpack, making sure not to forget anything. After dropping the spare keys into the mail slot on my way out, I would be locked out of the apartment forever.

Confident that I had everything I was supposed to have, I locked the apartment behind me, dropped the key, and headed out on my last walk through the city, down to the harbor where my plane waited and my meeting was scheduled to take place.

As it turned out, Charlie's idea of alternative financing was rather commercial in nature—very commercial, actually. His plan included having a very large advertisement painted onto the side of my plane.

The person I was meeting was an American woman from a multinational advertising agency that was representing the global launch of the Wasabi Willy's Family Sushi Restaurant franchise. Do you remember that restaurant? I am not sure I could ever forget it. It was where Edward had taken me for lunch almost a year earlier back in Juneau, Alaska.

If you remember the place, you might also recall from the tales of my Alaskan adventures that it was actually a really great restaurant once I got past the huge neon sign with the giant blob of maniacally smiling wasabi in a sumo-wrestler loincloth. So, because it was a place that I actually liked, and because they were willing to pay my way around the world if I let them put an ad on my plane, I had no problem doing whatever they wanted me to do to promote them. Besides, they were also going to give me free sushi along the way, so it was kind of a win-win situation.

I tried to listen carefully to the woman as she explained the various details of the arrangement that Charlie had hammered out with them, and the responsibilities I would have to fulfill in order to secure their financial backing and keep my around-the-world-flight a reality. I only half-listened because I needed the other half of my brain to keep a wary eye on the graphic artist who was busily painting some advertising on the side of my plane.

The woman went on and on about endorsements, guest appearances, and grand opening schedules while I smiled and nodded.

"Whatever it takes, I am happy to do it," I told her.

"Perfect," she said. "Now, as I mentioned earlier, I am only the Icelandic representative of the advertising agency, so you'll have to finalize all the details and sign the contracts when you visit one of our larger branch offices in Europe. But I hope, for now, that I have provided you with everything you need to know, and have answered any questions you might have."

"Yes, definitely," I replied, still looking over nervously at the graphic artist who was putting the final touches on the artwork.

"Awesome," she said, and she stuck out her hand. "Then have a wonderful day and safe travels. We'll be out of your hair in a jiffy and let you get on your way."

She packed up her papers and handed me an envelope full of copies of the various contracts for my records. I stuffed those into my backpack and stood back to wait for the final unveiling of the new artwork for my plane.

The graphic artist stood on his tiptoes and carefully peeled away the protective paper and tape from the fuselage of my plane. He jumped off the pontoon and back onto the dock.

"Voila!" he said proudly as he stepped back to admire his work.

There it is, I thought, smiling weakly at the sight of the giant blob of smiling, sumo-wrestling wasabi that made me cringe the first time I saw it in Alaska a year ago. The only difference now was that it was painted on the side of my plane in bright green, and now it would smile at me maniacally every time I climbed into the cockpit.

"I could go for some sushi right about now," the little voice in my head commented.

Some Further Reading (if you're interested)

<u>Kitty Hawk, North Carolina</u>: Kitty Hawk is (of course) a real place. It is a small town on the east coast of the United States where, as detailed in this book, Orville and Wilbur Wright made their first powered aircraft flights in the nearby Kill Devil Hills in the dunes overlooking the Atlantic Ocean on 17 December 1903. Some might argue that the Wright Brothers were not the first to make powered flights. Others might argue that had the Wright Brothers not done it, that eventually someone else would flown first. But what cannot be argued is that the world we live in today is a world of flight and it all leads back to a cold and windy day when two brothers from Dayton, Ohio flew a rickety wood and paper plane across the dunes for all of twelve seconds. And the rest, they say, is history.

<u>The Halifax Explosion</u>: On the morning of 06 December 1917 the a French cargo ship carrying tons of explosives headed for the war in Europe collided in Halifax harbour with another vessel, caught fire and eventually exploded. The blast killed thousands of people, flattened buildings, set others on fire, and left some of the stone buildings of Halifax blackened on one side to this very day. As mentioned in this book it was the biggest man-made explosion in history until the first atomic bomb was detonated nearly thirty years - and another world war - later. Check out the Canadian Broadcast Corporation's excellent website about this event at: www.cbc.ca/halifaxexplosion

<u>Halifax Fairview Lawn Cemetery (Victims of Titanic Disaster)</u>: Because of Halifax's proximity to the site of the Titanic disaster, it was only natural that ships from this port were dispatched to recover bodies floating at sea following the sinking of the doomed ocean liner on its maiden voyage. A total of four ships steamed out of Halifax on a mission to find and recover bodies from the disaster. These ships recovered hundreds of them, of which some were buried at sea and others brought back to Halifax. Of those brought back to Halifax, some were picked up or shipped home to their families. Others, including many unidentified bodies, were buried in three separate cemeteries in Halifax itself. Fairview Lawn Cemetery is one of these and contains a section of headstones of Titanic victims. Try Googling "Halifax Fairview Cemetery Titanic" to see pictures of the graves and the cemetery itself. Also check out the Nova Scotia government's excellent website on the Titanic and her connection to Halifax, Nova Scotia: http://titanic.gov.ns.ca/

<u>Earhart Street in Gander, Newfoundland</u>: As noted in this book some of the streets in Gander are named after famous aviators, an homage to the town's history as the crossroads between Europe and North America during the early years of commercial aviation in the 20th century. Earhart Street runs through a quiet residential neighbourhood just as described in this book. Try using Google Street View at one of the intersections at either end of the street to see the simple black and white street sign and the rest of the neighbourhood.

<u>Gander, Newfoundland on 9/11</u>: As described in this book, thousands of passengers on 28 separate planes were diverted to Gander following closing of North American airspace in the aftermath of the attacks in New York and Washington. Check out the book "The Day the World Came to Town: 9/11 in Gander, Newfoundland" by Jim DeFede to hear some of their stories and read about the warm welcome that these surprised and unexpected visitors received.

<u>Vikings Discovering America</u>: Leaving aside the fact that the Americas did not have to be "discovered" in the first place since there were already plenty of people living there, Canadians have long known that it wasn't Columbus who discovered America. It was the Leif Eriksson, of course, and he and his fellow Vikings landed there five hundred years before Columbus. In the 1960s the remains of one of their settlements was discovered and excavated at an area of Newfoundland now known as "L'Anse aux Meadows". Try Googling this for more information about the Viking presence in North America.

<u>Icelandic Pronunciation</u>: Icelandic is a fascinating language with some pronunciations that are unusual to foreigners. You might be interested to check out some real Icelanders pronouncing the various Icelandic names and words from this book at www.forvo.com. Names like Ásta and Pétur, for example, are not pronounced quite like you might expect them to be if you're a native English speaker like I am.

<u>Icelandic Last Names</u>: The Icelandic system of last names works just as is described in this book. But it's not as unusual as it seems because this is a system that Iceland shares with the other Nordic countries like Norway, Sweden or Denmark. Unlike those other countries, however, Iceland has continued to use this system into the modern age.

<u>The Icelandic Naming Committee (Mannanafnanefnd)</u>: Believe it or not Iceland does have a governmental body that regulates which names are allowed in Iceland and it operates very much as described in this book (although there are occasional pressures to change it from time to time). Try Googling "Icelandic Naming Committee" to see different websites and news reports about this strange and wonderfully Icelandic committee.

<u>Icelandic Skyr</u>: Never forget! Skyr is not yoghurt! Check out www.skyr.is (in English too) for everything you ever wanted to know about skyr, including recipes and where to buy it outside of Iceland.

<u>Long Summer Days in Iceland</u>: The third week of June brings the longest days of the year in the Northern hemisphere and because Iceland is so far North this means that the days are *really* long. As most people know, if you go far enough north the sun won't even set at all on these days but just sort of dip down to the horizon and then back up again. Fortunately for Icelanders they are not *that* far north but around the 21st of June the sun sets in Reykjavík somewhere just after midnight and rises again just over two and a half hours later. And in-between the sky never really gets very dark. Check out www.sunrisesunset.com and generate your own calendar for Reykjavík in June.

<u>Sulphur-Smelling Tap Water</u>: Iceland is incredibly lucky to have access to free hot water that comes straight out of the ground for use in radiators or showering or whatever else you might use hot water for. In some parts of the country the sulphur smell is quite noticeable but don't worry, for some reason you don't stink after you're done your shower and dry yourself off.

<u>The Imagine Peace Tower</u>: On a small island in Reykjavík harbour is Yoko Ono's tribute to her late husband, John Lennon, in the form of a tower of light that is lit

each year from October 9th (John Lennon's birthday) until December 8th (the day he was shot and killed). The light shoots thousands of metres into the sky and is visible for miles around. Try Googling "John Lennon Peace Tower" to see some pictures of this amazing and touching tribute to the slain Beatle.

Literacy in Iceland: Iceland eliminated illiteracy in the late 1700s and has remained a "universally literate" nation ever since. This is not surprising since even the early Vikings who first settled in Iceland 1100 years ago were already a highly literate people, as is evidenced in the sagas which were written a couple hundred years later. Icelanders are also highly educated as well. Check out www.iceland.is/the-big-picture/people-society/education for some more information about literacy and education in Iceland and the fact that "*Iceland's universities attract hundreds of foreign students each year and many courses are taught in English. The country is well known for strong programmes in Icelandic language and literature, glaciology, and geology.*"

Aluminium and Energy Production in Iceland: This issue forms one of the central themes of this book and is very much an on-going debate in Iceland. In this book I have barely scratched the surface of the various questions that are critical to this discussion and it shouldn't surprise you that the arguments put forward by all sides are much more complicated than they might appear at first. I have to admit that I have absolutely no idea how I would decide to do things if it were up to me. On one hand it is absolutely true that an aluminium smelter using clean energy is vastly better for the environment than one burning fossil fuels, but building hydroelectric dams and geothermal plants on an enormous scale in Iceland damages the environment, not to mention that the smelters themselves pollute Iceland's clean air and water, as do the fossil-fuel-burning ships that bring raw materials there and take the aluminium away again. If people recycled more, that would lessen the need for new aluminium to be produced (I read somewhere that the energy required to produce the aluminium in a single soda can could run your television for four to five hours). But the operative word in that sentence is "if" and until people *do* recycle more, it's probably better to do as little damage to the overall global environment in the meantime, right? And so on, *ad infinitum*. You can see how arguments like these can get completely out of control. I've thought a lot about it I still don't know what the right answer is, but if you want more information from two of the major sides in the debate you can check out the website of one of the major environmental groups: www.savingiceland.org. You can also check out the website of Alcoa Aluminum (who featured in this book): www.alcoa.com/iceland/en/info_page/home.asp

The Blundstone Boot Company: The Blundstone Boot Company of Australia is also a real company who have made amazing (and much copied) boots since 1870. These boots will feel good on your feet from the very first moment that you put them on. Check out their website at www.blundstone.com.

Elves, Trolls and Hidden People: Depending on who you ask the belief in elves, trolls and hidden people in Iceland is either a legitimate and wide-spread phenomena or it's something that Icelanders exaggerate for the sake of tourists. I suspect the reality is something in-between. In such an alien landscape as Iceland has it's not difficult to believe in unseen beings. There is even an Elf School in Reykjavík where foreigners can learn about the various kinds of supernatural beings who inhabit the Icelandic countryside. Try Googling

"Iceland Elves", "Huldufólk" or "Iceland Elf School" to find out some more information about Iceland's unseen citizens. Also check out www.alfar.is which is the website of the town of Hafnarfjördur which boasts the highest concentration of Huldufólk in Iceland. The website gives information as well as offers walking tours.

Blind Spot Test: The optical blind spot discussed in this book is a real phenomena that can be very easily demonstrated. All you need to do is Google "Blind Spot Test" and you'll get plenty of results that will help you find your blind spot by simply looking at a pair of dots (or letters or whatever) and closing one eye.

Bobby Fisher - Boris Spassky Chess Match: Fans of chess know all about the infamous 1972 World Chess Championship played in Reykjavík between the American chess prodigy Bobby Fisher and the Soviet reigning champion Boris Spassky. Played at the height of the Cold War the match was as much about the clash of political ideologies as it was about chess. But in just under two months and twenty one games Fisher defeated the Soviet champion and capitalism prevailed.

Reagan - Gorbachev Reykjavík Summit: Due to Iceland's unique geographic location it was the ideal spot for meet-ups between the two Cold War superpowers. And so it was that in 1986 the leader of the free world, U.S. president Ronald Reagan, met up with the leader of the non-free world, Soviet premier Mikhail Gorbachev, in a small white house in downtown Reykjavík to discuss various Cold War kinds of issues. History tells us that capitalism ultimately prevailed in that showdown as well. It just took a few more years. Try Googling "Hofdi House" to see where this historically significant summit took place.

Iceland Public Swimming Pool Shower Policy: Most Western visitors who go swimming in Iceland can tell you about the strict no-bathing-suit policy enforced in Iceland's public swimming pools. Try Googling "Iceland Swimming Pool No Bathing Suit Shower" to see some pictures of the funny signs that show visitors which zones to concentrate on when washing themselves.

The 1973 Heimaey Volcanic Eruption (Westman Islands): The volcanic eruption described in this book that took place on the island of Heimaey in the Westman Islands is a real event that completely changed the landscape of this tiny island and its fishing harbour. Try Googling "Iceland Volcanic Eruption 1973" to see some amazing photos of the eruption and its aftermath.

Puffin Hunting: As crazy as it might sound, the method of hunting puffins described in this book is absolutely for real - so is the fact that Icelanders eat puffin. Try searching "Gordon Ramsay Puffin Hunt Iceland" to see some videos of television chef Gordon Ramsay trying his hand at puffin hunting (albeit considerably further back from the cliff edge than many Icelandic puffin hunters dare to go).

Icelandic Parliament: The ancient Icelandic parliament described in this book is an amazing example of how advanced the supposedly barbaric Vikings were. The parliament was located a beautiful but desolate location known as Thingvellir where the North American and European tectonic plates meet and are slowly growing apart at a rate of 2 or 3 centimetres a year. At the base of the imposing cliffs an Iceland flag now flies at the location of the original Law Rock. Try Googling "Thingvellir" for more information and photos of this amazing and historic place.

<u>Hákarl (Rotted Shark)</u>: I wish that I could tell you that the Icelandic dish made from buried rotted shark is not a real thing, but unfortunately it is. And it is... not for the weak of stomach. Try Googling "Hakarl" to read more about this interesting delicacy is prepared and to see what it looks like.

<u>Geysír</u>: One of Iceland's most visited tourist spots is an area east of Reykjavík where the source of the English word "geyser" is located. Unfortunately, the original Geysír geyser is not as active as its nearby smaller partner the Strokkur geyser and eruptions are infrequent. Fortunately for the tourists the Strokkur geyser erupts every few minutes. And for anyone with a camera that means plenty of opportunities to get a perfect photo, included the much coveted "water dome" type photos showing the eruption just as the water balloons up but before the surface breaks. Try Googling "Geysir" for plenty of pictures of this.

<u>Eyjafjallajökull Volcanic Eruption 2010</u>: For a few interesting weeks in the spring of 2010 an eruption of Iceland's Eyjafjallajökull volcano spewed ash into the high atmosphere which blew downwind and completely shut down European airspace. Try Googling (or YouTube) "Iceland Volcano 2010" to see some unbelievable photos and video of this eruption.

<u>Icelandic Sagas</u>: As Konrad rightly points out in this book, what is interesting about the Icelandic sagas is the fact that they are written in normal prose, instead of some artsy poetic verse that makes most people nod off to sleep or simply stop listening. Every Icelander is familiar with the sagas and is thus connected with their long history in a way that most nation's citizens are not. And the easy-to-read writing style is surely the reason why. You can read the sagas (including those featuring the outlaw hero Grettir who is mentioned in this book) for free online at the Icelandic Saga Database: sagadb.org

<u>The Blue Lagoon</u>: Just off the road on the way to the airport from Reykjavík is the world famous Blue Lagoon spa where visitors can swim in naturally heated geothermal water and try a variety of spa treatments, including floating massages. Check out their website: www.bluelagoon.com

<u>66° North Clothing</u>: It warms my heart to type the final words of this book and talk about something that I really believe in. Lean close and I will tell you a deep and wonderful secret... you will never own a better jacket (or sweater or fleece or whatever) than something you buy from 66° North. Don't buy it just because of their clever advertising (Google "66 North Clothing" to see some of these). And don't be scared by the price tags - it's worth every penny, I assure you. Check out their website: www.66north.com

On the off chance that you enjoyed this book, please allow me to try and entice you into reading another one by providing a sample from Kitty's continuing adventures:

Kitty Hawk and the Hunt for Hemingway's Ghost

Book Two of the Kitty Hawk Flying Detective Agency Series

Chapter One

It was so impossible to believe that I even had trouble convincing myself sometimes. But I was actually doing it. I was actually flying around the world. And if I doubted it and thought that perhaps it was all just a dream, all I needed to do was look out of the windows of my trusty De Havilland Beaver to see the spectacular and ever-changing landscape of North America passing beneath me.

Not that it had been easy, of course. Getting this far had been an unbelievable amount of work. Much more than I'd expected when I first daydreamed up the idea over a couple cups of coffee in my parents kitchen back in Tofino.

Fortunately, my parents helped me out with a lot of the planning and preparations. Excruciatingly detailed flight plans had to be drafted. Telephones calls had to be made and letters sent to various governments and local authorities. Complicated arrangements had to be made to ensure that I always had fuel no matter where I was. Every single stop along the way had to be planned out and settled in advance, including possible alternatives in case of emergency. And all of this required navigating a nightmare of bureaucratic red tape that I could definitely not have done all by myself.

Then there was my plane. That had to be prepared as well of course. And I could have never imagined all the work that would be required to get it ready.

First there was the plane itself. My parents insisted (and rightly so) that the entire plane be checked thoroughly to make sure everything was in the best possible shape for the long flight ahead of me. Fortunately, there was a company in Seattle who specialised in aircraft maintenance for the De Havilland Beaver so my parents and I flew down to spend a few days there while they checked my plane over and made various modifications. My father even arranged for the mechanics to spend a day with me going over various basic maintenance and repair operations with me while I furiously scribbled everything down in one of my notebooks.

Next were the additional fuel tanks to extend my flying range. Without those I wouldn't be going anywhere because several of the 'legs' of my planned route around the world were longer than the normal operating range of the De Havilland Beaver. Without additional fuel tanks and the extended range I simply couldn't do it. Fortunately for me (again), a company just an hour's flight away from Tofino specialised in custom-built fuel tanks and was able to install one for me.

After all of these modifications to my plane I then had to get used to flying it all over again. The added weight of the extra fuel subtlety altered the flight characteristics of my trusty De Havilland Beaver, which took some getting used to, but of course I'd flown with a ton of gold on board before so the added weight and slight sluggishness of the plane was nothing I hadn't experienced before.

Finally there was the emergency preparations. A friend of my father's who had been flying De Havilland Beavers for more than thirty years took me through every possible emergency situation we could think of and taught me how to handle myself and the aircraft under various extreme circumstances. He also helped us install special transponder beacons and navigational gear in the plane, in addition to all the other emergency gear. A life raft and life vests in the passenger compartment. Spare parts for the plane. Emergency food supplies. Flare guns. Everything you could possibly think of plus a bit more.

"It's not the things we've thought of that worry me," my father had told me. "It's the things we *haven't* thought of." And he was right, of course.

All of these modifications and supplies were not cheap and the whole trip was made possible by a donation from Charlie and his brothers from the charity trust fund they'd set up using the stolen gold from the Clara Nevada. I'd stayed in touch with them since our adventure through Alaska and the Yukon but I have to admit that Charlie was the best e-mailer of the bunch of them and it was with him that I maintained an almost daily correspondence.

The planning and preparations for my solo flight around the world seemed to flash by in a complete blur. I'd chosen March 17th as my departure date because that was the same day that Amelia Earhart had begun her own flight around the world back in 1937. And March had seemed a long way away back in the fall when I first had the idea to make the flight but it was Christmas before I knew it, then Valentine's Day, and March was soon to follow.

I wasn't on a deadline, however. My flight around the world wasn't a race to try and set some new speed record or something. Part of my plan was to make stops along the way and visit places that I'd always wanted to see. All in all the whole flight would take the better part of a year to complete but I was still determined to set out on March 17th if I could do it. And thanks to my father and mother, and Charlie and his brothers, and my best friend Skeena and my father's friends and everyone else who chipped in to help, by March I was ready and found myself lined up for take-off out on the water near the seaplane base in downtown Tofino.

It seemed like half the town had come out to see me off. My parents were there, of course, plus Skeena and her family (and she has a big family, with more cousins and aunts and uncles than I'd ever been able to keep track of). In the crowd on the pier cheering for me when I arrived there were a lot of familiar faces from around town as well as a few unfamiliar ones, including a lot of tourists who were visiting Tofino for the annual whale festival (an event celebrating the annual northern migration from Mexico of something like twenty thousand grey whales who just swim right past us every year on their way to feeding grounds in Alaska). There was even a reporter from the Vancouver Sun who had flown over to take my picture and interview me for a story in his newspaper.

It was all very overwhelming for me. I felt like a celebrity with people taking pictures of me from all sides with their camera phones and slapping me on the back to wish me luck as I waded through the crowd. I don't even know how all of them even knew about my flight. Clearly my epic undertaking had caught people's attention.

To the cheers and well wishes of the crowd of more than a hundred people I said a tearful farewell to my parents and Skeena and climbed up into the cockpit of my trusty De Havilland Beaver. Waving goodbye I started the engine and taxied out onto the water to make my final checks before take-off.

I was a bit nervous, I have to admit. My father and I had been down to the plane early that morning to check everything out and taxi it over to the downtown seaplane base to re-fuel it for the flight. I knew everything on the plane was in perfect order and that it was ready to go, but was I ready? As I put my hand up on the throttle lever I realised that I wasn't going to see my beautiful home in Tofino for months.

Ahead of me on the pier people held up signs that said things like "GOOD LUCK KITTY!" or "WE'LL MISS YOU!" and the reality of what I was about to try and do suddenly hit me. On paper while I made all the plans it was easy to think of the flight as some distant theoretical thing but now it was real and so many months away from home off in distant exotic lands seemed like a lifetime.

Was I ready for it?

"You can do this," I whispered to myself and pushed the throttle forward. The engine grumbled roughly for a moment then quickly smoothed out into a nice clean roar as I raced across the water and began to pick up speed. For a moment I half-expected to see the tip of Amanda Phillpott's kayak emerging in front of me, aborting my take-off, but she was nowhere to be seen and soon I was airborne and climbing up into the sky above the beautiful islands and inlets of Clayquot Sound. Down below the crowd on the dock cheered (I couldn't hear them, of course, but I could see them) and waved their arms to say goodbye. I waved back through the cockpit window and wobbled the wings of the plane to say farewell.

This is it, I thought. There's no turning back now.

A MESSAGE FROM THE AUTHOR
(a.k.a. I Like Root Beer)

I like Root Beer. For me there is no other beverage that is quite as magical and mysterious and inexplicably smooth as a cold mug of Root Beer. From the very first sip this enchanting brew tingles your palette with a plethora of blissful sensations and slides slippery cool down into your stomach as it warms your heart. And don't even get me started talking about that sublime frothy icy mess that we call a Root Beer Float.

When I was younger I fancied myself a bit of a Root Beer connoisseur, drinking my favourite brand A&W from tall, narrow champagne flûtes where the ice clinking against the side of the thin glass created a magical tinkling ambiance as I looked down my nose at all the other inferior Root Beer vintages. As I grew older and began to travel across the globe I naturally was inclined to seek out the very best Root Beers that the world had to offer. Surely somewhere deep in some ancient temple in the heart of the Mongolian desert there was a hitherto unknown type of Root Beer brewed by a secretive order of monks using ancient methods passed down through generations.

Sadly, as I was to discover, Root Beer is a North-American thing and you don't really find it elsewhere in the world. The closest I got was in the jungles of Sierra Leone which smell a bit like Root Beer and diesel oil. (In fact, most non-North-Americans to whom I have introduced this magical elixir have cautiously taken small sips then made a sour face, stating that "it tastes like medicine". Perhaps because the root that gives Root Beer its name was originally used as medicine - typical for North-Americans to turn medicine into soft drinks, right?)

I was crushed. If there was no Root Beer out there in the whole wide world, then what was the point of leaving my house in the first place? No one really needs to leave the house, after all. Everything you could ever need can be delivered right to your front door, including pizza and Root Beer and books and everything else you can find on amazon.com. But as it turns out the world is a pretty great place even without Root Beer. There are a million amazing things to see out there and as many more ways for all of us to see them, as our heroine and friend Kitty Hawk finds out in this book and the ones that will follow.

Whatever you want to call it, "holidays" or "vacations" (I prefer to call them "adventures" and thus lift them out from the realm of the mundane because I believe that it's always an adventure any time one of us dares to go out and see just a little bit more of the world), I always like to try and live life with what I call a "Hemingway Complex". I even once wrote a travel book using this as a title.

And what exactly is a "Hemingway Complex", you ask?

Well, some people might describe Ernest Hemingway as being "larger than life". But to say that is not entirely accurate. He was merely larger than other people's lives. He was certainly larger than my life, for example, but he fit quite comfortably into his own. My life isn't extraordinary like that of the great Ernest Hemingway. I've never run with the bulls or been in wars or hunted German U-Boats in the Caribbean while drinking cocktails. But to me living life with a Hemingway Complex means living in pursuit of the impossible. And it's the only way that I ever seem to do anything interesting. Like writing the very book that you now hold in your hands.

Thank you very much for taking the time to read my book. Don't forget to check out the latest happenings in the world of Kitty Hawk at www.kittyhawkworld.com and if you're interested also head over to www.secretworldonline.com to check out some of the songs that I write and record in my spare time in an effort to try and convince people that I am much busier than I actually am.

Talk to you again soon... in the next adventure.

Made in the USA
Columbia, SC
05 February 2020

87538324R00124